BY ZAC TOPPING

Wake of War
Rogue Sequence

WAKE

OF

A NOVEL

WAR

ZAC TOPPING

Tor Publishing Group
New York

This is a work of fiction. All of the characters, organizations, and events portrayed in this novel are either products of the author's imagination or are used fictitiously.

WAKE OF WAR

Copyright © 2022 by Zac Topping

A Forge Book
Published by Tom Doherty Associates/Tor Publishing Group
120 Broadway
New York, NY 10271

www.torpublishinggroup.com

Forge® is a registered trademark of Macmillan Publishing Group, LLC.

ISBN 978-1-250-33132-8

Our books may be purchased in bulk for promotional, educational, or business use. Please contact your local bookseller or the Macmillan Corporate and Premium Sales Department at 1-800-221-7945, extension 5442, or by email at MacmillanSpecialMarkets@macmillan.com.

First Edition: July 2022
First Mass Market Edition: May 2024

Printed in the United States of America

0 9 8 7 6 5 4 3 2 1

For Susan, my muse.
My guiding light through the dark.

WAKE
OF
WAR

I
WELCOME TO THE WAR

20 July 2037

The TC-27 Chariot banked hard to port and began spiraling toward the ground, the g-force pinning Specialist James Trent to his seat. The sudden drop caused a terrible weightless feeling to slither up his guts and for some reason made his feet tingle. The others packed in around him were handling the frantic descent in their own ways; eyes squeezed shut, lips quivering in rapid prayer, white-knuckle grips on rifles and seat straps. Like it would do any good. Might as well suck on a lucky rabbit's foot for all the difference any of that shit would make.

But on the plus side, after hours of being crammed on the aircraft, at least it was finally going down.

The main lights blinked out and LEDs in the floor switched on showing the way to the exits. The indicator over the emergency jump door was still red though, which was good because no one had parachutes equipped.

Compensators hissed and the airframe stabilized. There was a sudden flattening feeling as the craft slowed its drop and Trent's guts were pressed down into his feet. Much more of this and he'd retch.

Trent tried to play it cool, focusing on anything other than the drop. He looked up at the ceiling, taking note of the interior of the craft which was completely naked, all the exposed wiring and piping and coolant lines running along the skin of the craft. A real genius design that was. Sure, it probably saved production costs, but it wouldn't be hard for some disgruntled soldier to get up out of his seat and start yanking on shit and destroy vital flight systems.

He'd seen some guys lose it before. One too many deployments to combat cities and they came back all scrambled up. Did all kinds of crazy things. Wouldn't be much of a stretch to imagine someone like that just up and deciding to go out with a bang.

The TC-27 dropped again. A quick, sickening lurch for two to three seconds and Trent knew they fell another few hundred feet closer to terra firma. He felt his throat tighten, a bead of sweat forming on his brow, and knew his complexion must be somewhere between yellow snow and filthy bathwater. He closed his eyes and tried to swallow it down.

Suddenly the ship sagged, slowed, then with surprising ferocity crunched down on solid ground. Shock systems sent power to the landing gear, which shook the craft like it was in a blender. Reverse thrusters roared to slow the heavy piece of machinery until the brakes could take over and bring the entire thing to a stop.

Trent peeled his eyes open in the sudden silence that filled the cargo space as the flight systems powered down. The lights came back on and a pair of flight assistants in dark gray jumpsuits came out of the cabin and began assisting soldiers off their craft. Trent unclipped his harness, loosened the damned chin strap that was way too tight, and dragged his rucksack out from under the seat. He strapped his rifle onto his chest rig, slipped into the aisle, and walked toward the rear of the craft where the bay doors had folded open.

His boots thumped down the grated metal gangway as he disembarked.

The heat was the first thing to hit him. A dry, heavy air that squeezed around him, forcing sweat to immediately soak through his combat uniform. He squinted against the brightness of the early summer sun.

The airfield was huge, but only a handful of aircraft were on it. A few other TC-27s were parked by a maintenance bay nearby, and a pair of AC-65 Wasps sat on the opposite end of the runway staring out like hungry predators basking in the afternoon sun, their sleek armor and inverted grav-engines angling down and back like the wings of their namesake, 30mm cannons poking out the front. With the Federal Reserve collapsing and the government spending freeze in place, Trent hadn't expected to see them here. He'd heard somewhere that the entire payload of an AC-65 was somewhere near three million dollars, American. Even if they were just intended as a show of force, it was good to know they were there.

Everyone was rounded up and marched across the tarmac into a hangar where they began the in-processing ritual. Trent shuffled along in line, constantly shrugging the weight of his rucksack in search of a more comfortable position, which was apparently impossible. After a while the line stopped moving and someone gave the order to *smoke 'em if you got 'em*. A moment later a cloud of carcinogenic smog hovered over everyone's heads. Trent bummed a cigarette from the guy next to him, cupped his hands over it while the guy lit for him, and nodded thanks.

No one spoke. There was a silent sense of dread that lived just under the veil of military enthusiasm. Trent let the smoke out through his nose and gazed at the towering mountains surrounding the valley. The mountains that were home to the enemy, the violent militant faction known as the Revolutionist Front who were stoking the flames of rebellion while the country was imploding.

Trent finished his cigarette and was called forward. The soldier behind the counter was another specialist, tapping away on a touch pad. She looked up at Trent as he approached. "ID and Nat-Reg."

Trent gave her his ID card and she entered his information into her pad. A printer whirred and spat out a few sheets of paper that she gathered up, stuffed into an envelope and thrust toward Trent. "Specialist Trent, James Oliver. Assigned to the 117th Infantry. Head over to supply for loadout. Enjoy your stay in the valley. Next."

"Wait, I'm sorry, you said infantry?"

She glared at him. "That's correct."

"I'm supposed to go to a supply unit," Trent stammered, throat going dry.

"The needs of the Army, Specialist. And the Army needs you in the infantry. Now move along."

Trent took his file, reeling from this unexpected development, and went over to supply where he was issued tactical body armor, a various assortment of interchangeable ballistic plates, a med kit, and 210 rounds of ammunition in seven separate magazines. He signed for everything and moved off to the waiting area where he was assured someone from his unit would retrieve him shortly.

He bummed another cigarette and tried to calm himself. Fucking infantry. No way. He hadn't practiced basic combat tactics in months, and even then it had only been half-assed attempts to appease qualification paperwork. But here he was in a real combat zone with real fighting and real enemies, not holographic targets with score meters ticking away like a fucking video game.

Gunfire cracked outside the perimeter wall no more than a few hundred meters away. Trent's head snapped around, heart hammering in his chest, and that awful tingling feeling shot through his feet again.

"You'll get used to it," said one of the soldiers sitting nearby in a faded, dirty uniform. "Soon enough you won't even notice it."

Trent tried to relax, however the hell he was supposed to do that. The gunfire continued to pop sporadically for another minute before it ceased. No one on the airfield or anywhere on the FOB seemed to care. It was just another summer afternoon in the valley.

Not much later, a GV-6 Prowler—one of the military's all-purpose utility vehicles—rolled up to the holding area. Trent recognized his new unit numbers stenciled on the grille and waved it down. The truck crawled to a stop as a soldier climbed out of the passenger-side door. He had dark skin and dark eyes that stared at Trent without emotion. He wore the rank of specialist and his name tape said SIMARD.

"You the new armorer?" Simard asked.

Trent handed Simard his files. "I'm Trent. You guys are the 117th?"

Simard handed the files back without looking at them. "You got it. I'm Simard, this is Jenson." He gestured to the private sitting behind the wheel, a young white man, couldn't be more than eighteen years old. His bottom lip stuck out and a string of brown spit ran down his chin. He waved.

"Come on," Simard said.

Trent crammed himself into the back seat. For such large vehicles there was surprisingly little room inside. Trent's knees were jammed in tight and the rigid upright seat back was at such a severe angle it practically had him leaning forward. Comfort was clearly not part of the military design.

Jenson shoved the transmission in drive and hit the gas. They pulled away from the airfield and onto regular blacktop, passing rows of Quonset huts and bunk pods as they crossed the FOB.

Simard twisted in his seat and faced Trent. "You ever been to combat before?"

"No. Not until today."

A grin spread across Simard's face. "You ain't been in combat yet. But it's cool, I got you. We were all pumped to get here at first. Ain't that right?" He looked at Jenson.

"That's fuckin' right," the private said. "Gonna serve justice to the rebels an' all that shit."

Simard continued. "All that shit. That's all it is, Specialist Trent. What do you think about that?"

"Just Trent," he said. "Or James. You don't really think things are gonna go bad here, right?"

"Why? You scared?"

"No. I mean . . ." Trent swallowed a lump in his throat and recovered. "I'm not here for glory is all."

"What are you here for, then?"

Truth was Trent had enlisted for the Military Granted University Scholarship, but somehow didn't think that would sound cool to admit. So far in his three years of service he'd been able to maintain easy gigs on comfortable East Coast stations, far from any combat. Another year and he'd be free of the Army's bullshit, and free to subject himself to an all new type of bullshit at the University. But the prospect of working in an office with climate control sounded much better than working in the ditches for the rest of his life. Thing was, that sentiment was sometimes hard to get across to other soldiers who would forever be grunts and ditchdiggers and were happy about it. Every time he admitted that he joined the military for anything other than killing he was ridiculed and looked down upon.

Simard broke the silence, sparing Trent the admission. "I'm just fuckin' with you, man. We ain't hard-asses here. Shit's all a joke in my opinion."

"Wanna know why I joined?" Jenson asked. He continued without waiting for an answer. "To get my plumbing cert." He laughed at his own joke, belting out a backwoods kind of chortle.

"You ain't layin' shit, Jenson," Simard said, turning back around. He hung his elbow on the open window. Outside, more barracks trailers flashed past. A few units were standing outside in formation. "Anyway, Trent," Simard continued. "This is Forward Operating Base Spearpoint." He waved out the window. "Too many dicks, not enough equipment, no end in sight. But hey, at least we got someone to fix our busted-ass weapons now."

"Yeah man," Jenson said. "There's some chicks on base, but every one of 'em's got at least a hundred dudes houndin' after 'em."

"Would you fuckin' stow it?" Simard cut in.

Jenson shut up and focused on the steering wheel.

"Anyway," Simard said, "you're in Alpha Company, Fourth Platoon, Third Squad. Got it? That's us. And as far as things not getting bad, you're outta luck. Intel says the RF just put out a new video, only this one wasn't a PR statement like the usual." Simard paused. "Joseph Graham just declared war on all government forces in the city. Which means this shit is real as it gets and we're in it for the long haul, so watch your step cuz this place is a shithole."

"Yeah man," Jenson said. "Bet you still notice the smell? Don't worry, that'll go away."

"The smell doesn't go away," Simard said. "You just get used to it."

In the back seat, Trent fought down another bout of sickness. The Revolutionist Front wasn't playing around. Joseph Graham was the charismatic and completely psychotic leader of the Revolutionist Front who'd already earned himself a top spot on the government's most wanted list for his role in orchestrating numerous crimes against humanity. Graham, who'd once been a backwater preacher and cult leader, had managed to use his gift of persuasion to lure enough fellow crazies out of the woodworks to put together a substantial following that eventually turned into a legitimate rebel army. A rebel army camped out in the mountains surrounding the valley Trent currently found himself trapped in as a new member of a front-line infantry unit.

From the driver's seat, Private Jenson reached back and offered Trent a cigarette.

"Welcome to Salt Lake City."

2
THIS SHIT IS REAL

The 117th Infantry Battalion's Headquarters Company was in a repurposed maintenance bay on the far side of the airfield. Inside was a labyrinth of plywood offices, dim lighting, and humming electronics. Trent stepped over the cables snaking across the floor as he made his way to a radio desk and handed his file to the lieutenant behind the counter.

The LT glanced at the folder and slid it into a rack of other files. Behind him a radio operator was manning the comms and checking a map mounted to the wall with sections of the city circled in red, blue, and green. There was a lot of red.

The LT sipped his coffee and glared at Trent. "Armorer, huh?"

"Yes, sir."

"We'll see." He turned to the radio operator. "Holdridge, get Staff Sergeant Grader on the horn and let him know his weapon tech is here."

"Copy that, sir," said the private.

A few moments later Staff Sergeant Grader pushed through a doorway in back, wiping grease-stained hands on a rag that he tucked into his back pocket as he approached. The man was lean with narrow shoulders and thin wrists, hair slightly longer than regulation with bits of gray starting to show at the temples. He adjusted a pair of black-framed glasses as he looked over his new charge.

"Specialist Trent," he said. "You're our new armorer?"

"Roger that, Sergeant."

Grader extended his hand. "Welcome to Salt Lake City."

Trent shook. "Thank you, Sergeant. Glad to be here," he said, knowing how stupid it sounded.

Grader stared at Trent for a moment. "Yeah. Well, come on, I'll take you to your shop."

Your shop. That sounded good. Sounded important. If Trent handled this right maybe he wouldn't have to leave the perimeter, maybe he'd be too valuable to risk in combat.

Staff Sergeant Grader retrieved his sidearm, then led Trent out of Headquarters and across the compound to a row of stacked shipping containers. He stopped at one at the end, yanked the latches up, and pried the doors open. They squealed in protest like they'd been closed for a long time.

"Last unit left these for us," Grader said. "But we've been understaffed so they've been . . . unused, to put it politely. You'll have to do some cleaning and organizing, but it's all yours." He stepped into the container and hit the power. An electric hum rang through the walls as the lights powered up. Trent peered in.

It looked like someone had dropped the trailer from a thousand feet up and rolled it down a hill. Mounds of moldy trash, broken pieces of ancient equipment, dust and broken lights, storage racks tipped over, contents spilled all over the floor. Trent was pretty sure he saw a rat run into the shadows.

Grader frowned at the mess. "I know it's not much, but it's yours now."

"Who's been maintaining the unit's weapons?" Trent asked.

"There's a support element from the Third Mountain we've been outsourcing our equipment to. They'll be glad for the break. But you've got a lot to do. I'll work on getting our stuff sent back here, as well as line up the queue we've already got on hand." Grader frowned again. "It's, uh, a lot. So . . . I'll let you to it. If you need anything, you know where HQ is, and my hooch is just over there." He pointed toward the bunk pods. "You report to me directly. We don't hold formation in Fourth Platoon so you're responsible for policing yourself. I expect you here by zero eight hundred."

"Weekends off?"

Grader looked at him.

Trent cleared his throat. "Sorry, Sergeant. Zero eight, got it."

Trent was up the next morning before sunrise and took it upon himself to go for a run. It was quiet and the FOB felt empty, which was rather disconcerting considering they were apparently surrounded by the enemy. He jogged past a guard tower along the perimeter wall with two soldiers tending an auto-.50-cal and spotted a few automated drones circling above and felt a little better.

Trent finished his run and got back to his bunk pod to find Simard sitting outside smoking a cigarette.

"You trying to make us look bad," Simard said, taking a long drag.

Trent shrugged, unclipped his rifle. "Just habit."

"That shit'll pass," said Jenson as he stepped out of his pod cradling a thermos of steaming coffee. "Ain't no one out here to impress."

Trent sat on the front step and set his rifle against the door. Jenson poured coffee into some Styrofoam cups and offered them around. The three of them sat drinking coffee and smoking as the sun rose above the Wasatch Mountains to the east.

"This whole war thing isn't so bad, after all. I mean, so far," Trent said.

Simard cocked his head. "Don't tell me this is your first fuckin' tour."

"This is my first fuckin' tour."

"Damn," Jenson whistled through his teeth. "They sent us a virgin armorer."

"Says the private who just got out of drill," Trent countered.

Jenson rubbed his eye with a middle finger.

"Really though," Simard said. "You been in long enough to make specialist but this is the first time you been deployed to a combat zone? How the fuck you manage that?"

Trent swirled his coffee, wondering how much he should say. No sense in being coy. "Truth is I joined for the scholarship," he said. "Been trying to get assignments near Trade Districts so I can have a leg up when I get into the University. Mostly administrative stuff so far so it hasn't been too hard to put in for non-combat transfers. I guess it was only a matter of time."

"So you wanna be a big shot when you grow up, eh?" Simard said.

"I, uh . . . I don't know." Trent stood and stretched.

He didn't want to keep going down this line of conversation so he went into his pod to grab his toiletry bag and a towel to head for the showers. He thought about taking his uniform down to the shower stalls but decided to leave it. Showers weren't too far away, he'd be back quick enough.

When he stepped back outside he found Jenson and Simard standing bolt upright, arms folded behind their backs, faces locked on some point off in the distance. A soldier stood in front of them in full combat uniform, rifle slung across his chest, a patch with the rank of staff sergeant on his breast. The name tape said CREON. At seeing Trent emerge from his hooch, Creon's hands came off his hips and crossed over his chest.

"The plot fucking thickens," the staff sergeant said. "Get at parade rest, soldier."

Trent snapped to position like Simard and Jenson.

Creon narrowed his eyes on the three of them. "Let's go over this again. I see one unsecured weapon, and now *three* soldiers standing around with their dicks in their hands."

Fuck. Trent's rifle. He could see it in the corner of his eye, leaning against the outside of his trailer. Well outside of arm's reach, well outside of regulation.

"That's my weapon, Sergeant," Trent said.

Creon took a step closer. "What's your name, soldier?"

"Specialist Trent, Sergeant."

"You're new here."

"Roger that, Sergeant."

"Listen here, Specialist. I see two soldiers without weapons and one who left his weapon out in the open for any yokel fuck to grab." Creon jabbed a finger toward Trent's rifle. "That weapon is your life. It's as much a part of you as your own swinging dick. That goes for all of you. For every soldier in this theater of combat. The fuck do you expect to do when you turn the corner and find a Revolutionist pointing a gun at you and you've got nothing but a fucking triple foam foo-foo latte in your soft-ass hands?" He glowered at the three of them.

Trent didn't know this Creon from a hole in the ground but he'd been in the Army long enough to know you don't speak when a senior non-commissioned officer goes on a tirade.

"The three of you are lucky I've got shit to do or I'd have you pushing dirt until I got tired. Secure that weapon and fucking shape up. Lives are on the line. That is all." Creon stared at them for a moment, then turned on his heel and stormed off.

The three of them waited until he was out of sight before relaxing.

"Fuckin' dick," Jenson spat.

"Sorry, guys," Trent said scooping up his rifle and clipping it to his chest.

"Sergeant Creon's an asshole," Simard said, lighting another cigarette. "He lives for that shit. Like he joined just so he could play the hard-ass." He nodded at the shower bag in Trent's hand. "Hurry up and we'll show you the chow hall when you come back. And don't forget your fuckin' weapon."

The chow hall was a pre-fab structure like the hangars at the airfield only smaller. Having only eaten prepackaged MREs since he'd arrived on the FOB, he was eager to see if what they had on offer was any better. It usually wasn't, but one could always hope.

They shuffled through the door at the far end of the half-domed building, waiting in line with all the other soldiers, melting into the crowd of tan uniforms and mumbled conversation. They grabbed trays and moved down the serving line. Trent eyed the offerings with suspicion, but accepted a scoop of goopy egg-substitute, some greasy bacon, diced potatoes, and a cup of vat-grown strawberries. The coffee was standard-issue brown water. He doused it with flavored creamer.

The hall filled quickly with troops, some in dirty and stained combat uniforms just coming in from night patrols, others in training shorts and T-shirts smiling and taking their time. The officers sat together at a table near the far end of the room, senior NCOs at a table nearby.

Trent, Simard, and Jenson sat at a table near a flat-screen showing the news back east. New York was hosting delegates of the European Union at the Javits Federal Building this week. Protests in Washington. Rebels fighting in Texas. A hurricane was heading for the Florida coastline.

Trent choked down a sip of coffee. It all seemed so far away even though he was just a few states to the west.

The news cut to a story about the rebels in Utah and every head in the chow hall turned as one. The anchor put on a serious face as he looked into the camera. "The Revolutionist Front released an official statement yesterday declaring '*open war on all government forces and their sympathizers in the Salt Lake Valley,*'" he said. "The statement was accompanied by a video of rebel leader Joseph Graham along with several captives, presumably at one of their many hidden camps in the Oquirrh Mountains. Analysts have confirmed the following footage *is* real and warn viewers of its content." The camera cut to a shaky video of a balding, middle-aged man in fatigues surrounded by armed rebels somewhere in the forest. Kneeling in front of them were two soldiers and one police officer. They were blindfolded and had their arms behind their backs.

Joseph Graham looked into the camera as he spoke. "When in the course of human events it becomes necessary for one people to dissolve the political bands which have connected them with another . . . a decent respect to the opinions of mankind requires that they should declare the causes which impel them to the separation," he said. Trent recognized the words from the opening of the Declaration of Independence.

"President Haymond has led this country into chaos," Graham continued. "He proved himself unworthy to lead when he backed out of the Global Trade Accords to protect cabinet members' business profits, closing our borders and plunging the economy into ruin. He proved unworthy yet again when, in response to protests from the American people, he appointed the warmonger, General Les Schroeder, as secretary of homeland security and enacted martial law. Then came reinstatement of the appallingly archaic Conscription Act without congressional approval. This long trail of abuses and usurpations invariably led to the outbreak of open and justifiable hostilities that have continued to escalate to this day. We have called for his removal, but he does not listen, and his loyalists cannot hear through their armor, nor over the crack of their rifles."

Trent felt called out there and swallowed a lump in his throat, then looked around the chow hall. Frowns and furrowed brows all around.

"Governments are instituted among men and women," Graham droned on through the television, "deriving their power from the consent of the governed, that whenever any form of government becomes destructive of these ends, it is the right of the people to alter or abolish it, and to institute new government.

"America is dying," he said. "But even as it takes its last breath, a new America is waking. We will not rise by clinging to a sinking ship. Let the capital and all it stands for sink into the swamp it was built upon. For we, the people, the path to salvation lies in the west, in the Federation of Pacific States where a *new* seat of power for a *new* government is being built from the blood and sweat of those willing to fight for it.

"As of today, the Revolutionist Front joins the Coalition of Free State Militias in the fight to protect the west in this fragile time." Joseph Graham paused, narrowed his eyes at the camera. "The stain of the old government shall be wiped from the land."

Graham stuck his hand out and one of the rebels put a pistol in it. He pressed the gun to the back of the head of one of the captive soldiers. The camera cut out and went back to the anchor. At least the media had the decency to not show an actual execution, but they'd shown enough. The hall was silent as the anchor segued to the weather.

While Trent forced down the rest of his meal, Staff Sergeant Creon came through the doors, pushed his way through the crowd, found a table of soldiers in combat uniform, and appeared to give some orders.

The soldiers stood, cleared their trays, and filed out of the chow hall. Creon gave the hall a final scan, then followed them out.

"That's First Platoon for you," Simard said through a mouthful of potatoes. "Bunch of hard-asses."

"Creon's in Alpha?" Trent asked.

"Sure is. He's one of First Platoon's squad leaders. Thinks he's at the Siege of Baton Rouge. They love that shit, though."

Trent made a mental note to avoid them at all cost.

They finished their meals, dropped their trays in the collection bin, and stepped outside, lighting customary post-breakfast cigarettes.

Trent checked his watch. 0730. "I should be getting to the shop," he said. "I'll catch you guys—"

Something whistled overhead. A half second later a concussive blast rocked a stack of shipping containers across the street.

Trent felt the impact more than heard it.

Another screaming round overhead, another blast, this one shredding a water collection tank. Trent, Simard, and Jenson dove to the ground as shrapnel rang off the walls of the chow hall and obliterated a portable shitter.

Trent's ears were ringing as more thumping blasts rocked the FOB. The base sirens powered up in wailing, banshee tones as soldiers poured out of the buildings and took cover in the nearby shock bunkers.

Heart hammering, Trent watched as more rounds came down on the FOB, slamming into huts, punching craters in the road. There was something surreal about the whole thing, like living a scene from a movie.

Then the booming stopped. The sirens powered

down, the soldiers crammed inside the bunkers slowly came out.

Trent climbed to his feet, took a daring step out into the open.

"Holy shit."

Quick Reaction Forces raced to the gates. A squad of Prowlers drove by at high speed, soldiers racking weapons in the turrets, armored trucks loading up troops to go out and hunt down the attackers. Mini-drones rose above the FOB and zipped out over the city.

"Jesus Christ," Trent said under his breath. And just like that Trent had his first taste of war.

The RF kept up the random mortar and rocket attacks for the next few weeks, making Trent's job of getting the shop in proper working order all the more difficult, since every time there was an attack he had to stop what he was doing and take cover, then report for roll call to verify he was still alive. But he eventually got it together.

Trent stood at the door admiring the orderly contents: the stacked shelves, the clean workbench, the work orders filed away in plastic sleeves on the wall, the weapon racks filled with rifles for repair. Crates had been delivered from the Third Mountain Division and stacked in back containing the 117th's overstock of broken equipment, some of which he'd already repaired and sent back into the field. The work was constant, but he had a good rhythm now and he was determined to prove his value to the Army right where he was.

Trent switched the lights off and locked the doors.

He glanced at his watch. Dinner chow had come and gone three hours ago so he tamped down the hunger by lighting a cigarette. Free from the confines of his duty, he didn't quite feel like going to sleep so he strolled off into the dark.

He found Simard on guard duty in a tower along the southern perimeter. Jenson was asleep on the floor of the tower and twitched awake at the sound of Trent's approach, recognized his friend, and rolled back over.

Simard leaned on the wall, cigarette between his fingers. An M381 belt-fed machine gun sat next to him on a bipod. It faced out over a ghetto they'd named Shanty Town situated across the highway. The slum was pitch dark save for a few small fires here and there, no way to tell if they were controlled or accidental. The smell of molten rubber drifted on the breeze.

They stared out for a long time before Simard broke the silence.

"It's weird," he said. "Should feel like home, 'cause it sort of is, ya know? But it's not." He took a long drag on his cigarette. "It certainly doesn't fucking feel like home anyway."

"Yeah, it's weird."

"Man, I need some trim," Simard said. "If I get desperate enough I might go talk to Kinneson over in Headquarters."

"I can't imagine she's into black guys," Trent said.

Simard waved him off. "Who gives a shit if she's from Kentucky or wherever the fuck? Those are the ones that get a taste and never go back." He jabbed his cigarette to punctuate his point. "They got that saying for a reason."

"Fair enough. Still a slippery slope, though, man.

Get caught fraternizing and you're fucked. Or get her pregnant and really be fucked."

Simard seemed to think that over for a moment. "True," he finally said. "You got a girl back home, Trent?"

"Yeah, actually," Trent said.

"And?"

"And what? She's back home. I'm here."

"You got a picture?"

Trent hesitated, then pulled out his Nat-Reg card. Tucked into the sleeve behind it was a three-by-five color photo. He unfolded it and showed it to his friend. Simard peered at the picture.

"That's Alley," Trent said.

"Damn, bro. What's a smoke-show like that doing with an Army bum like you?"

Trent took the photo back and looked down at it. Alley was there smiling up at him, dark hair pulled back in a ponytail, big sunglasses covering her face. She was leaning back on a beach towel, propped up on her elbows, pushing her chest out in a way that she knew drew attention to her body. The photo was taken the week Trent left for basic training. She went to the beach with some friends and took it just for him, she told him in the letter. At first the picture sent waves of primal desire pulsing through him; then he wondered who'd taken the picture, who else was there that day to spend time with his girlfriend. He began to think about all the other guys at the beach jacked up on muscle enhancers and spray tans, hunting for lonely women. But there was nothing he could do about that so he buried the thought and let the picture remind him of good times.

"We met in high school," Trent said. "Somehow I

was smooth enough to convince her to go on a date with me. We've been together ever since. She's interning for some advertising agency in New York now. Kinda why I joined the Army. Didn't want to be a bum and couldn't afford a job outside the Labor Division." Trent paused, glanced at Simard, worried he'd come off as a snob. Simard made no indication he noticed. Trent continued. "Figured I'd enlist and get the benefits before I got conscripted and left with nothing. I enlisted for her. For us, really." He ran his thumb over the photo and felt that familiar stirring in his gut.

Simard lit another cigarette. "Damn, bro. You should just let that shit go." He blew smoke through his nose. "You know Jody's plowin' it out right now."

"The fuck, dude." *Jody* was the colloquial name given to any guy who slept with soldiers' wives and girlfriends while they were away at war. That kind of thing happened so often it'd become something of a running joke in the military. Not a real funny one, however.

"Hey, just being honest, man. That's how it goes. Tight body like that, girl with a good job . . . you're gone now. You think there ain't some next dude lined up? You been in long enough to know how this shit works."

Trent knew quite well, had seen it dozens of times with other soldiers, but he held tight to the idea that it couldn't—wouldn't—happen to him.

"Alright," Trent snapped. "What about you?"

"Yeah, I got something back home. Got a few kids somewhere, too."

"Really? How old?"

"Doesn't matter. I was young when I started. Never

got the permits for any of 'em. And the last one was my third."

"Damn, man," Trent said lighting his own cigarette. "That's violation of Pop-control. You got snipped?"

"Fuck no. His mother never claimed him as mine. It was her first so she's good. She wants to marry me when I get back and have another. Been trying to avoid that conversation like the plague. I'm up to my fuckin' eyes in fines for the first two, let alone what kind of nightmare it'd be to file for second-marriage extension." He paused, grew silent. "But who knows. After this deployment, as long as she's naked I'll probably do anything she says."

Trent stared at his friend as he tried to think of something to say.

"Good luck," was all he came up with.

In the corner, Jenson snorted and rolled over in his sleep.

The next day Trent had the shop open early. Sergeant Grader stopped in to drop off breakfast in a foam box. Fake eggs and bacon, starch cubes with salt and pepper. Trent thanked him. Grader surveyed Trent's workload, nodded and left.

Trent hunched over the workbench staring down at a pile of parts from a turret gun that'd been smashed apart during a vehicle rollover. He had to scrounge for spare parts and hone a few pieces just to meet tolerances. The government had no money to spend on new equipment and what money it did have went to cities already involved in heavy resistance like Dallas, Denver, and Minneapolis. Even then, spending was at a minimum. With severely fractured federal funding, the nation was going belly up.

Trent grabbed a pack of cigarettes off the counter and lit one. He glanced idly at the foam tray of food-like stuff, now cold and completely unappetizing.

The sound of boots outside brought Trent around. Sergeant Jameson and Corporal Everett from Third Platoon stepped in. They looked worn out, their uniforms gone gray from dirt and sweat and continuous wear. Scruff on their faces well outside regulation. Their eyes were bloodshot and lined in pink from days without sleep.

Jameson came forward. "What's up, Trent?"

"Living the dream, Sergeant."

"I bet."

Trent shifted uncomfortably on the stool. "What can I do for you guys?"

Jameson nodded to Everett and they unclipped their rifles, handed them over. Trent stuck his cigarette in his lips before grabbing the weapons, racked the slides to make sure they were cleared, and gave them both a quick look over.

"What's the issue?" he asked.

Everett looked to Jameson. Jameson sniffed, shrugged, and leaned on the counter.

"Had a couple misfeeds in the field," he said.

Trent nodded. "Okay. They cleaned?"

The sergeant's tired eyes slid up to Trent's. Trent made a placating gesture, set the rifles down, and plucked the cigarette from between his lips. He offered the pack to the infantrymen. They accepted and lit their own. "You guys getting a lot of fighting out there?"

"Some."

Trent paused, the shop filling with heavy silence.

"I'll take a look at them," Trent said. "You got backups?"

Jameson nodded. "We got a few guys down on casualty call. We can use their weapons for now, but these'll need to be fixed quick."

"I'll see what I can do, but I can't guarantee a return time. Got a lot of weapon systems here to manage." Trent waved at the stacks of rifles, machine guns, and grenade launchers piled in the back of the shop. The shelves were packed with pistols and random parts from vehicle and drone-mounted weapons as well.

Jameson shrugged again, rubbed at his eye with a dirty knuckle. "Sure thing."

Trent grabbed a work order form and filled out the appropriate info, noting each rifle's serial number, the time and dates of the requested work. Sergeant Jameson and Corporal Everett hung around finishing their cigarettes.

"So," Jameson said. "You hear about the CID coming here?"

Trent looked up. The Central Intelligence Department worked psy-ops and covert shit. Spies, basically. If they were coming to Salt Lake it meant things were serious. Or they were about to be.

"Damn," Trent said. "I didn't know that. Where are they?"

"Engineers are building a compound for them at the north end of the FOB. They'll have their own camp attached to us. We've already been given orders to start bringing locals in for questioning."

"Questioning? The CID's going to question civilians?"

Jameson pulled a face. "I know, right. It's already

got the yokels all fuckin' riled up. You hear that shooting at night?" He waited for Trent to nod. "They know shit's coming down. Makes it dangerous for us." He glanced at Everett.

The corporal finally joined the conversation. "Yeah," he said bobbing his head up and down. "It's real dangerous now. Getting worse by the day. Each time we go out they got more weapons."

Trent shook his head. "Wait, the CID, though, they're already here? Questioning captives?"

"Sure are," Jameson said. "They got 'em held in some basement somewhere on post. Won't tell anyone where, but sometimes you can hear screaming from underground."

"Comes up through the drains," Everett said. "Fucking creepy."

"But the locals," Jameson said. "They know it and they don't want to be taken. They think *we're* bad guys so they keep shooting at us and make it worse for themselves. Like I said, they're trying to outgun us."

Trent saw the look that passed between Jameson and Everett.

Jameson cleared his throat. "So, uh, Trent . . . we got a small favor to ask of you."

Shit.

"When you take a look at those weapons, do you think maybe you could do a little something with the trigger mechanism? Like, modify it? Make the burst selection full-auto?"

The cigarette almost fell out of Trent's mouth. "Sorry guys, that's against regulation. You know that. I could lose my armorer's license. And my rank."

Everett stepped closer. With Jameson leaning against the bench and Everett covering the doorway,

Trent got the sneaking suspicion he was being boxed in. He swallowed a lump in his throat.

"Uh, Sergeant, Corporal. Let's just think about this."

"We have," Jameson said, steel in his voice. "Fuck regulation. Written by pussies behind desks." He pressed his palm to the greasy workbench. Trent's eyes tracked it, then came back up to Jameson's. "Maybe if it was your ass out there past the wire every day and night getting shot at you'd think about this differently." The sergeant straightened, let some of the grit out of his expression. "Look, Trent. It's not like we're asking you to do anything crazy. Just modify the burst selection. That's all. Realistically, it'll be on semi anyway unless shit hits the fan and then regulations won't fucking matter." He dropped a heavy hand on Trent's shoulder and squeezed. Everett took a step closer. "You understand, right? You'll do this for us? To save soldiers' lives."

Trent wanted to say no. He wanted to convince these men that breaking the rules was a bad idea. But he couldn't figure out how to justify it in any way that could possibly sway a pair of fighting infantrymen. And if he couldn't convince them, then why should he try to convince himself? They had a point. Trent was just a rear-echelon guy, safe behind the perimeter walls. Who was he to say *no, I won't help you stay alive*?

Trent let out a breath he hadn't realized he'd been holding.

"Okay. Fine. I'll make the modification."

Jameson smiled. Everett took a step back.

"Excellent," Jameson said coming off the bench. "We head back out tomorrow night. We'll be back before then. Thanks for the cigarette." He slapped Trent on the shoulder and the two of them began to leave. As Sergeant Jameson got to the door, he stopped and turned around. "And, uh, don't say anything to anyone about this, right?"

"Right."

Jameson nodded. "Good. You may see a few more of our guys come by, too, once they hear about what a great job you do with repairs. I expect you'll show them the same professionalism."

Trent resisted the urge to swallow another lump in his throat. "You got it, Sergeant."

Jameson slapped the shipping container wall and stepped off.

Trent looked down at the pair of rifles on his bench and tried not to think about what the CID was doing beneath his feet.

3
A RIGHTEOUS PURPOSE

Sam Cross made her way through camp aware of all the eyes on her. She knew what they were looking at was not what they saw. Not a nineteen-year-old girl from Texas with a scar on her cheek, not the Remington 700 hanging from her shoulder, not the confident killer she was determined to become. What they were looking at was one of Joseph Graham's Chosen, there among them stalking through their ranks.

Two weeks ago she'd been called up from the reserves in Tooele, a small forgotten town to the west along the edge of the Salt Flats where new recruits waited anxiously to join the ranks of the Revolutionist Front. Joseph Graham had come down and hand-picked her himself, watching, unbeknownst to Sam, as she scored hit after hit on targets eight hundred yards out despite the wavering sight picture from the heat and wind coming off the Flats. The spectacle that day had spiraled, Sam's peers retelling the story over and over with new details each time, hyping her legend before she ever fired a single shot in combat. And now, after fourteen days of waiting around at the mountainside camp, Sam had been summoned.

She made her way through the tents, through the trees and the shadows of the forest, past the huddled groups of rebel fighters waiting for their chance to get down into the valley and give the government pigs what they deserved. She skirted around the clearing where no one was allowed to venture for fear of being spotted by military drones or satellites. Stealth was most important at this point since the American military had established a fortified base in the valley and the RF were still only hiding out in the mountains. So there were rules to follow. Just three days ago a new, wide-eyed recruit had stumbled through the clearing in midday and earned himself twenty lashes in front of the entire camp. Even through the gag in his mouth Sam had heard his cries of pain. Weakness. He deserved every moment of it.

The command tent was at the top of a hill next to a camouflaged radio tower with an old Chinese-made stealth jammer hardwired into the base, blocking transmissions from being located by bouncing dummy signals to every reflective surface within a hundred miles. The military knew the RF were there, just not where exactly. Hence, stealth and discipline.

An armed guard at the entrance to the tent saw Sam coming and challenged her with a password. Not like she didn't belong there in camp, but Joseph Graham was a smart—and more importantly, cautious—man. He changed codes almost hourly and gave each person he called for a different one to ensure that no one showed up who didn't belong. This kept potential spies from nosing information or would-be assassins from getting too close.

Sam gave the correct password and the sentry pulled the tent flap open to let her in. It was a large space, like a small building made of multiple tents sewn together. Several people inside paused to look as she entered. It was hot in there, not enough power to run the air-conditioning, jamming equipment, and radios all at the same time. A fan worked in the corner, flapping the edges of some maps on the table in the middle of the room. A weapon rack was tucked in one corner holding several Russian AKs and a few old American M4s.

Sam identified who appeared to be the person in charge. "I'm Sam Cross," she said. "I was called to see Joseph Graham." She tried not to let the pride show too much. Better to act as if she was right where she belonged and not some giddy child in the presence of greatness. She'd spent enough of her life dealing with people who thought of her as nothing more than a pretty, helpless little thing. But times had changed.

The commander looked her over, his eyes stopping on her Remington. It was an older rifle, like most of the RF's gear, but it had already become her signature piece of equipment. A model 700 chambered for .308 ammunition, bolt-action, ten-round magazine adapter, with a 12x40 Mule-Optics range-finding scope and custom long barrel that gave Sam the extra reach she needed to be confident shooting upward of a thousand yards if needed. It was an extension of her own body and it had once, many years ago, belonged to her father.

"One moment," the commander said before disappearing behind a flap. The others in the tent watched her while she waited. It made her uncomfortable, but she had to remind herself that they were looking at her with respect now and not the contempt and disregard she'd once thought was all she deserved.

The commander came back. "He'll see you now. This way," he said, gesturing to a back room. Sam left them to their planning.

Joseph Graham was seated behind a desk, the

space dimly lit by small, yellow lights giving the feel of candlelight. There were old books on his desk that Sam wondered if he'd actually read or just had out for show. *Of course he read them, don't be stupid,* she thought, suddenly afraid that he could tell what she was thinking. He watched her from behind a pair of large reading glasses, his green uniform crisp and clean, his neatly trimmed beard showing specks of gray that gave him an air of wisdom. The frown on his face could've been careful regard or displeasure, both of which made Sam even more nervous.

Stop it. You're here because he picked you. You're not a helpless child, so stop thinking like one.

Sam lifted her chin. "Sir, Sam Cross reporting."

Joseph Graham breathed deeply through his nose, then gestured to the empty seat in front of his desk. Sam slid into the chair and tucked her rifle between her knees.

"I've been contemplating the idea of purpose," Graham said, his eyes locked on Sam, searching. "It's the driving force in our lives, the reason we get up each morning and continue to draw breath, the reason we stand tall in the face of overwhelming opposition. 'He who has a why to live for can bear almost any how.' Do you know who said that?"

"No, sir."

Graham watched her quietly for a moment before continuing. "We have a great task ahead of us, securing a stable region to build a new order, safe from the old government's poisonous touch. We have a chance to do something that hasn't been done in almost three hundred years, something that is long past due. There are strong leaders in place already working to establish a foundation for the new America in the heart of California, but we must protect them, give them time to grow. It will be difficult, but the pain is necessary to achieve victory. Do you know why you're here, Samantha Cross?"

"I was sent for, sir."

Graham urged her to continue with nothing more than a look.

"I was chosen," she said.

"Yes," Graham said. "You were chosen. Chosen by me when I went down to the training grounds to see the brave men and women who have *chosen* to join the fight against tyranny and oppression, who have *chosen* to be a part of the reformation, to tear down the old and build anew. That is the purpose of this war, the purpose of this rebellious army. But we are an army of individuals, each with our own purpose." He paused, then said, "Tell me about your family, Samantha."

Fear clamped an icy hand around her throat. That feeling of helplessness, weakness, came rushing up and almost won, but Sam squeezed the rifle in her hands and locked it down. She was not that child anymore. "My family," she said, "died when I was young."

"I would dare to say you are still young," Graham said. He pulled out a file and began flipping through it. "August 2, 2032," he said. "Five years ago. They came to your family farm in Amarillo, Texas, to claim your brother for conscription. Tell me about that day, Samantha." He set the file down, laced his fingers together, and stared at her through the glinting lenses of his glasses.

Sam clenched her jaw, memories flashing through

her mind. The military trucks trailing clouds of dust as they raced toward the house. Pa yelling. John being dragged away. The shooting, running, watching her house smolder while she hid in the hills. "I was fourteen," she said. "I ran and hid while they murdered my family."

"You regret that," Graham said. "Running away."

"Of course. I mean, yessir."

Joseph Graham climbed from his chair and came around the desk to place a hand on Sam's shoulder. She felt the strength of his resolve radiating from him. "You were but a child when you witnessed the murder of your family," he said. "A great and terrible thing. You were scared, understandably so. Many wouldn't have even had the courage to flee, but you did what you had to to survive. To live so that you may see vengeance brought upon your tormentors, and in doing so help bring about a new order."

"Yessir. I've thought of nothing else since that day."

"And you're not scared anymore," Graham said.

"No, sir, I'm not."

He nodded. "Then there is your purpose. That force down in the valley isn't made of men or women. They're not sons or daughters, brothers or sisters. They are willful servants to a tyrannical regime, content to obey their imperial masters who order death and destruction upon their very own people. We will not allow them to subjugate us. We fight for a new order, at all costs, and any who stand in our way are not worthy of life.

"You, Samantha Cross, are no longer a frightened child, but an instrument of vengeance, the silent hand of death. With that rifle, you will be my reaper in the valley. Are you prepared for that great responsibility? Are you ready?"

Sam thought of her father gunned down on the front lawn, her mother dead inside the house, and her brother taken away forever. "Yessir," she said. "I'm ready."

4
THERE ARE ALWAYS CONSEQUENCES

Trent had been filling out paperwork at the shop when shooting broke out near the perimeter and Staff Sergeant Grader called to pass on the order for every able body to get to the walls and provide force protection. The FOB was short-staffed and they needed everyone they could spare. Now Trent was hoofing it toward the nearest tower, boots slapping dirt, MX in his hands, equipment pack bouncing heavily on his back. He tried to control his breathing, time it with his footfalls. The strap of his helmet dug into his chin.

Breathe in, breathe out. Boots pounding.

The gunfire seemed to come from every direction. The walls suddenly didn't seem so protective. He got to the tower, ran up the steps. His legs were burning, heart hammering. Took him a second to catch his breath.

On the wall Private Gibson and Corporal Macken from Third Platoon were firing indiscriminately; Gibson with his MX, and Macken on an M37 heavy machine gun. The weapon was deafeningly loud, links and spent casings raining down around their feet as Macken pivoted and sent an ungodly amount of rounds across Interstate 80 into Shanty Town.

Trent slapped Macken on the shoulder and shouted over the pounding machine gun. "The fuck are you shooting at?"

Macken stopped shooting, twisted his head to look over his shoulder. "Saw muzzle flashes!" He was shouting louder than necessary. Trent's ears were ringing just from the few seconds he'd been standing there, he could only imagine the damage that was being done to Macken's ears. Then Macken leaned into the sights and opened up the M37 again.

"Are you sure?" Trent yelled. "You're not even identifying targets! Hey! Calm the fuck down, you're wasting ammo—"

A bullet rang off the tower. A tracer from somewhere in Shanty Town streaked by just above their heads.

"Jesus!"

Trent shouldered his MX. Muscle memory took over; barrel up, cheek to sights, selector switch to semi, finger on trigger. Squeeze.

The MX kicked, one spent casing flipping up and out of the breach, spinning off over the edge of the wall. A brief moment of panic as he realized he, too, hadn't bothered to identify a target. But the moment passed and the rest came easy. He pulled the trigger, felt the recoil, pulled it again. It was exhilarating, his heart was racing. He felt an awkward smile spread across his face, pulling on his chin strap. A strange sensation, since he knew there was nothing funny going on. He kept firing until the last round was spent, the last casing sailed off, bolt locked to the rear. He dropped the empty magazine, traded it for a new one. Thumbed the bolt release, felt it slam into place, another round locked and ready to be fired.

But he didn't let loose. It had gone quiet. Macken cracked open the slide cover on the M37, slapped another belt of ammo in place. Gibson was staring wide-eyed down the sights of his MX. The shooting had stopped. Silence, save for the ringing in Trent's ears.

Across the highway, Shanty Town was still. The first huts were maybe two hundred meters out and from that distance, it didn't look like they'd done any damage at all. Trent watched, waited for more muzzle flashes. Nothing came. Nothing moved.

Then a small four-door car came speeding out of the ghetto. It shot out from a narrow lane, bounced over the rutted dirt path that led to the highway, screeched onto the blacktop, and sped off toward the west. Trent, Macken, and Gibson watched it leave.

"They're headed to RF territory," Macken said. "I bet those were legit rebels."

Gibson slapped his buddy on the shoulder. "Damn, dude, we just had a no-shit firefight with the enemy."

"Fuck yeah," Trent said as he lit a cigarette with a shaky hand. Macken and Gibson did the same. They stood behind the tower wall laughing and smoking, each of them fighting to hide the nervous comedown. For all the celebration, their eyes kept scanning over Shanty Town.

Trent dropped his pack and unzipped it. He pulled a cleaning kit from an inside pouch and tossed it to Macken. "Here, get that 37 cleaned. I'll go grab you some more ammo cans."

Macken handed the kit to Gibson. "Here, *you* clean this. I'll keep an eye out." He scooped his MX from the weapon rack. Gibson didn't argue, just bent to wipe down the machine gun. Trent left them in the tower, exhilarated, and thankful he was safe behind the walls of the FOB.

* * *

After the fighting broke out, the FOB shut down communications with the outside world. No phones, no video chat, no email. Not even handwritten mail was sent out until Intel could filter the facts for the media. Called it Operational Security, but really, it wasn't much more than cultivating propaganda. The news on the East Coast would spin it in some way to push President Haymond's agenda. Fear was a great motivator for spending, too, and America needed to get back on the global market.

Now, three days after the citywide attack, Trent and Simard sat outside the armory shop playing a game of Poor-Man's Poker while the FOB settled back down.

"You know what's weird to think?" Simard said, cigarette bobbing between his lips as he fanned out his cards.

"What's that," Trent said, checking his own shitty hand.

"To think that at some point our experience here is gonna end."

Trent looked up. "I, for one, actually look forward to it."

"I don't mean in the valley, I mean life. Existence in the universe and shit."

"Okay."

Simard dropped a five-spot on the crate they'd set up as a playing table. "No, I'm serious," he said. "Think about it, everything you know comes from what you experience in life. Once you die, it's all over, it might as well have never existed."

"Jesus Christ. Call." Trent matched the bet.

"Like, think of your favorite movie." Simard discarded a pair of cards, drew two more, then looked at Trent, waiting.

Trent exchanged three cards, not holding much hope of getting anything good. "You want to know my favorite movie?"

"Yeah."

"*Tides of Woe,* I guess."

Simard took a drag from his cigarette. "Damn, dude. I thought you were one of the happy-go-lucky ones. That shit's depressing as fuck."

"Don't kid yourself, I'm a glutton for anguish," Trent said. "Why I joined the Army. Your bet."

"Well anyway, just think, at some point you won't ever be able to watch that again because your turn here in this universe will be over. Done. Vanished into fuckin' nothing."

Trent set his cards down. "You always talk like this when you play cards?"

Simard shrugged. "I don't know why I think like this sometimes."

"From the shooting, maybe?"

"Nah. It's what we came here for, right? You know I had to give an official statement after the attack the other day? We shot up a car by the east tower. I just ran up there with some guys from a unit out of North Carolina and we lit this fuckin' sedan up."

Trent tried to think of something to say. The usual *better them than us* mantra didn't taste quite right. "You ever wonder if we're in the right here?" he asked instead.

Simard raised an eyebrow at that. "You mean stopping a bunch of crazies who think dragging federal loyalists into the street and executing them will change the way the president thinks?" Simard said. "These fuckers are nuts and they're tryin' to destroy the country, not save it. Rapid City's under rebel control and look at that place. Fuckin' bodies swinging from streetlamps on the news every night. Trails of refugees heading for the Canadian border. Pulled down all those statues of presidents they used to have downtown, blew up huge chunks of Mount Rushmore like that'll change anything. The place is a symbol of what the rebellion really is. Mass murder, rape, human trafficking. No police, no local government, no law, just like they wanted and it's fuckin' hell. Imagine that across the entire country."

Trent chewed on that for a minute. "Yeah. I guess so. I just hope this war is a path to resolution and not just, like . . . America's death throe, like Graham said." He paused to give Simard a chance to agree, but Simard said nothing. "I just hope I'm on the right side of history," Trent finished.

Simard leaned back in his chair. "You're looking way too far into it. You said you joined the Army because you want to go to college, right? Army's gonna pay for it. Just worry about that if it makes you feel better. All that other *what-if* talk is just gonna fuck you up. Remember, you can't do any good for anyone else until you take care of yourself first, right?"

"Well if that's how you're looking at it, maybe you *should* go fuck Kinneson," Trent said, trying to lighten the mood and move on from the topic.

Simard made a face like he was weighing the pros and cons. "Yeah, well . . ." His gaze drifted over Trent's shoulder. "Ah shit. Heads up, here comes Sergeant Wade."

"What?" Trent twisted, saw the platoon sergeant

marching toward them. A broad-shouldered Black man in his early thirties with a permanent scowl, Sergeant First Class Wade struck an imposing figure. He didn't bother with all the screaming and yelling some of the other NCOs seemed to love, mostly because he didn't need to. With the look on his face and his brisk, confident stride, people just knew he was tough. And he was marching straight for Trent and Simard.

Sergeant Wade came to a halt, muscles shoving his arms out so they hung away from his body like an action movie star. He glowered down at the two of them.

"Specialist Trent," Wade said.

Trent stood from his chair, almost knocking it over, standing at parade rest. "Yes, Sergeant."

Wade slid his gaze over the cards on the table, then back to Trent. "Captain Holmstead needs to see you in his office. Come with me."

"Roger that, Sergeant." Trent grabbed his MX, clipped it to his chest rig, and followed Wade to the captain's office.

There was no conversation on the walk, no more detail about what the captain wanted. Trent wondered if he'd have to give a report on his actions the other day. Maybe he'd get a medal for his heroics.

Heroics.

For what? He didn't do anything anyone else hadn't done that day. Something else then. He tried to remember how long it'd been since his last promotion. Was he up for Sergeant? Excitement quickened his steps so he walked alongside Sergeant Wade. Quietly, Trent imagined the promotion board before him, asking questions, nodding solemnly at his profound answers.

Wade led Trent through the plywood maze of the

administration offices and came to Captain Holmstead's door. He knocked twice. Through the plywood Trent heard the captain's voice call them in.

Wade pushed the door open and let Trent through.

Captain Holmstead sat behind his desk, First Sergeant McGuinness stood in the corner. Sergeant First Class Wade moved to the other corner. Trent felt nervous at all the rank in the room, but he was ready to prove himself. It occurred to him suddenly that his section chief wasn't there. Odd, Sergeant Grader should've been the one to lead Trent into the room.

And then he saw what was on the captain's desk.

Lying on top of the polished surface right next to the brass name plate was the disassembled receiver and trigger mechanism for one of the MXs he'd modified for Third Platoon. His heart sank. Skin went clammy. Throat instantly dry.

Captain Holmstead leaned his elbows on the desk, pressed his fingertips together. "Do you know what weapon system these parts are from, Specialist Trent?"

Trent snapped to the position of attention, struggled to find his voice. "Yes, sir," he said. "They're from an MX."

The captain nodded. "The Armatec Industries M10 carbine. Five-five-six by forty-five millimeter NATO, air-cooled, gas-operated, magazine-fed compact assault rifle produced in Norfolk, Virginia. This model's been battle-tested in almost every environment known to man. Took Armatec ten years just to perfect the design for a military-grade assault rifle that can function with lethal consistency in a compact, maneuverable design. Each weapon costs the government two thousand American dollars." Captain Holmstead stared at Trent. "Do you notice anything wrong with these pieces?"

Trent fought the urge to vomit. "Yes, sir."

"And what is wrong with them?"

"The firing mechanism has been modified to allow the weapon to fire on full auto, sir."

"Who modified them, Specialist?"

Calm. Breathe. "I did, sir."

The captain leaned back in his chair. The ceiling fan hummed overhead, fluttering the edges of some papers on the desk; the soft murmur of radio conversations vibrated through the thin wooden walls. Trent stood rigid, fists clamped to his sides, eyes locked on the wall just above the company commander's head. He could feel Wade and McGuinness's statue-like presence looming behind him.

Captain Holmstead continued. "Three days ago the enemy made a concerted effort at driving American forces out of the valley. During that fighting, several squads from Third Platoon completely ran out of ammunition in the middle of the engagement and had to retreat prematurely, leaving the rest of the fire teams undermanned. Did you even once consider the possibility of this inevitable outcome before you vandalized government equipment?"

"Sorry, sir, no."

"Don't fucking apologize now, Specialist," Sergeant Wade snapped.

Trent didn't know what to say, so he said nothing.

"You didn't consider it," Captain Holmstead said. "That kind of lack of foresight and selfish action is not tolerated in the 117th. You are hereby stripped of the rank of specialist, and demoted to private first class. The cost of replacement parts for the weapons you've altered will come out of your pay. Also, since you can't be trusted to continue working in the armory . . ." He saw the expression on Trent's face, lifted his hand. "Although I'm sure you'll learn your lesson here, it would be too tempting for others to come to you in the future with more special requests and I don't want to foster the kind of environment that could persuade my troops to make poor decisions again. You'll be reassigned to First Platoon under Staff Sergeant Creon."

Trent's heart pounded in his chest, felt like the ground had disappeared beneath him.

"You'll be fulfilling the duties of a general infantry soldier for the indeterminate future of this deployment," the captain said. "We will outsource weapons maintenance and repairs to the Third Mountain again until the unit acquires a new armorer. Hopefully, this lesson will serve to teach many others about following orders. As for you, you'll adhere to the military code of conduct and serve with the utmost integrity from here on out, is that understood?"

"Yes, sir." Trent choked on the words as they scratched their way up his throat. He felt dizzy, a thousand thoughts racing through his head and not one of them coherent. He tried to go back in time, imagine himself saying no to Jameson, picturing the sergeant walking away angrily as Trent upheld the integrity of his charge. Didn't do any good, though, since he couldn't go back in time. Nothing would undo what just happened. He was no longer the 117th's armorer.

Now he was infantry.

"That's all, Private Trent."

Trent snapped a crisp salute, turned on his heel, and forced his legs to carry him out of the room. Sergeant First Class Wade followed him out.

"Hold up, Trent," he said.

Trent stopped.

Wade reached up and plucked the rank from Trent's chest. Stuck a new tab in its place. Trent didn't have to look, he knew what it was. He'd been that rank before.

"Now you can go, Private," Wade said. "Sergeant Creon will be expecting you."

Trent was in a daze, his deployment flipped upside down. "Roger that," he mumbled.

He spent the rest of the afternoon gathering his things from the shop and clearing out his bunk pod, slowly, delaying the inevitable. It was just before dark when he finally found the courage to head for First Platoon's barracks. One thought kept going through his head, spinning like the ceiling fan in Holmstead's office.

I'm infantry now.

5
AIN'T NO EASY RIDE NOW

Trent tipped the fuel can upside down and emptied the contents into the metal burn barrel he'd been ordered to pull from the latrine as part of his welcoming detail to First Platoon. He took the lighter from his pocket, flicked it a few times before igniting a wad of old magazine papers, then tossed them into the barrel. He watched the image of Candice Holiday—last year's hot movie model—singe and curl up as the rotten sludge began to smolder. He tossed more wadded paper into the barrel and then stuck a length of rebar down into the muck and stirred as the contents burned down to ash. The concoction of shit and piss and fuel gagged him, stung his eyes and turned his stomach.

Across from the row of plasti-mold stalls that made up the latrines, lines were forming for breakfast chow outside the dining facility. But Trent had been ordered to empty the latrines before he was allowed to eat, so he wrenched the metal rod back and forth and did everything he could to not look at the boiling stew.

The breeze shifted, a cloud of black smoke twisted around him. He coughed, gagged so hard he almost vomited. A few people in the chow line looked over. Trent spat. How quickly things had turned. He'd had it made, an easy gig on the FOB, combat pay without the combat. Hell, Sergeant Grader had pretty much let

Trent handle himself. It had been easy street. A cake-walk.

Then he went and fucked up and his cakewalk be-came a trudge through shit. Literally.

Trent gave the rebar a twist and felt a new level of anger rise in him.

"Private Trent."

Trent cringed. There was no need to emphasize the rank. He turned to see a heavy-framed southerner named Corporal Bodine coming over from the chow hall. He was dusting bread crumbs off his uniform as he closed on Trent.

"Ser'ant Creon wants er'body in the war room by zero nine," Bodine said in his thick southern accent. "Finish what yer doin' an' don't be late."

A week ago Trent was the same pay-grade as this motherfucker. "You got it, Corporal," he said. The breeze shifted and Bodine scrunched his nose, waved a hand in front of his face. "Jesus Christ," he said be-fore trudging off.

Trent stood by the latrines, one hand on the rebar sticking up from the muck, a spiral of greasy smoke twisting on the wind. He checked his watch: 0843. Guess he'd miss breakfast again.

Trent pushed his way through the aisle and found a seat near the end of the row with the rest of Second Squad, where he'd been assigned. The steel chair scraped the floor as he settled in next to Private O'Malley, an eighteen-year-old out of upstate New York. O'Malley was one of those kids who was excited to get into the shit so he could go home and tell badass stories to impress his friends. He had the regulation buzz cut, wore his dog tags at all times, and would constantly say things like *I hope I get to shoot at someone,* completely ignoring the point that if he were in a situation where he could shoot at someone it was highly likely someone would be shooting back.

"You stink like shit," O'Malley said.

Trent grunted. "This whole place stinks like shit."

Bodine sank into the seat next to Trent. All of First Platoon was cramming into the war room that was really only meant for small-scale briefings, but today seemed to be something important. Staff Sergeant Creon stood at the end of the row, arms crossed, keeping an eye on his squad. Other squad leaders stood around the perimeter ushering in soldiers. First Lieutenant Vickers and Sergeant First Class Lancer hovered at the front of the room with a blank screen mounted to the wall behind them. A single fan turned back and forth in the corner, uselessly. There were no windows, no air conditioning, and the sun's heat was radiating through the arched metal roof.

Once the last of First Platoon had filed in and found seats, the doors were closed and the lights flicked off. The screen blinked on showing a map of Salt Lake Valley. SFC Lancer called the room to attention, then stepped aside for Lieutenant Vickers.

"Listen up, gentlemen," the LT said, pulling a clicker from his pocket. "The 117th is being tasked to take back sections of the city in a joint operation with several other infantry units as well as some Marine elements, being called Operation Aggressor. Alpha Company's First and Second Platoons will be working with units from Bravo and Charlie to clear sectors in West Valley, South Salt Lake, and into Taylorsville." He thumbed the clicker and several yellow circles appeared over the sectors just mentioned. "You'll be working toward West Jordan and the regional airfield. The goal is to push the RF back and set up command posts and traffic control points with the intent of establishing permanent forward camps throughout the valley. Intel believes the RF are planning to try and establish their own fortified base at the Vircon mining complex in the southwest sector. We need to ensure they do not succeed, but we cannot afford to deploy troops that far out without first clearing the city and establishing supply lines. Salt Lake is the key to their foothold in this rebellion. We take Salt Lake, we squash the Revolutionist-fucking-Front."

A roar of approval from the audience. O'Malley elbowed Trent, smirking.

"You'll need that motivation," Lieutenant Vickers said. "This is going to be a long haul. The RF are looking for a fight, they want to prove themselves. This is where we put an end to their enthusiasm." The screen zoomed in, showing a close-up of a few city blocks, clouds of black smoke rising from fires centered at major intersections. "The first objective is designated Sector Bravo," Vickers said. "APCs will be taking you downtown where you'll clear blocks building by building. Once the area's been secured, an Army engineer unit will rally to your location and begin constructing a fortified CP that will become a permanent camp. We'll be moving out at zero hundred hours under cover of dark. With the late hour and the citywide curfew in effect, we hope to minimize civilian casualties. There are still innocent people out there who need order restored. We are not here to inflict misery on them. Keep that in mind. Gentlemen."

With that, Lieutenant Vickers turned off the screen, tucked the clicker in his pocket, and marched off.

The lights came back on and SFC Lancer stepped up. "First Platoon, you have nine hours to prep and get your shit in order. Be ready to stage at eighteen hundred, ready to roll out at zero hundred. Headhunters, this is the long haul. Best to assume you won't be back to the FOB for quite a while. We're moving out to establish new camps, you can probably guess who'll be running them. Prep yourselves mentally. Dismissed."

Before he even bothered to pack, Trent went straight to the phones to call Alley. The line out the door seemed to stretch for fucking miles. He waited for almost two and a half hours in the sun before he finally made it inside the facility, signed a clipboard and was sent to a booth. He sank into the plastic chair tucked between the plywood dividers, leaned over the counter, and picked up the phone, one of the antiquated types that still had cords. Every conversation was routed through OPSEC monitoring. Part of the standard-issue deployment packet was a sheet with all the things you weren't allowed to say or talk about. There was even a section with prepared generic responses in case someone asked about a sensitive topic.

The system registered a user and connected Trent to a contracted dispatch company. A Canadian accent on the other end asked for the contact number and thanked him for his service before connecting the call. It rang several times, long enough for Trent to feel the beginnings of a bad mood welling up at having had to wait forever just to get a voicemail. He sat hunched in the cubicle, heel pumping anxiously as the call connected.

"Hello?" A woman's voice answered. It ended with the rise of inflection that indicated a question. Obviously, she didn't recognize the number.

"Hi, Alley."

"Oh, Jimmy. Hi."

An awkward, long silence through the line. Not quite the response he'd been hoping for.

"So, uh . . . how are you?" Trent asked.

"I'm good, Jimmy. How are you? You safe?"

"Yeah. Well . . . yeah." He wasn't sure how to go about this, but he felt like he had to tell her he was going to be away for a while. And possibly in mortal danger. "Look, uh. I can't really say much, but I might not be able to call you again for a while."

Again, silence.

"Alley?"

"Yeah," her voice crackled through the phone. "It's just . . . getting hard."

"What's that mean?"

"You not being here. It's not easy."

Anger flared in Trent's chest, his heart quickened. "Yeah, well it's no cakewalk here, either."

"I'm sorry," she said. "I can't even imagine."

The anger melted away. Trent took a breath. "I didn't mean . . . it's fine. I'm just under a lot of stress here." He hadn't told her—or anyone back home— that he'd been demoted. He felt ashamed, which made him feel angry, and that anger was bubbling to the surface a lot quicker these days. This was the last chance he'd get to hear Alley's voice for some time, he didn't want it to be a fight. In fact, it could be the last chance he'd ever get to hear her voice. The reality hit like an ice shelf breaking off in his gut. He decided to steer the conversation to more pleasant grounds. "How's your summer going?"

She seemed to perk up at that. "Good. I started a new job."

"Oh that's great, where at?"

"It's a secretary position at Allied Insurance in Manhattan. Full-time with benefits. Dad knew some people there and got me in."

"Man, that's great to hear. You like it so far?"

"Sure," she said. "The work keeps me busy and the staff are nice. I'm getting in with some really influential people, too."

Something unsettled in Trent. A feeling of distance, maybe. The realization that his girlfriend, his life, was outside his reach, but others were there to fill his place. Vaguely, he remembered his conversation with Simard. "That's good, Alley. That's really good."

"I'm actually getting ready to go to the beach for a long weekend," she said. "Jess should be on her way over soon, so it's actually good you called before I left."

"Tell her I said hi," Trent said. "What beach you going to?" He was already picturing her tanned body under the sun, bikini clinging to her curves. He could almost smell her hair and the lotion.

The phone thumped like Alley was moving around. "Oh, uh, we're going with some friends from work to a beach house in Jersey. Brady's got this place right on the water. There's a bunch of us going and—"

"Who's Brady?"

"—the weather's supposed to be beautiful, so I'm pretty excited. I haven't really had a chance to go to the ocean this summer with the new job and all. I'm on this outreach committee that's been working a lot of weekends."

"Alley. Who's Brady?"

"What? Oh, he's just a friend from work."

"Is he also on this outreach committee?"

A pause, movement somewhere in the background. "Yeah, he's a junior partner so it's his project. It's a good connection for me—"

"Does Brady have a girlfriend?"

"What's that matter? It's not like, you know, anything like that."

"But you're going to his beach house."

"Jimmy. Come on, this isn't easy for me. I miss you every day. It's good for me to keep an active social life. Look, Jess is going to be here soon and I have to get ready. Call me as soon as you're able to, okay?"

He squeezed the phone, heard the plastic creak in his fist. If he clenched his jaw any harder his teeth were likely to shatter. "Yeah. I'll call you. I love you."

Static in the earpiece, commotion in the background. "Okay, Jimmy. Miss you."

A click and the line went dead.

Trent sat there for a moment fighting down the rage welling inside. Maybe he was being irrational. Maybe he wasn't. Nothing like being two thousand miles away stuck in a fucking burning trash-pit of a city getting ready to go kill-or-be-killed and thinking about some yuppie fuck spending the weekend with his girlfriend. *Brady*. What kind of name was that? Guess it didn't matter what kind of name you had if you were a junior partner with loads of fucking cash and a beach house in Jersey. Guy probably had dozens of women lined up to fill his pad. And Alley was another on his hit list.

Someone tapped Trent on the shoulder.

"You alright, Private?" asked the soldier working the tent. "Line's disconnected."

Trent slammed the phone on the hook. "Yeah, I'm just fucking fine." He rose from the booth and stormed out.

Trent spent the rest of the day prepping for the mission and trying not to think of home. He'd managed to pilfer some tools from his armorer's kit before signing it over to the battalion, and now they were jammed into his ruck, which was close to bursting with extra shirts, underwear, socks, a spare uniform, a sleeping roll, rain gear, a few extra water bottles, a toiletry kit, some field manuals, and MREs. He had to brush the dust off his tactical vest since it'd been sitting under his cot for most of the deployment thus far. As he looked at it propped against his ruck, he knew those easy days were over. He could only imagine what it would look like soon enough. He checked the armor plating, checked the snap connections, tightened the straps of the flex-weave shoulder pieces. The hydration bladder was filled, the drinking tube looped over the shoulder. Quick-release MX mount clipped in place. Rifle cleaned. Magazines loaded.

Now Trent sat outside the Quonset hut and waited, chain-smoking cigarettes and thinking about Alley. He imagined her getting in the car, driving up to the beach house. Pictured her running up to Brady, wrapping her arms around him. A not-so-innocent start to a weekend of half-naked fun. Then Trent's imagination turned on him like a sadistic devil on his shoulder whispering in his ear. More images flashed through his head.

A stranger's hand on Alley's bare thigh.

Alley sitting on Brady's lap.

Trent remembered the nights he'd spent with her, the two of them up until dawn making love, their bodies sweaty, sliding together, the alcohol numbing their senses. Only it wasn't Trent's face, it wasn't even Trent at all. Now it was some asshole named Brady.

Trent sucked the cigarette down to the butt, dropped it to the sand and stamped it out with the heel of his boot. All around him soldiers from First Platoon were gathered and waiting under a canopy of stars blurred by the blanket of smoke hanging over the valley, a general sense of anxiety drifting through the ranks. It was still miserably hot, each of them sweating through their uniforms as they watched for the APCs.

When the armored vehicles finally arrived someone shouted and everyone jumped to their feet. Staff Sergeant Creon came down the line, double-checking his soldiers.

"On your feet, Headhunters," he shouted. "Get aggressive, it's time to show these rebel fucks the extent of our displeasure." Soldiers barked the standard approval. Sounded like a bunch of idiots practicing karate punches. The first of several APCs stopped in the road before the Quonsets, air brakes hissing. The heavy armored doors dropped open and soldiers began filing in.

Trent lifted his tactical vest, slid it up and over his shoulders, then struggled to get his ruck on over it. A bit of shimmying and he got everything in place, clipped his MX to the chest rig, and turned to get on the nearest APC.

Staff Sergeant Creon was standing in the way.

"Private Trent," he said. "Time to man up and prove your worth. Don't fuck up or jeopardize my squad or I'll leave your sorry ass out there in the streets, you hear me?"

Fuck off, you cocksucking piece of shit. "Roger, Sergeant."

Creon glanced over Trent's gear, tugged on the shoulder straps, then shoved him toward the APC. Trent's boots thumped up the ramp. He ducked through the doorway and squeezed into a web seat, his ruck pressed against the wall shoving his torso so far forward he was practically bent double. His MX dangled between his knees, barrel pointed to the floor. Small bulbs in the ceiling lit the tight space in harsh orange light. It smelled like diesel and engine exhaust. A vent somewhere overhead pumped hot, stale air. More soldiers piled in and everyone was shoved deeper and deeper inside. Finally pressed in as tight as they could go—shoulder to shoulder, knees jostling for room, elbows dug into ribs, straps and belts biting into skin—Creon waved down the line and climbed in. A mechanical whine and the ramp lifted, closed, locks slamming into place.

A brief moment of panic as Trent felt his hands go numb, head swimming, the pounding in his chest threatening to burst his heart. He closed his eyes, fought down the claustrophobia. He tried to breathe, sent his imagination somewhere pleasant, like an open meadow or a sandy beach. Immediately, his mind saw Alley there, smiling, reaching for him. Then someone else—some handsome, rich fuck—stepped in, grabbed her hand, and tugged her away.

A fist thumped into Trent's knee. "Don't be a bitch."

Trent opened his eyes. Bodine sat to his left, looking at him. "Fuck you, Corporal," Trent said.

Bodine nodded. "That's the spirit."

The lights winked out and red LEDs came on. Everyone looked like they were covered in blood. Harsh shadows swarmed over human faces, turning soldiers into demons. Black sockets where eyes used to be. Skeleton hands clutching rifles.

Trent blew a breath through puffed cheeks. His head was swimming. He reached for the drinking tube on his left shoulder and sucked down some warm water.

Engines powered up, the APC lurched, and they were off, the soldiers inside swaying and bouncing. The unsettling feeling of movement without the visual affirmation did nothing for Trent's panic attack. Somewhere up front through the hatch, radios beeped and clicked, voices called out orders.

The APC drivers were apparently taking the scenic route across the FOB as they stopped, started, stopped, started. Trent tried to figure which gate they were heading to, but it was impossible. Then an overhead speaker announced they'd finally left the FOB and were passing through civilian territory. Staff Sergeant Creon shouted over the engines.

"Listen up," he said. "Get your heads right. Curfew's in effect so anyone on the street is considered hostile. Watch your sectors of fire, identify your targets. Don't just go fucking shooting everything. We're here to tame the Wild West, not play in it."

Nervous laughter. A couple grunts.

"Now, triple-check your shit, weapon status amber."

Clatter of gear as everyone readied.

Trent fidgeted with his chin strap, checked the

snaps on his armor. He pulled the primary magazine from his cargo pocket and shoved it in the MX until it clicked, kept the selector switch on safe, no round in the chamber.

Then the speaker came on and told everyone they were in enemy territory and pushing through to Sector Bravo, ETA three mikes.

Everyone shifted nervously, ready to exit the confines of the armored transport. Staff Sergeant Creon crouched by the door, craned his head to look at the squad. "Headhunters, weapon status red. Stand by to exit." The APC came to a jolting stop and Creon had to reach for a webbing strap on the wall to steady himself. "Stay on my six," he said. "Form up on my position."

The locks *thunked* and the ramp dropped open. Creon was the first out, and then everyone twisted off their seats and poured out behind him. Bodine punched Trent in the knee one more time then ran off. Trent swallowed the fear and let adrenaline take over. Legs pressed him up, stumbling under the weight of the ruck. His boots pounded the ramp then hit pavement. He followed Bodine toward the sidewalk.

It was dark, streetlamps blown out, trash everywhere. Side streets were blocked off by piles of debris and stacks of burning tires. Vague forms darted through the shadows.

Trent splashed through a puddle of sludge, stumbled, fought for balance and slammed into a wall. Bodine was in front of him and already formed up behind Creon. O'Malley hit the wall behind Trent and slapped him on the shoulder. Somewhere ahead, gunshots popped, muzzle flashes appeared from windows and alleyways. Soldiers still in the street raced for cover behind cars and dumpsters. In a matter of seconds, First Platoon was in position and ready to press forward.

The enemy gunfire was slow and sporadic. Undisciplined. The rounds didn't seem like they were coming anywhere close. One squad formed up on the far side of the street and returned fire with concentrated and controlled bursts. The enemy gunfire faded quickly.

Creon called over his shoulder. "Fucking amateurs. Watch your corners. Let's go." He peeled off, found a doorway to the building on their left. Signaled for Bodine to kick it in, then followed behind as they slid inside. Trent came up behind Bodine again. They moved down a dark hallway checking doors and clearing corners until they came to a flight of stairs. Creon crouched, rifle pointed up. He motioned for Trent to come forward.

"Take point," he said.

When Trent paused, Creon grabbed him by the shoulder and shoved him up the stairs. Trent almost fell, but found his footing and raised his rifle. Bodine slapped Trent on the shoulder, letting him know he was on Trent's six, and they ascended. At the top they came to a ninety-degree turn down another hall. Lights flickered above, illuminating the stained carpet and cracked walls. As they began moving down the hall, a door opened at the far end and a man in a white tank top and boxer shorts stepped out holding a handgun. Trent dropped to one knee and aimed his rifle.

He froze. Rules of engagement said anyone on the street was deemed hostile, but they weren't on the street. He stared at the man, the man stared back, and in the blink of an eye, hoisted the pistol and pointed it at him. Trent's finger went to the trigger, pulled.

Nothing happened.

Shit fuck fuck I didn't chamber a round.

The light machine gun behind him ripped open on full auto, spraying the hallway. Bullets punched through the walls and shattered a window throwing the curtains out into the night. The man in the boxer shorts was thrown back into the wall, then slumped to the floor leaving streaks of blood on the peeling paint.

Bodine yanked Trent up by the drag strap on the back of his body armor. "Don't fuckin' take a knee," he said. "Jus' shoot the motherfucker."

Trent pulled the charging handle on his MX, loading a round in the chamber. Bodine shook his head and shoved Trent aside to take the lead.

They finally found a roof access and scrambled up. Two soldiers took rear guard covering the doorway while Creon led the rest of the squad to the edge where they could look down on the intersection in the middle of the block.

They could see squads moving in the street below, pressing toward the intersection. About a hundred meters ahead of them, people were scrambling over the trash piles to shoot at the advancing soldiers.

Creon took point. "Bodine, I want that M37 raining hell on those motherfuckers to the west." Creon gestured off to where a group of rebels were huddling together behind some parked cars getting ready to try to flank the troops below. "The rest of you cover First and Third squads. Identify your targets and take them out. I want enemy bodies in the street."

Everyone braced along the wall, picked out movement in the dark, and aimed their rifles. Trent squinted through his iron sights and tried to calm his breathing. Bodine dropped the M37 into position next to him and, at Creon's order, everyone opened up. Tracer rounds flashed down, sparks pinging off cars and cement. Trent zeroed in on a man with a Russian rifle firing at Third Squad. He aimed, released a breath, and squeezed the trigger.

The man fell onto a pile of trash and didn't move again.

The radios were going off, voices calling out enemy positions and their numbers. Trent found another target, a pair of fighters sliding through the shadows trying to move around their position. He aimed, took one of them out. The other dropped his weapon and ran off into the night.

They picked off more rebels as the night went on, while the other squads cleared the block at the ground level. Trent kept up and did his part. He thought of Alley. Thought of another man's hands on her. Leaned into the anger. After a while, it was like nothing. Which was good, because it was going to be a long night.

6
VENGEANCE AT HAND

Sam hitched a ride out of the mountains along a hidden road that led down into one of the slums at the edge of the valley. From there she'd linked up with another driver who took her into the city and brought her to the RF cell, secreted away in a warehouse district, where she was to meet with the field commander and get the details of her mission.

The driver pulled around back and two sentries standing watch from a loading dock gestured to them, indicating it was safe to get out. As soon as Sam shut the door the driver sped off, apparently eager to get out of the area.

"I'm here to see Commander Torres," Sam said, slinging her rifle over her shoulder.

They led her through the warehouse floor, past the workers pretending not to notice the armed rebels keeping watch from the scaffolding, past the towering shelves of plastic-wrapped materials, and down into the basement where another set of guards let them through a blast door left over from the Escalation Crisis back in '32. Beyond that was the field command center.

"Commander Torres, this is the new sniper," one of the guards said.

Sam wouldn't have been able to pick him out of the crowd as the commander, but she figured that was the idea. Made them harder to spot out in the open. Same reason none of the RF wore uniforms or insignia. Torres was tall and lean, the kind one gets from a life of surviving outdoors. Sun-darkened skin, deep creases around permanently narrowed eyes, long graying hair swept back into a ponytail. He came over and looked Sam up and down.

"You're Sam Cross?" he asked.

"Yessir," Sam said.

"Well, welcome to the fight, Cross," Commander Torres said, then motioned someone else over. "This is Rob Barrett," he said. "He'll be your teammate and spotter."

Rob Barrett was maybe a year or two older than Sam, in his early twenties at most. Short-cropped hair, square jaw. Broad shoulders. He wore a T-shirt and green cargo pants tucked into his boots, a sat-watch on his left wrist, a holstered pistol on his right hip. He stood with shoulders back, chest out. A strong posture, but not unnatural. An athletic type. A fighter. He extended his hand. "Nice to meet one of Joseph Graham's Chosen," he said.

"I'm Sam." She made sure to give a firm grip.

"I thought you were a man," he said. "I mean . . . well, when I heard your name, I just . . . I didn't . . . shit, I'm sorry." His face flushed, making his blue eyes seem even brighter.

"Rob's an honest man," Torres said, cutting short the awkward moment. "And he's quite the shooter himself, I'm confident you'll make an excellent team. Come." He led them over to a table with a map of the valley spread out on it. "Our mission here is to prevent the military from gaining control of the southeast sector. We're working on a plan to secure the Vircon mine in the name of the Revolution and use it as our own permanent base of operations in the valley. Once we do that, we'll have the footing we need to withstand the military forces, drive them out and liberate the city of federal occupation. But in the meantime we have to put pressure on the government pigs and keep them from gaining any more control of the city while we get things in order. That means fighting in the streets, face-to-face, up close and personal. We have teams in the city ready to go, some even already fighting back the oppressors. That's where you two come in.

"Your mission is to provide overwatch to the teams as needed. You'll be on the move running and gunning. It's a hard job, and a dangerous one, but you've been chosen for a reason." He put a hand on each of their shoulders and looked them in the eyes. "It's not just Joseph Graham counting on you, but the entire Revolution, and every soul down in that valley tired of the imperial overlords pushing their faces in the dirt. Remember that. Remember your purpose."

"Where you from?" Rob asked once Commander Torres had left them to settle.

"Texas," Sam replied as she dropped onto a cot and started field stripping her rifle.

Rob waited for her to say more. When he realized she wasn't going to, he continued. "I'm from California," he said. "Sacramento, actually. I was going to school in LA but quit when they declared martial law after the Philadelphia riots. Didn't want to just stand around and do nothing. Then when they started conscripting people again, well, I figured it was better to choose my own side. And, you know . . . I wasn't going to support a president turned dictator. Couple of people I knew were talking to these guys who were heading out to Nevada to join the resistance. They got wind I placed in a few long-distance shooting tournaments back home and next thing you know, I'm with the Revolutionist Front, out here taking the fight to the enemy. I even saw Joseph Graham once." Rob cleared his throat. "From a distance, though. Not like you saw him."

Sam wiped the bolt, oiled it, and slid it back into the rifle. She'd never really been comfortable talking with new people, even if Rob was friendly enough and not bad to look at. But that wasn't what she was here for.

He went on. "So, uh . . . why are you here? I mean, why do you want to fight?"

"I have my reasons."

"Fair enough. Lot of people here got their reasons they don't want to talk about. Anyway, we're glad to have you. Not too many snipers in our ranks. Mostly farmers who know how to shoot, but we take what we can get. I gotta ask, though, how old are you?"

She pinned him with a stare. "Nineteen."

"So . . . I mean, how did you . . . where'd you learn to shoot?"

"On the farm."

Silence again. He rubbed the back of his neck, opened his mouth then closed it. Sam realized she liked watching him squirm, then felt bad because of it. "It's alright," she said. "I'm just messing with you."

A grin spread across his face.

The curtain to their small living space drew back and one of the RF sub-commanders poked her head in. "Commander Torres needs you in the field," she said. "Military's on the move toward the West Valley sector, got a grid for you two to scout out and hold down until further orders. You have ten minutes. A car will be outside to take you into the city." She pulled the curtain closed as she left.

"I guess it's time," Rob said.

Sam met his eyes and wanted to smile, but found she rather liked the strong, silent game she'd been playing with him. But this wasn't a game. They were about to go out and meet the enemy.

7
A DANGEROUS CONTRACT

H oly shit."

Markus lowered the binoculars. From the overlook on the side of the mountain the mega-sprawl of Salt Lake stretched out below, the city packed tight into the valley, towering skyscrapers to the north surrounded by an expanse of overcrowded ghettos that spread right up to the base of the mountains. Millions of people crammed into that space. And beyond that, the flat gray water of the Great Salt Lake shimmering in the distance.

"We gotta drive through this shit?" Len asked as he lit a cigarette.

"If we care to meet the terms of the proposed contract, yes, we drive through this shit," Markus said.

"No different than Omaha," Temple added, rolling his neck and stretching after the long drive. "More mountains though."

Tripp was scrolling through news feeds on a touch screen, one leg hanging out the passenger-side door of his truck. "Looks like rebel activity's ramping up in the southwest sector. Military's enforcing a citywide curfew to weed the rebels out of the civilian populace and NRC's reporting another thirty-six people killed just last night in random fighting."

"Got our work cut out for us here, Chief," Rourke said as he stood at the edge of the overlook, sending a stream of piss over the side. The big guy was always itching to get in a fight.

"Our only concern is getting to—and then protecting—the Vircon facility," Markus said. "We're not contracted to fight the war."

"That must be the Vircon mine," Dieter, Markus's second-in-command, said, pointing across the valley to the crater carved into the western mountains.

"In the southwest sector," Tripp added.

Dieter pulled out a map and spread it over the hood. "We should stay on highways as much as possible," he said. "We can connect up with Interstate 15 here, cut over to 48, and that'll take us to the mine."

Markus checked the path Dieter traced. "Sounds good. We'll take lead, you guys stay tight on our six. No way to tell what's going on down there until we get in it. I want everyone close, don't get split up or separated. We hit the shit, we punch through and regroup later, clear?"

They were clear.

"Good. Let's load up and get out of here."

The crew checked their gear and weapons, then jumped back in the trucks. Break time was over.

The change from mountain road to crowded slum was instant. The pickups slid out of the forest and into a tight, cramped ghetto of run-down huts cobbled together from corrugated aluminum, flapping tarps, and rotten plywood. Streets that had once been paved were reduced to crumbled paths, rivers of sludge oozing along the curbs. The smell was rancid, raw sewage and garbage roasting in the sun.

People lurked at the edges, wandered through the street. Old cars rattled up and down the road. Children chased mangy dogs through trash-filled alleys.

A group of men huddled together at the street corner turned their eyes away as Markus and his crew drove past.

They hit the on-ramp to the highway and picked up speed.

Markus grabbed the radio. "Keep it tight, guys."

"Roger."

Dieter pointed out the turn and they swung off the highway and rolled through an industrial sector that abruptly turned into more crowded housing, tight and unwelcoming. Parked cars lined the streets, a few on cinder blocks, others nothing more than burned out shells. Graffiti marked the sides of buildings. Gang territory.

They passed a group of young men who unsubtly brandished the weapons in their hands. Markus spotted a pair of Uzis, a shotgun, and some American M4s. Several of the men made signs with their fingers.

Markus keyed the mic. "Stay sharp. Don't engage unless they initiate."

Then they were through and onto open road again.

They passed a small airport, and Dieter checked the map to confirm it was the South Valley Regional, not the international airfield that had been claimed by the Army farther north. They swung southwest and drove through more crowded ghetto before pulling onto a dirt road that took them all the way to the Vircon Industries mine.

They stopped outside the gate, which was not much more than a thin sheet of steel on rollers. An access door next to the gate opened and a man in a gray paramilitary uniform stepped out. He had a sidearm strapped to his thigh and a clipboard in one hand. On top of the wall, a pair of riflemen appeared and trained their weapons on Markus and his crew.

"I thought they said this place was in need of security?" Dieter said. "Seems like they're doing just fine."

The guard came up to the window.

"Who's in command here?" He asked in a thick British accent.

"I am," Markus said.

"State your name and business here," the Brit said.

"My name's Markus. This is my crew. We answered the bid for the private security detail."

The guard threw a glance at the ragged pickups and arched a brow. "That so?"

"That's so."

"Right then, let me verify." He plucked the radio from his belt and called it in. A moment later they were cleared and waved through the gate.

Inside the compound was an expanse of flat, hard-packed dirt and gravel with office trailers and a few permanent buildings. The perimeter walls stretched out to the north and south, a secondary perimeter within the compound marking off the logistics and headquarters area. Construction vehicles and flood-lights ringed the edges. For all the area within the compound, the British security element seemed scarce. It was a lot of ground to cover. Maybe that's what his crew was here for. A joint operation could be a pain in the ass, however.

Markus was scanning for defensible positions with optimal sectors of fire when he saw the mine.

Ahead of them a vast hole plunged down into the depths of the earth, carved layer by layer until an abyss had formed in the side of the mountain. Down in the pit, cranes and work trucks hauled the rock and metal, the sheer size of the mine dwarfing everything within. Behind the gaping wound, the western mountains stretched into the sky.

The Oquirrh Mountains. Rebel territory.

They pulled up to the Vircon headquarters and cut the engines. Markus had the crew wait with the trucks while he went inside, where he was met by a receptionist and brought down to a conference room.

Seated at a long table in the middle of the room were a man and woman, both scanning images displayed on the interface built into the surface. They looked up as Markus and the receptionist entered.

"Pardon me," she said. "This is the gentleman here for Mr. Sellers."

The woman at the table was probably in her early forties, short professional hair tucked behind her ears, business-casual attire. She poked the screen and the images disappeared. "Annika Sellers. Nice to meet you," she said, getting up to shake hands. Her eyes flicked over Markus's dirty clothes, pausing a moment on the pistol at his side before coming back up as she presented a professional smile.

"I assume you're here for the security detail?"

"That's right," Markus said.

She must've seen the look on his face as he made the connection with the last name. "Ned Sellers is my father, as well as the chief operations officer of this facility," she said. "I manage accounting."

The man next to Annika Sellers remained seated. He leaned back in his chair, crossed his arms over his chest, and nodded at Markus. "More guns the better, I suppose," he said.

"This is Phil Orsten," Annika Sellers said to Markus.

Begrudgingly, Orsten also stood from his seat. He was a short man, trimmed in a fine suit that he seemed to wear like a badge of honor. Unlike Annika, his face creased with distrust. "More mercenaries," he said.

There was a drawn-out silence as Markus clenched his jaw. He resisted the urge to curl his hands into fists. There were things in life he could let roll off his back, but being labeled a mercenary wasn't one of them. There were lines he and his crew didn't cross, even in the dog-eat-dog world that America had become. Things like murder, kidnapping, extortion were beyond his line. Those things were, however, not beyond a mercenary's. There was a difference and this asshole knew it.

"Ned Sellers is busy at the moment," Annika said, breaking the obvious tension. "Why don't you and your crew settle in and join us for your briefing after dinner."

Orsten waved it off. "Fine, let's show you your quarters."

Markus went back outside to gather his crew as Orsten led them to a maintenance bay at the north end of the compound not far from the HQ building. They stepped inside, Orsten flipped a switch, and a loud *thunk* echoed in the space as the lights kicked on. A wide concrete floor with several military all-purpose vehicles sat in a row before them.

Rourke whistled through his teeth. "Those are military Prowlers."

"Decommissioned and repurposed," Orsten said. "Purchased by Vircon. They're yours for the duration of your contract here. Armory through there," he pointed to a doorway on the left. "And bunks through there," he pointed to another door next to it. "Everything in one building so you're ready at a moment's notice. Any case, I'll leave you to settle in and we'll see you back at headquarters for your official briefing and dinner. Gentlemen." Then Orsten left.

Markus marveled at the equipment. The Prowlers were in mint condition with full armoring painted black, turret hatches, and double-shielded glass. Radio antennas and a radar pillar poked up from the rear hatches. Three of them, each fully kitted for mobile assault. Must've cost a fortune. The crew began poking around, opening the doors and trying out the seats. Tripp disappeared into the armory.

Dieter came over to Markus. "You know, this is a lot of costly equipment to just let some mangy mercenaries come in off the road and play with."

"Yeah." Markus knew what his second-in-command was thinking.

"Like they know something we don't," Dieter went on. "Something we're not going to like."

Len came out of a room in back and shouted across the bay. "Hey! Guys! They got fuckin' *showers* back here. What did we do to deserve this?"

Markus rubbed his temples. "Not what we've done, what we're going to have to do."

They met for dinner just before sundown. Orsten showed them to the dining room where they were seated around a large table and served sushi and steamed vegetables on fine china. The crew eyed their plates with caution. Markus gave the chopsticks a try while Rourke grabbed at the rolls of fish and rice with his bare hands. Tripp and Len argued about the necessity of putting the napkin in their laps while Temple sipped tentatively at a proffered glass of wine and Dieter was already asking for more. At least they'd showered beforehand. Long hair slicked back, beards trimmed and the dirt scraped from their hides, they were a parody of civilized class.

After dinner they were ushered into a conference room with a large screen mounted above another long table. A man they hadn't met yet was at the head of the table with Annika Sellers swiping through some files on the interface. He had the crisp look of money about him; fine suit, neat hair, and a hint of arrogant self-importance on his face.

"This is Ned Sellers," Orsten said making the introduction. "Chief operations officer of Vircon Industries mining facility."

Markus shook.

"Pleased to meet you," Ned Sellers said. "You and your crew come highly recommended. My friends over at Dynasec told us about the job you did for them in Corpus Christi. They might've gone under if not for your efforts there. We're glad to have you here."

A man in a gray security uniform entered the room carrying a small tablet. Probably in his mid-thirties, he moved with the confidence of one who was experienced with command.

"Gentlemen, this is Captain Reyes, head of the corporate security team for Vircon," Sellers said. "Reyes, this is Markus and his crew."

Markus saw the look in Reyes's eyes as they gripped each other's hands. Uniformed professionals never really did get on well with freelance operators.

"Got a last name?" Reyes asked in a sharp accent.

"None you need be concerned with," Markus countered. "What's with the British element here?"

"Vircon is a London-based company," Orsten said. "Reyes here is former SAS. The rest of the security team comes directly from HQ. Gentlemen," he said gesturing at the chairs.

They unclenched hands and took their places at the table.

Sellers nodded to Orsten, who pulled a clicker from his pocket, and the room went dark. The screen lit up with a satellite image of the valley and he began the briefing.

"Salt Lake Valley is a five-hundred-square-mile tract of land jam-packed with over four and a half million people, all as-of-yet undecided as to which side of this civil war they want to support. For the time being, the state's political persuasion leans toward the Federation of Pacific States. Essentially whatever California decides to do, Utah will as well. The federal government doesn't want that, but there's not much they can do about it right now since they're busy quelling dissention across the Midwest and around DC. In the turmoil and confusion, the rebel movement known as the Revolutionist Front has taken up residence in the Oquirrh Mountains to the west." He hit a button and red highlights lit up the range on the left side of the screen.

"And the US Army has settled in at the Salt Lake International Airport to the north, renaming it Forward Operating Base Spearpoint." A blue square blinked on indicating the Army base at the top of the screen.

Orsten continued. "This is us, Vircon Industries' mining facility." A green blob appeared along the eastern edge of the Oquirrh Mountains, practically between the Revolutionist occupied territory and the American Army base. "We have reason to believe that the RF have their eyes on our operations here. If they're able to commandeer this facility the financial implications would be crippling to what remains of the federal government and their forces here trying to remove the rebel threat from the area. The RF have no love for Old America, and Joseph Graham—their leader—has ties to political party members in the Pacific Federation, specifically in California where talk of a new government is starting to take hold. We've reached out to military leaders with our concern but they're bogged down, understaffed, and this facility is just too far away from the airfield for them to be able to maintain adequate supply lines. At least until they're able to push the RF out of the valley."

"What kind of economic impact are we looking at here?" Markus asked.

"That leads us to Vircon's mission . . ." Orsten punched a command into the interface built into the table. The screen changed again to the Vircon Industries logo, followed by a slide presentation consisting of images of construction equipment, stockpiles of raw ore, and graphs of company production. "This is the world's largest open-pit mine," Orsten stated with pride. "Which produces—annually—over two hundred thousand tons of copper, three hundred thousand troy ounces of gold, and three million troy ounces of silver. We have our own smelting station here at the north end of the compound where the raw material is prepared for shipment and distribution. It all gets rather technical after that, but the point is Vircon is quite literally a gold mine. So . . ."

He paused, adjusted his tie. "It's your task to ensure the safety and security of all executive staff and the facility while mining operations continue. Your contract is with Mr. Sellers directly, separate from the company directive, although you'll be working closely with the company's own security detail here through Captain Reyes. Work will not be slowed by this war. We will press on and meet the demands of our buyers, and under no circumstance will we allow this facility to fall into the hands of the rebels."

Orsten sounded confident but given the state of the region, Markus knew the man was underplaying the situation. "Do you believe it's going to get bad around here?" Markus asked, trying to gauge their understanding of the risk. "And just how soon that may happen?"

"That depends," Reyes said.

"On?"

"On the whims of a psychotic revolutionary leader and a military force subject to its government's economic constraints."

"That's succinct," Markus said, settling back in his chair.

"Point is," Sellers said from the back of the room, all eyes turning to him. "You'll be paid handsomely and you're under no obligation to continue, but you must make your decision. If you choose to decline our offer then say so and you can leave now. With your old battered trucks, of course."

"You haven't discussed compensation yet," Markus said.

"Quarter million each," Sellers responded without flinching.

"Length of contract?"

"Six month initial, renegotiate after that if necessary."

Markus took a moment to meet the eyes of each member of his crew. He could read his men without a word. They gave their answers.

"Alright," Markus said. "I want to sit down with Captain Reyes and get a solid tactical briefing. I'll need time with your engineers, facilities crew, whoever has knowledge of the physical structures of this place, anyone with local contacts in the area. We need to know everything they do. We'll need maps of the compound, a tour of the facilities with full access to the entire site, the works." Markus saw the way Captain Reyes stiffened at the request.

Ned Sellers leaned back in his chair. "Very well."

Markus nodded. "Where do you want us to sign?"

Annika Sellers slid the contract to him. He scanned the pages briefly, then signed.

"Excellent." Ned Sellers rose from the table. "I'm confident in the continued success of this mine. Gentlemen." He left, Annika Sellers and Phil Orsten in tow.

As soon as the door closed Reyes spun on Markus. "Let me make this clear, cowboy. I don't like this one fucking bit. I don't have time for any American gunslinger bullshit. We may be limited in number but this is a professional operation here. You mind Sellers, I'll handle the facility. That said, they may think things are all bloody well but it's only a matter of time before it goes balls-up."

"Good to know," Markus said. "I'll find you once we've settled in. I imagine we've got a lot of work to do."

"Right." Then he, too, left.

"Well," Tripp said, stretching in his chair. "We're in it now, boys."

Markus couldn't help but wonder at the potential cost, but the only thing to do was prep and hope for the best. The screen on the wall kept cycling through the presentation. The satellite image of the valley came around again, with the opposing forces highlighted in bold colors, the mine smack in the middle. Markus hoped he'd made the right call.

8
UNINVITED GUESTS

Trent fought a losing battle against exhaustion. No matter how hard he tried to force his eyes open they kept sliding shut, leaving him looking somewhere between drunk and brain-dead. He'd hear gunshots and jerk awake to find the rest of the squad unreactive and realize it was just his imagination. Then sleep would come back and whisper sweet nothings in his ear.

Someone kicked Trent's boot, startling him awake all over again. It was Specialist Sawyer, the platoon medic. "Here," he said holding out a small bottle of pills. "They'll help while you acclimate to the sleep cycle."

"Thanks," Trent said, popping two and pocketing the rest. He washed them down with a swig from the drinking tube on his shoulder. Maybe it was his imagination or maybe the pills worked incredibly fast, but Trent suddenly felt awake. He sat up a little, wiped his face, and scanned out the window of the abandoned business center they'd camped out in overnight. The street was empty, buildings pocked with bullet holes. Strange how everything looked different in the haze of early morning.

"Platoon's moving out in ten," Sawyer said. "Heard the LT passing the order to the team leaders a minute ago. Best not to get caught sleeping."

"Thanks again," Trent said. Everyone else in First

Platoon seemed to look for reasons to be pissed at him since he'd joined them after his demotion. Stain like that could be hard to get rid of, but Sawyer was alright.

Shortly after Trent got his blood moving again, Creon materialized from the shadows like some kind of shark from the murky depths and seemed almost disappointed to find Trent awake and alert. The staff sergeant grunted and moved on, rousing the rest of the platoon. They gathered in what used to be the lobby of the business center, all red-eyed and eager to move.

Lieutenant Vickers led the brief. "We're moving out to link up with the 488th at a waste management site ten klicks from here. Once there we'll hold tight until engineers can rally and make it into a permanent command outpost. That's ten klicks on foot, Headhunters, straight through hostile rebel-controlled neighborhoods. APCs are rerouted to Bravo Company to the east so we're on our own for this hike. The shit we've seen so far has just been gangs and gullible yokel assholes who think fighting the American military is a good idea. Considering all I hear outside right now are crickets, I'd say we corrected that line of thought for them." A couple quiet laughs. "However, I expect that to change today," the LT went on, cutting the laughs short. "In the game, Headhunters. Fall out to your team leaders."

The hike through the city in broad daylight was one of the most nerve-racking things Trent had ever done up to that point. Why they hadn't marched through the night while the curfew was in effect was beyond him. Now people walked the streets and crowded the sidewalks. Cars zipped by, either speeding up or veering off when they noticed the squads of soldiers moving through their neighborhood. The buildings seemed taller, closer, every alley a perfect spot for an ambush. There were people on rooftops and balconies watching, talking on phones, whispering to each other. One guy with an AK-47 even waved to them like there was no cause for concern. Trent felt completely exposed. He checked his corners and tried to remember muzzle awareness. Follow the guy in front, keep moving.

By the time they reached the waste management facility Trent felt like a high-tension wire ready to break. As if to signal their arrival, an AC-65 Wasp flew overhead, circled the facility, then disappeared to the north. The 488th had beaten them there and welcomed them through the gate. Lieutenant Vickers got a briefing from their platoon leader while Sergeant Creon assigned the squad to pull security along the perimeter. Trent swallowed two more perk pills as he and Bodine settled in on the roof of a single-story utility building overlooking the city to the south. Contrary to the lieutenant's prediction, the rest of the day was uneventful. Trent didn't know if he should be thankful for that, or concerned because of it.

Later, he and Bodine—as well as the rest of First Platoon—were relieved of guard duty by members of the 488th and allowed some real downtime. Pretty much everyone used it to sleep. They were woken up just after sundown and Creon had everyone gather in the makeshift ready room inside the massive incinerator building for another briefing. Apparently the day's lack of excitement had also concerned the leadership.

"Intel has reason to believe the RF are using the neighborhood to house their fighters while they conduct reconnaissance activity in the area," Creon said.

"The fact we didn't get hit today tells us they're most likely gathering intel before they move. We don't like that and we aren't going to wait for them to finish. They believe hiding among civilians protects them. It might protect them from artillery fire and air strikes, but it sure as hell isn't going to stop the 117th from getting in their shit." A round of enthusiastic agreement from the platoon. Trent swallowed a lump in his throat.

Creon continued. "We'll be going into the apartment block here," he traced a circle on the touch screen the 488th had set up. "Splitting up into teams to cover more ground and clear multiple buildings at once. A ground team will be on standby with Prowlers ready to grab any squirters. The goal is to gather our own intel, so snatch and grab gear, suspected RF or RF sympathizers. Zip cuffs and nonlethals if possible, we are going into people's homes, not all of them are bad guys so use discretion. That being said, do not hesitate to kill a motherfucker if they make a move."

O'Malley was smirking at Trent again. "We're gonna get to catch us some bad guys," he said as the briefing ended and everyone went to ready their gear. "Finally see one of these rebels up close."

"That's if we find any," Trent said.

"Don't be a bitch," Bodine butted in. "We're gonna find something one way or 'nother."

Night settled, the curfew went into effect, and the streets emptied once again. Trent was in Creon's team, designated Hound Two. He had a feeling Creon kept him close in order to keep an eye on him, being the in-experienced infantryman that he was. It didn't make Trent feel any better, just one more thing to worry about. The second team, designated Hound Three, was across the street and getting ready to breach the automated doors to the first floor of the tenement block. Bodine took point on this side of the street with O'Malley, Private First Class Jones, and Trent stacked behind.

Lieutenant Vickers gave the go-ahead from his position with the standby team, designated Hound One, and both teams breached the tenements. Trent stayed close on Jones's six as they moved through the main floor lobby and to the stairs, their boots crunching over broken glass and trash. The elevator was apparently broken, with caution tape stuck to the damaged car door, but they wouldn't have taken it anyway.

Up the stairs to the first set of apartments, where Creon halted the team. He flashed some hand signals Trent only half understood and Bodine stacked outside one of the doors in the long hallway. Intel had given the team leaders specifics on priority targets so they didn't have to go into every apartment, and hopefully any rebel hiding nearby would freak and bolt for the street where the LT's team would snatch them up. It was sort of like sending a fox into a hen house to see what happens.

Creon checked everyone was in place, grabbing Trent by the drag strap and shoving him tight against the wall behind Jones, then held his hand up and made a knife motion. Bodine stepped out, loaded up, and kicked the door in. The flimsy security bolt tore free, the door swinging hard into the wall, splinters of wood flying into the space beyond. O'Malley was the first through, then Jones and Trent.

"Get on the ground! Get on the fucking ground!" O'Malley shouted at a man lounging on the couch in his living room. The man's eyes went wide and he made to get up but O'Malley and Jones tackled him to the floor. They zip-cuffed him, kneeling on his back and twisting his head around so hard Trent worried they'd break his neck. He didn't know what to do so he just stood there holding his MX until he heard Bodine's voice from down the hall shouting at someone else. He came back out with a woman and two girls, ushering them into the living room where Creon ordered them to get prone. He placed Bodine and O'Malley with them and had Trent and Jones drag the man down the hall away from his family.

"Get your fucking hands off my family!" the man shouted. He twisted, dug his heels into the floor, and tried to get away, but Creon drove a fist into his gut and doubled him over. They tossed him on the floor in one of the bedrooms and rolled him over. Jones covered the door and Trent watched as Creon crouched down next to the guy.

"You RF?"

The man avoided eye contact with Creon.

"I asked you a question," the staff sergeant said. "For your family's sake, I suggest you answer it."

"No, sir," the man said, the fight apparently gone right out of him. "I ain't RF."

Creon grabbed a handful of the man's hair and tugged. "You wouldn't lie to me."

"No, sir, please . . . don't hurt my family."

From the living room, Trent could hear them crying, the mother hushing the young ones who kept calling out for their parents. His heart was hammering, his knees weak, sweaty fingers clutching the rifle in his hands. He was breathing heavily, like he'd just run ten miles.

"Your family will be fine," Creon said. "So long as you tell me the truth. Are there any RF in this building, or any RF sympathizers? Help me out and we'll be out of here. If you don't, if you lie to me I'll know it and then, well . . ." He let the rest of his meaning hang in the air.

The man was crying now, curled over on his side, hands bound behind his back, a knot of hair clenched in Creon's fist. Trent felt humiliated for the man, and for himself to be a part of this.

"Sergeant," he said before he could stop himself.

"Start searching the room, *Private,*" Creon said.

Trent wiped sweat from his face and went to the dresser in the corner, started digging through their stuff, going through drawers and tossing clothes on the floor. He felt like a criminal invading this family's personal space. If he did this back home he'd go to prison. Out here, he was just following orders. If this guy wasn't RF before he just fucking might be after this.

"This is how it works," Creon said. "We know there are enemy sympathizers in this building. We know someone knows, so we will keep asking until we find out. If you're telling me you know nothing then I'll have to go in the other room and start asking your wife. Then your daughters. Do you think they'll tell me the same story?"

The man was clearly struggling now with his thoughts. Trent suddenly wondered if the man really did know more than he was admitting.

"Okay," the man said. "There's a guy on the next level who drives for them."

Trent and Jones exchanged a look.

Creon let go of the man's hair, helped him sit up against the bed. "Apartment number?"

"Unit D-34. He lives alone, should be home now."

"Of course he should," Creon said. "Curfew's in effect." He stood, keyed the radio. "Hound One this is Hound Two, over."

"Hound Two, go ahead."

"Got a lead on a civilian target in unit Delta Three Four."

"Copy that, Hound Two. Rerouting Three now. Good work."

They heard Hound Three breach the unit one level above them, heard the shouting and thumping as the suspect was apprehended, boots back out into the hall and down the stairs. Once Team Three confirmed they had the package, Creon cut the man's zip cuffs and gave the order to move out. They left the apartment in shambles as they shuffled back out into the hallway. Trent's last glimpse was of the family huddled together and crying on the living room floor, and he felt some small piece of himself disappear.

9
JOKES, JODY, SNATCH AND GRAB

A couple of guys from CID came in on an AC-65 to interrogate the civilian First Platoon had captured. The craft had barely touched down before the spooks were out the doors and crossing the landing zone, bracing against the wash of the grav-engines and disappearing through another set of doors. No one had seen them since.

Those who weren't on guard duty sat around lounging on their cots, playing cards, trying to soak up the downtime before it was snatched away again with another mission or some meaningless detail, as it often was. Trent was thumbing through a book he'd found in the waste management facility's old break room, a dog-eared copy of *The Shadow of Capitalism* by some professor in the early '20s, while the rest of the guys were arguing over what they thought the CID was doing to that civilian.

"I bet he's strung up by his fuckin' balls, bro," Ramirez was saying.

"Nah," Jones said. "They don't fucking torture *everyone* they come across."

"What, you think they just ask him nicely?"

"That's probably exactly what they do," Trent added.

"How the fuck you figure?"

Trent marked his place and set the book down. "First of all, that civilian just got black-bagged right out of his home. Then he's in some room, tied to a chair, can't move. God knows what he's heard about us, about what the big bad Army does to people who cross us. If nothing else he's seen movies. Then a couple of dudes come in not in regular uniform, don't say a word. I bet that civilian started spilling his guts before the CID even had to ask."

Ramirez and Jones stared at Trent, smoke rising from the cigarettes between their fingers.

"He's right," Sawyer said as he stretched out on his cot nearby.

"Yeah, I guess you got all the answers from reading books, huh?" Jones said.

"Some," Trent replied.

Corporal Bodine chose that moment to come back from the shitter, lumbering into the group with his toiletry bag in hand. "Lotta good they'll do ya out here, Private. Fuckin' book ain't gonna help you remember to chamber a round."

They had a good laugh at that, the story of Trent's first night on assault had spread through the platoon like wildfire. Any little thing did; no one was safe. That alone helped Trent not take it too personally.

"Besides," Bodine went on. "Why you readin' that garbage anyway when there's perfectly good nudies right here." He plucked one of the porno mags from the box under his cot and tossed it at Trent.

Ramirez snatched it out of the air. "That's where you been hiding 'em," he said. "I've just been picturing your mom for the last week."

Bodine shoved Ramirez out of his chair to whooping laughter.

"Keep it down unless you want to get put on detail," Sawyer said.

"You don't fuckin' talk about my mom, motherfucker," Bodine said.

Ramirez picked himself up off the floor. "I wish I was fuckin' your mom . . ." He ducked another punch. As he danced away from Bodine he asked, "You think Jody fucks moms, too? Or just wives and girlfriends?"

Bodine gave up the fight and plopped onto his cot, which creaked under his weight. "Jody fucks whoever he wants," he said. "Everybody knows 'at. Fact o' life. He's probably givin' it to your girl right now."

Private First Class Coville, who'd been quiet the whole time, spun off his cot and kicked over a rations box, spilling the contents across the floor.

"The fuck, dude?" Ramirez snapped.

Coville's hands clenched into fists, eyes watering, something happening to his chin. "I got a letter . . . before we left," he said, an obvious quiver in his voice. The jokes stopped, everyone fell silent, watching. "Amanda left me," Coville said. "For some piece of *shit* yuppie college fuck back home." This he said while looking at Trent. "So shut the fuck up about Jody, you fucking assholes!" He wiped his nose and stormed off. Sawyer got up and went after him.

"Well shit," Bodine said.

Ramirez righted his chair, sat down, and opened the magazine. "Sucks for him, man."

Trent sat there, thumb tucked in his book, staring after Coville. He was from Tallahassee, Trent knew that much. Other than that Coville was a quiet type, followed his orders and never really added much to the conversation. Maybe that wasn't enough for his girlfriend. Or maybe Jody really did fuck girlfriends whose boyfriends were off at war. Trent thought of Alley, wondered if she was with Brady, whoever the fuck he was. It was pointless to think about, but he couldn't help it. There was nothing he could do. He tossed the book aside. Didn't feel like reading anymore.

That night Trent dreamt of Alley cheating on him. One of those dreams that doesn't end, the plot never changing course as most dreams do, an endless loop in his own mind.

The cold shock of the cot being kicked brought him out of it. Trent twitched, started awake. Corporal Bodine was standing over him shaking his head. "You were whimpering like a bitch," he said.

Trent rubbed his eyes, thankful that it was indeed just a dream. "Fuck you, Corporal."

"Sergeant Creon wants us all for another briefing."

"What time is it?" Trent could see through the plated security windows high above that it was dark out, but his internal clock had been thoroughly fucked since he left the FOB. There was no such thing as proper circadian rhythm in the infantry.

"It's time to git yer ass up. All o' you," Bodine said, going to the other cots and kicking the others awake.

Lieutenant Vickers had everyone gather in the old break room where Trent had found his book. Sergeant Creon was there, arms crossed and scowling as usual.

"Listen up, Headhunters," Lieutenant Vickers started. "The civilian we apprehended has agreed to give up the RF scout he drives for. They're scheduled to meet this morning and CID wants to do a snatch and grab. We'll cordon the area and provide support. Once they secure the target we'll escort them back here where it will no longer be our business what the CID does from there. Your squad leaders will have specifics for your teams. Be ready to move in fifteen mikes. Dismissed."

Turned out they were headed to a part of the city known as the Vice Block, where so many illegal and seedy things went on no one would be likely to notice a Revolutionist moving about. Trent was placed in Creon's team again as they entered the block and cleared a single-story house, then posted up inside the walled-off front yard. Hound Three was across the street, and the other teams on the far side of the block were tucked out of sight and ready to pounce. The CID guys were in two different cars parked along the side of the road. Radios set to stealth volume, everyone hunkered down and waited.

The sun still hadn't come up yet but it was getting close, blue-gray showing to the east. In the street, the last stragglers of the night stumbled back to whatever hole they'd crawled from, slinking into shadows and curling up in alleyways to hide from the coming day. Trent's knees burned from crouching behind the gate but he wasn't about to risk moving or making noise and being the reason the mission failed.

A car turned the corner, a blue four-door sedan with a white front quarter panel. The driver's car. CID had tagged the guy with a subdermal tracker, seized his bank accounts, and sent him back to get his car with the specific instruction to meet the RF scout as normal.

The call, no louder than a whisper, came through the earpiece telling all units to stand by for extract. Trent watched the car drive past his gate and then down the road out of sight.

He could hear the car decelerate, splash through a puddle, then stop, the motor still running. Sweat dripped down Trent's face, his MX felt slick in his hands. Hot as hell even first thing in the morning. There was a good chance the scout had a backup plan for things like this. Maybe even an ambush of his own if the RF had somehow found out their driver had been taken in the night. Anyone in that apartment block could've called. No way to know. Not until it all went down.

There was the sound of a car door opening then thumping shut. Sudden screeching of tires, engines revving. Brakes. Shouting. Trent blinked sweat out of his eyes and tucked the stock of his rifle into his shoulder. Any second now. The muscles in his legs screamed to move. He could almost sense the rest of the teams getting ready.

Then the call came through the comms. "Headhunters, *go go go!*"

Trent looked over his shoulder to see the team spring up as one and pour through the front gate.

"Watch the street," Bodine hollered as he yanked Trent to his feet and went through the gate and out onto the sidewalk. He had his machine gun up, sweeping the buildings as he turned the corner to link with Team Two. Trent followed, his legs tingling as blood rushed back into them. He trained his MX on the alley he thought he'd seen someone retreat to, waiting to hear shooting any second. Voices shouted familiar commands and he knew he was surrounded by the rest of First Platoon as they closed off the area. The two CID cars came screaming up and the Prowlers from the 488th came out from behind the abandoned convenience store around the corner where they'd been staged.

Creon waved everyone into the back of the vehicles and First Platoon piled onto the trucks, then the convoy sped off, leaving the Vice Block wondering what in the fuck just happened.

The Prowlers roared through the streets, splashing through standing sewage and bouncing over potholes, everyone doing their best to hang on and watch their muzzles. Trent was in the back of the trail vehicle and watched as a car sped up behind them. The turret gunner was sweeping rooftops and didn't see it.

"Hey Bodine!" Trent shouted. "Are they following us?"

Bodine checked, pointed his M37 at the windshield and the car slowed down, but didn't turn away. "Probably," Bodine said. "Keep yer fuckin' weapon on 'em and if they try anything shoot 'em!"

"Try anything like *what*?"

"Christ!" The Prowler hit another bump and they almost went over the back. "If they git too close or if they start shooting, shoot the fuck back!"

"This is fucking crazy," Trent said, but his words were lost in the ripping wind. The car followed them for some time and then suddenly turned down another street and disappeared.

Then the entrance of the waste plant flashed past and they were back inside the camp. Trent lowered his weapon as the soldiers from the 488th closed the gate behind them. The Prowlers stopped and everyone jumped off, slapped each other's backs, high-fived, lit cigarettes, and watched the CID guys drag a black-bagged figure out of one of the cars.

"Holy shit, that's a real-life fuckin' rebel," Ramirez said.

They had the man by both arms cinched behind his back as they led him inside the building by the landing pad. Not two minutes later a TC-11 small transport craft came in and scooped them up. It rose over the plant and zipped north toward FOB Spearpoint.

"Bet that's not how that motherfucker thought his day was gonna go," Jones said, inciting a round of laughter. It was cut short when Creon called the platoon together for head count and after-action review. They were warned the RF were likely to retaliate so everyone was on high alert, full combat gear at all times and don't go anywhere without a buddy. Last thing anyone wanted was to be captured in turn by the RF. Trent remembered the video in the chow hall of Joseph Graham about to execute the soldiers in the forest. That would be the easy way. The RF also did much more horrible and slow things to people when they were angry. Creon made sure to remind everyone of this, then dismissed them. And just like that it was back to business.

10
SOMEONE HERE TO SEE YOU

"Sir, you might want to come see this."

Ned Sellers pinched the bridge of his nose, then begrudgingly closed the laptop in front of him. "I'm not accustomed to being interrupted in my office."

"We need you at the gate, sir," Markus said. "There's someone here."

"Who is it?"

"The RF, sir."

Sellers's mouth opened then snapped shut. For a moment, a look of growing panic tried to command his features, but it was gone and in its place the arrogant confidence of a corporate executive.

Markus escorted Sellers to the Prowler parked outside the headquarters building and drove him across the compound to the gate that opened onto New Bingham Highway. Reyes was already there in the guard tower with a few of his men, rifles at the low ready.

As Markus pulled to a stop, Reyes split off from his men and came over to help Sellers out. He ignored Markus.

Sellers was cinching his tie and looking around. "Where are they?"

"They're outside," Markus said. "We didn't want to let them in for security reasons."

"How many?" Sellers asked.

"Just one truck," Reyes said. "An envoy. They want to talk. Figured we'd wait for you."

"Very well," Sellers said, straightening his suit jacket.

Markus unlocked the pistol in his drop holster and wrenched the access door open. Reyes flashed some hand signals to his guys on the wall and joined Markus and Sellers. They stepped through.

Barren fields stretched out before them toward the Copperton slums in the distance. A warm breeze carried the stench of rot and smoke from the city. The eastern mountains reached up from the horizon and Markus couldn't help but feel boxed in, like the entire valley was some kind of stage. Or arena.

And there before them was the truck.

Parked in the middle of the road, it was a battered old thing that blended right in with its surroundings. Passenger-side mirror was missing. Cracked windshield. Quarter panels of different colors. It seemed all four tires had air, at least. The passenger door creaked open and a middle-aged male climbed out, unarmed.

Markus stopped, stuck his hand out to Sellers to keep him close, Reyes posted on his opposite side.

The late morning air was dense with heat and silence.

"You the one in charge?" said the man. He was looking at Sellers. He had a dark complexion, lines running through his face, eyes narrowed, almost closed. Long gray hair pulled back into a pony tail. His green collared shirt was dust-covered and well worn. The man could have passed for a farmer. Probably *had* been one, once. Before he decided to become a rebel.

"I'm Ned Sellers, chief operations officer here,"

said Sellers. "I'm in charge of this facility." He stuck his chest out, tilted his chin up. "And who are you?"

The man stuck his hand out. "Commander Torres of the Revolutionist Front." Sellers hesitated. "You'll have to excuse the lack of decorum," Torres said. "We don't wear uniforms. This is a guerrilla war we're fighting."

"What do you want?" Sellers said. He left Commander Torres's hand hanging.

Torres dropped the hand. "I'm sure you're aware of the present situation in the valley. You know that the American government sent its military here to gain control of the region. You also know, I'm sure, that you have a profitable business here that stands to be disrupted by that."

"This business is in no danger of interruption," Sellers cut in. "And I'm well aware of the goings-on here. I know the military set up base in the airport, I know they're scouring the city looking for rebel fighters, and I know that you're hiding in the mountains hoping for revolution. All of this matters little to me. The mine will continue to operate as normal, despite whatever disagreements you have with the government."

Markus shot a glance at Sellers, saw Reyes do the same. Sellers was acting confident, but Markus wasn't so sure he truly understood the weight of the situation.

"True," Commander Torres said. "We do hope for revolution. And it will come, but it won't be easy. There'll be fighting, and lots of it. The Revolutionist Front doesn't want to see the unnecessary suffering of innocent people."

"That why Joseph Graham keeps posting his executions on the public net?" Reyes countered.

Torres's eyes shifted to him. "Those who choose to stand against the revolution will meet the fate they deserve. Everyone has a choice; the repercussions of that choice are on them."

Sellers slashed a hand through the air. "Look, cut the bullshit, Commander Torres. What do you want? You didn't come here just to waste my time with conversation."

"Your compound," Torres said. "It's in a perfect strategic location. Fortified and self-powered, it exists separate from the main grid. If you allow us to use the compound as a base, we can assure you protection from the federal pigs—"

"Absolutely not," Sellers said. "Vircon will have nothing to do with your political battles. We don't need your protection. We have our own measures to ensure continued operation. There's nothing else to discuss. Sorry you had to come all the way here for nothing. I'd wish you good luck in your endeavors, but . . ." With that, Sellers turned on a heel and marched back toward the access door.

Markus waited, watching Torres for any indication of aggression. Reyes waited, too. The rebel commander narrowed his already pinched gaze on Sellers's back, then looked at the two armed men before him.

"Arrogance won't mean shit once the fighting starts," Torres said before he too turned and marched back to the pickup. Markus waited for the truck to pull a U-turn and head for the Copperton slums before turning away himself.

He caught up with Ned Sellers once they were back inside the compound.

"Sir, perhaps we should consider the possibility that normal operations might be affected by the fighting that's very likely to happen here. How realistic is it that Vircon will send support?"

Sellers gave Markus a quizzical look. "Support? This is it. You are the support. You and him." He gestured at Reyes, who'd just joined them after giving orders to his crew on the walls.

"We have to be realistic here," Reyes said. "I think now's a good time to have a contingency plan for when everything goes bollocks."

"Agreed," Markus said. "That commander wouldn't have come here if they weren't ready to move. Whatever's going to happen is going to happen soon, and fast. We need to start prepping for fortification and emergency EXFIL."

Reyes nodded stiffly. "Right."

Sellers waved his hands. "Whoa, whoa, whoa, gentlemen. We're not preparing to take part in this battle and my employees aren't militia. Fighting happens all over the globe and business keeps going. It keeps going because of men like you and your crew, expensive crews that produce results. I'm sure that commander is rethinking things right now after seeing you here. We've given you weapons, equipment, vehicles, anything you need to defend our operation. So if, and that's an emphatic *if*, the RF make a move then you'll be all over them. Just keep watch on those mountains and we should be fine."

"Sir," Markus said, stepping in close and lowering his voice. "If you trust our experience and want us to handle things for you like we did in Corpus Christi, or Omaha or any of the other places and jobs you've never heard about for reasons of professional discretion, then you need to heed my counsel."

Sellers clearly wasn't used to taking orders. He

gripped Markus's shoulder like they were old buddies. "We'll secure our perimeter and do as we've been doing. That's that. I won't hear any more of it."

The sat-phone on Sellers's hip started beeping just then. He answered it, listened to whomever was on the other end for a moment, then stormed off, speaking harshly into the phone. Sellers flagged down a passing work truck, climbed in, and rode off.

Reyes stood beside Markus. "Thank God we have the valuable tactical insight like that of Ned fucking Sellers."

"No shit."

11
SHOTS FIRED

Sam settled into a shooter's position, lying prone on the roof of the apartment building; hand wrapped around the grip of the Remington, pointer finger stretched out above the trigger guard. She sighted through a hole in the brick façade and watched the Army checkpoint three hundred yards out, composed of one shock bunker capable of protecting against anything 7.62mm and under, a perimeter of three-foot concrete barriers, two military Prowlers with turret .50 cals, and nine personnel with MXs and body armor. The checkpoints had started to pop up all over as the military moved into different sectors of the city. More checkpoints than the RF was comfortable with.

Five stories up, their elevated position gave Sam full view of the street below where people were going about their daily business completely unaware of her presence. They were sheep grown used to the government pawns pushing them around. She wanted to despise them for being so weak, but Joseph Graham had said they would be blind and it was up to her to show them that they could fight. Her own father had refused to take sides, and it cost them dearly.

Sam pulled her cheek from the stock and rubbed her eyes. Two hours now she'd been on the scope and her mind was starting to wander. Couldn't have that. Not today, not now. Commander Torres's big push was almost at hand and she was intent on proving herself.

Rob was next to her now, watching the checkpoint through binoculars when the comm on his belt chirped.

"*Attention all units, this is Commander Torres. In the name of Joseph Graham and the Revolution . . . it is time. Commence the assault. Good luck and Godspeed.*"

They looked at each other. "Is that it?" Sam said.

A moment later gunfire began to crackle across the city. Sam could just make out the distinctive recoil of Kalashnikovs and the snap of military MXs. There was something heavy, too, pounding out big-caliber rounds at a steady rate. Had to be the Army .50 cals. The fight was on.

She got back on the scope to find the soldiers at the checkpoint clearly agitated and grouped inside the barriers; those who'd been outside the perimeter patrolling the street came running back. One of them was on a radio by the bunker, likely the one in charge, an officer or senior non-com. Sam ran a quick mental calculation and placed the crosshairs just above left-center of the soldier's head.

"One soldier right of bunker, two turret gunners in the open," Rob said, calling out targets.

The squad of RF fighters hidden in the storefront three buildings down began their assault and opened fire, the reports of their rifles echoing off the buildings. People in the street screamed and ran for cover. The roar of gunfire ripped through the air. Car alarms went off, lights flashing, horns blaring. The soldiers in the checkpoint crouched behind the barriers, reluctant to fire, heads darting around as they scanned the block. They hadn't identified where the shooting was coming from yet so they weren't firing back. Commander Torres had been counting on that hesitation to give the RF the initial momentum.

Sam watched a soldier holler into the radio while gesturing at his soldiers. His hand flashed out like a knife, sectioning off different locations in front of the checkpoint. Sam realized he was calling out sectors of fire. He was organizing the troops.

She eased her finger onto the trigger. Tried to steady her breath. Her heart was pounding. This was it.

She hesitated.

Rounds smashed into the checkpoint, dust and chunks of concrete flying in the air. Soldiers ducked, took cover, some either too brave or too stupid to get behind the barriers and just stood in the open gaping at the violence. It was all happening so fast. Only a few seconds ago the street had been quiet and now it was a battle zone.

Then the soldiers found their footing. A few of them popped up over the walls and fired back. A light machine gun opened up from the bunker, shooting indiscriminately. Someone climbed into the Prowler and let loose with the .50 cal, its heavy, rhythmic thumping raining devastation on the neighborhood. Buildings were getting hammered, bullets punched through glass storefronts and parked cars. Sam watched in horror as a few innocent bystanders were mowed down on the sidewalk. The soldiers were firing at everything in front of them now.

Why was she hesitating? Those fighters down there needed her support and she was freezing just like she'd done when she was a child. But she wasn't a child anymore, she was one of Joseph Graham's

Chosen and his words came back to her: *You are not afraid*. She reminded herself that these were the people who killed her family, and sighted on the .50 gunner.

Breathe in, out, pause. Finger brushed the trigger, squeezed. The rifle kicked.

The thumping stopped.

She scoped the Prowler and saw the .50 cal sitting dormant, the smoking barrel pointing upward, the operator no longer in sight. She swung the crosshairs over to a soldier standing by the bunker firing a light machine gun from the shoulder. She aimed, squeezed, felt the kick. This time she saw the spatter of red on the bunker wall as the machine gunner went down. Another soldier nearby saw it happen, ducked and began dragging the body into the bunker. A moment later, she came back out holding the machine gun. Sam dropped her, too.

Crosshairs up to the radio operator.

Fire.

The radio operator dropped, handset dangling by the curled cord.

It was starting to come easier now. Rack the bolt, on to the next target; a soldier out in front on one knee taking aim as he fired. Sam aimed for the bridge of the nose.

Before she could get her finger on the trigger, the .50 cal opened up again right as a car came speeding out of a side street, tires squealing, RF fighters packed inside. They raced toward the checkpoint firing out the windows. The .50 gunner swung about and ripped the car to pieces. Sam scoped the gunner, aimed quickly, and fired.

The gunner lurched, slapped at his neck. He let go of the .50 and fell down into the Prowler.

In the street, the car had veered into a parked truck and came to a stop. Smoke spewed from the hood. Two RF fighters crawled out and flopped to the pavement, covered in blood. Sam sighted targets quickly now, trying to keep the pressure on in order to give the fighters a chance to flee.

Another RF fighter popped out of a building almost right on top of the checkpoint, ran into the street, plucked something from her belt and threw it. Two seconds later the grenade went off in a blast of white smoke. A few soldiers fell behind the concrete barriers.

Just then, four more Prowlers came racing up from another street. They tore through the intersection and skidded to a halt in front of the checkpoint. Soldiers jumped out, weapons ready, firing as they pressed the RF back. Gunners popped out of the hatches and opened up with more .50-caliber machine guns. Mini-drones shot skyward, arced out over the block.

A hand pressed on Sam's back. "Time to go," Rob said.

She came off the scope, slid her tactical vest on, and rose to a crouch. She dropped the spent magazine, tucked it in her pocket, and slammed a fresh one into place. Rob tucked the binos in his cargo pocket, grabbed his pack and rifle, then they made their escape through the roof access door behind them.

They raced down a flight of stairs unconcerned about being seen or heard; people would be cowering on their floors at the sound of the firefight, and the Army hadn't pushed far enough into the block to run into them. Sam took the steps three at a time, leading with her rifle. Excitement, fear, doubt all pumping through her at once, but there was no time to consider any of it. Rob covered the rear with the M4. Flickering lights overhead made their movements feel stop-motion. At the bottom of the stairwell they pushed through a set of fire doors, moved down a hallway, and stopped at an exit door. Sam posted up and then nodded as Rob kicked the door open. Sam went through first, rifle out, covering the right. Rob went left, M4 at the ready.

In the street, people were running away from the sounds of gunfire. A quick glance showed no sign of military vehicles or personnel. Sam stepped out to cross.

Rob grabbed her by the vest, tugged her back behind a rusted-out car on cinder blocks and pointed to the sky. Sam looked up in time to see a mini-drone buzz past. After it disappeared over the buildings, she and Rob sprinted across the street and down an alley they'd scouted as an egress days ago.

They were supposed to fall back to the rally point at the corner of West Cherrywood and 4800 to be retasked if needed elsewhere, so Rob crouched next to a dumpster and pulled the handset from his pack, tuned the radio to the command frequency to check if the location was still secure. The handset squealed immediately, chaos on the net. He tried to decipher the multiple conversations shouting over each other all at once.

Sam scanned the street, wondering how many on their side were dying right now. She thought of the civilians who'd been gunned down on the sidewalk, clothes tearing in a hail of bullets, bodies twisted and falling to the pavement like their bones just disappeared.

She thought of her father and mother.

Had to or she'd lose momentum.

A voice came through the net suddenly, clear enough to make out; someone calling for help from an old Mormon sanctuary. They were pinned down inside. The voice crackling through the speaker was panicked, said they were almost out of ammunition. The soldiers were closing in.

Rob yanked a map out of his pocket, checked it. "That's only a few blocks south of here, we can help."

It was a bold move, taking the initiative without Commander Torres's order, but they had to do something. "Let's go," Sam said, anxious to keep moving.

They raced on foot, boots slapping, gear rattling as they cut down an alley, avoiding a pair of cop cars that were racing away from the fighting, and came out onto a side street where they could hear shooting nearby. Rob double-checked the map.

"Sanctuary's around the corner. Should be a parking lot here," he said pointing to the map. "Some building cover, possible egress if we keep our backs to this road here. What do you think?"

Sam looked at the map, then the actual surroundings. The gunfire was controlled, constant. Sounded like the soldiers were just keeping them pinned down. The radio on Rob's belt continued to call for help. "We won't see anythin' if we don't take the high ground," Sam said. "But we could get pinned ourselves if they find us. They didn't say how many troops are there?"

Rob shook his head. "Enough to pin down one of our squads."

"Right." Sam squinted up at a brick building on

the corner. Maybe three stories, not too high, but enough to give them good sight lines to overlook the lot on the other side. There were several alleys and side streets right there should they need to disappear quickly. "Up there. Let's go."

They found a fire escape on the side of the building behind some dumpsters and scrambled up, their footfalls echoing off the metal steps as they went. The sound of gunfire became louder once they reached the roof. Sam took the Remington from her shoulder, crouched over to the edge and looked down.

The Mormon sanctuary stood in the middle of a parking lot overgrown with weeds, surrounded by crumbling cement barriers and chain-link fencing. The front of the building was all shot up, twin pillars on either side of the towering arched doors cracked and splintered. Most of the glass had been shot out. The place looked like it had been abandoned long ago and was only barely standing.

Less than a hundred yards out an armored personnel carrier had driven through the perimeter fence and was inching closer to the front doors of the sanctuary, soldiers filing behind it as it approached. On the street directly below, more soldiers held positions behind a pair of Prowlers. As the APC crawled closer, the gunner in the turret let off a burst of rounds at the front doors.

"Why aren't they rushing the place?" Rob asked. "They've got enough troops. Christ."

"They want to take 'em alive," Sam said. "We don't have much time. Gotta make this count or they'll take us, too." She got on the scope, scanned across the parking lot, and sighted on the APC.

"Wait," Rob said. "Three-oh-eight won't do shit to that APC but piss 'em off. They'll turn on us quick."

"Well what do you want to do, Rob? We don't have time." Some part of her hoped he'd suggest leaving, let fate play out; another part of her knew she was being a coward.

"Take out the rear guard. Make them feel like they're being overrun. We have to get them to run."

Sam looked down. Two Prowlers parked on the curb, eight soldiers standing by, all of them watching the advancing APC. She glanced at Rob. "We have to hit them hard and fast."

Rob stuck the M4 over the edge. "Say when."

Sam swung the Remington to the street below, found what she assumed was a high-ranking soldier standing by one of the Prowlers talking on the radio through the open window. She racked the bolt, slid the first round into the chamber. Aimed at the man's shoulder with a downward angle that would put the round through his chest cavity, killing him instantly.

I am not afraid.

She fired.

Her target dropped. Had to move fast before the rest looked up and returned fire. She ejected the spent casing, shoved the bolt home and brought the cross-hairs to the next target, a soldier leaning over the hood with his back to her, and fired again.

Rob opened up with his M4, sending rapid-fire bursts down on the surprised troops. Rounds flashed and ricocheted off the pavement, off the armored Prowlers. Soldiers dropped to the ground instinctively, helmets jerking around trying to identify the direction of fire.

An idea came suddenly. Sam took aim at the tires of the Prowler and fired, heard the pop as the bullet penetrated the rubber, but the tire remained inflated. They were reinforced with run-flats. She'd have to lay down enough lead to completely shred the tire and overwhelm the safety feature in order for her plan to work. The Remington barked as Sam cycled round after round until the front tire finally blew out and the Prowler sagged. She shifted her aim to the rear tire, dumping rounds into it until it blew out and the truck leaned hard on its left. She did the same to the other Prowler.

The soldiers below were dragging their wounded into the vehicles, returning fire randomly into the buildings, firing at the intersection and alleyways. They still had no idea where Sam and Rob were, but that didn't stop them from shooting back. In the parking lot by the sanctuary, the foot soldiers scrambled back inside the APC as it made a slow turn and began crawling back toward the rear assault.

"Sam," Rob called as he loaded a new magazine. "More casualties" was all he got out before he started shooting again.

Sam understood. The APC would be fine under fire, but the soldiers wouldn't. They needed to force the armored vehicle into a casualty-evacuation role. She kept firing on the less armored Prowlers, taking out tires, firing into the engine blocks, splintering the reinforced windshields, anything she could do to immobilize them.

Rob kept shooting and reloading, empty magazines piling up at his feet. By the time the APC reached the battered Prowlers, there were only three soldiers still mobile. They dragged the wounded out to the support vehicle and loaded them into the back. A few soldiers slipped out from inside the APC and started returning fire. Sam watched as one of the injured pointed up to the rooftop. A moment later, the APC gunner popped out of the hatch and opened up with the turret gun. Sam and Rob dove back as the 25mm rounds pulverized the ledge. Sam could feel the shockwave from the heavy rounds pounding the building, the turret gun thumping with unrelenting force.

Then suddenly the shooting stopped.

Minutes went by before Sam dared to look up and saw Rob crawling over to the edge. The parapet was ripped apart, a gaping wound in the side of the building, brick and crumbled stone scattered over the black tarred roof. Streams of sweat carved dark lines across his face and dust fell from his shoulders as he rose to peer over. When his head didn't get blown off, he took a longer look. Sam watched him for a moment, ears ringing, heart pounding. It felt like time slowed, the edges dulled, and everything had gone numb. She hoped she didn't have to start fighting again.

Rob slid back against the wall. "They're gone."

"What?"

"They're gone, Sam. It fucking worked."

Sam forced herself up, Remington dangling in her hand. A tremendous effort just to move her feet, but she came to the edge and looked down.

The soldiers were gone. The APC was gone. There was blood all over the sidewalks, spent casings and ammo links all over the street. They'd left one of the Prowlers, which began to spark, light flashing out the windows. A second later it burst in a brilliant flash of blinding white light that forced Sam to turn away. The soldiers had dropped an incendiary grenade in the cab before they left.

Across the lot, the RF fighters who'd been trapped in the sanctuary dashed out the doors and escaped on foot, disappearing into a nearby slum.

"We should go," Sam said, fighting a tremble in her voice.

Rob climbed to his feet, gathered his empty magazines and stuffed them back in the pouches on his belt. Sam loaded her last full magazine into the Remington. They took their time getting down the fire escape.

The comedown hit hard. During the fight Sam's hands were steady . . . precise, but now they shook uncontrollably, threatening to expose her as weak and worse, as a fraud. For all the years she'd spent imagining killing the people responsible for her family's murder, actually doing it was unlike anything she could've prepared for, and it was showing. That wouldn't do, being one of Joseph Graham's Chosen. That honored title came with a heavy responsibility, so she stuffed her hands in her pockets as fellow rebels—as the media was fond of calling them—gathered around now, casting admiring glances at her as they waited for an update on the outcome of the offensive. As planned, they were gathered in the lower levels of the West Valley water treatment plant surrounded by dripping pipes and steaming boilers, miserably hot but well protected from military drone observation.

Commander Torres appeared on a platform above the crowd, his sub-commanders right behind him. The murmur of conversation died out, leaving only the hum of industrial equipment thrumming in the background.

Torres stepped forward, gripped the railing in front of him. "Today the Revolutionist Front showed the old government that its time here in the valley has run out." Cheers rising and melting into the ambient noise, weapons thrust in the air. Torres lifted a hand and the crowd fell silent. "Five key outposts and several military checkpoints in the West Valley sector fell at the hands of the Revolution today, but it came at the cost of many of our fellow brothers and sisters. Their sacrifice is not in vain, however. The government knows now that we are serious, and that we are not some second-rate militia with dreams of the apocalypse, but a strong fighting force dedicated to a new order that will stop at nothing until victory is attained.

"Every one of you fought with purity and purpose in your hearts, but there's one among you that must be recognized. One whose actions not only dealt a crushing blow to the enemy, but also saved the lives of numerous Revolutionists in the act." Commander Torres turned his gaze on Sam and motioned her forward.

She hesitated, wondering if he really meant to single her out in this crowd. Surely there were plenty of other people he could've meant. Rob's hand at the small of her back urged her forward and sent voltage up her spine. The crowd parted for her, their eyes on her as she climbed the stairs. She felt exposed on the platform next to Commander Torres as he brought her front and center.

"Samantha Cross," he said to the crowd. "Chosen by Joseph Graham himself, to be his Reaper in the Valley. The youngest sniper in our ranks at nineteen years old, driven by purpose, fueled by anger at the wicked regime, she has proven that our leader's wisdom and foresight are beyond all measure. He saw greatness in her and he was not wrong.

"Today, this young woman, this Revolutionist, dealt a hammer-blow to the enemy and made sure they knew they chose the wrong side. From her perch on top of a run-down apartment she pinned down an Army checkpoint defended by armored Prowlers, fifty-caliber heavy machine guns, armored personnel carriers, and a squad of highly trained soldiers while our assault teams conducted their attack. *Then*"—he paused and placed a hand on her shoulder as if presenting her like one of Pa's prized cattle—"she and her spotter crossed several city blocks on foot to rescue a team of fellow RF who'd been pinned down and surrounded. She was able to inflict such damage to the military unit closing in that they abandoned their mission and fled, leaving trails of blood as they went."

Sam fought the urge to swallow the lump in her throat, remembering the spatters of red on the pavement, the screams of agony and fear. She bit down on the inside of her lip in hopes of keeping her composure. She should be proud right now, not . . . whatever it was she was actually feeling.

"Take heart in the presence of Joseph Graham's Chosen," Torres said. "Know that good Americans like her are among us, and let that give you the courage to fight with all you have." He dismissed the audience, letting them return to their posts on the block.

"Sir," Sam said. "Rob was with me, too."

"Yes he was," Torres said, "but he is not Chosen, *you* are. Knowing that and seeing you here among them gives them strength." His rigid posture relaxed, his tone easing to a more conversational pitch. "I can see the burden weighing on you."

Sam looked up, startled, not realizing her thoughts had betrayed her.

"It's okay," Torres said. "It's a heavy burden, I know. Here, I have something for you." One of his sub-commanders handed him a tablet that he then handed to her. "Our leader wishes to speak with you. It's on an encrypted relay, completely untraceable. It's perfectly safe."

Sam took the tablet and Commander Torres gave her some space. She woke the screen, waited a moment as the image of Joseph Graham materialized. "Hello, Samantha Cross," he said, his voice turning butterflies loose in her stomach.

"Hello, sir." It was all she could do to keep the tremble from her own voice.

"You've done greatness for the cause today," Graham said. "I knew you would, I could see it in you, feel it when I stood by you, as all the others can feel it now. It's not fate that drives you, Samantha, but your own heart, your own will that determines your path and sets the example for others. And what a great path it's already becoming."

Sam cast a glance at Rob waiting at the bottom of the platform and wondered if he could hear. She wanted to be near him again, a bond already forming from the chaos of battle. The realization only made her more uncomfortable. "I'm just . . . doing what I must, sir."

Graham's image smiled. "I know. And I know it's difficult, because I was once like you; young and angry and filled with fear. I know what you feel. I know the pain of loss, too. Like you, I've seen the true face of what this country has become. It was during my incarceration at the Moab detention camp where I first saw the depth of depravity this nation had embraced."

Sam remembered reading about that in the recruitment forums. In his younger days Graham had spent a lot of time with counterculture groups who went to protests and instigated riots outside government facilities across the country. He rose through the ranks of several different organizations at once and landed on the authorities' radar. Not long after that, he'd gotten arrested for his involvement in the death of a congressman when some thugs dragged the man from his house and beat him to death in the street. Graham had nothing to do with it, but a few of them were former associates of his so when they were arrested they gave up some bullshit story about how Graham had ordered them to do it. It was all Homeland Security had needed and they threw him in the prison camp. While he was there his grandfather and sister died in a suspicious car accident and the rest of his family fled the country. Graham was eventually released, but he'd had enough. Sam knew the story, but to hear it from the man's own lips was something else.

On the tablet, Graham went on. "I saw in those cages the face of desperation; thirst and hunger and helplessness, everyone in there waiting for someone to save them. At first I, too, prayed for a savior. That lasted the first couple of months. Then I gave up hope and knew no one would come. But it was there in that most helpless moment that I realized a savior would not appear unless I made it so. While others cried, I forged myself into something more. I cast off my fear and, despite the chains, I took action and began laying the groundwork for what would become the Revolutionist Front. I chose to join the Coalition of Free States in their fight against the federal pigs, and I became something more, as you will become something more here.

"You see, the thing I learned was that it's alright to have fear, but it's not alright to be crippled by it. I didn't let it stop me from making a choice and doing what must be done. Because that is the essence of freedom . . . *true* freedom. We must do what is necessary. You must accept your path, Samantha, and carry that responsibility until it becomes weightless, and then you will be free. I know you will do this. Do you remember what we spoke of in my tent?"

"Yessir," Sam said. "We talked about purpose."

"Yes. Do you remember your purpose? Remember your family, your father and mother and brother?"

"Of course I do," she said, then added, "sir."

"The memory of your family is your light in the darkness. Let it guide you when doubt tries to corrupt your heart. And know that I'm proud of you, Samantha Cross." The link ended and Commander Torres came forward.

"He may not admit that our paths in life are destined, but his wisdom is . . . divine, yes?"

"Yes," Sam said after a moment.

He took the tablet, placed a hand on Sam's shoulder.

"You and Rob fought well today, but there's more to do."

The sound of footsteps running along a scaffolding brought Torres around. Rob sprinted up the steps, rifle ready as an RF fighter came out of the shadows gasping for breath. "Commander," said the fighter, hands on his knees. "One of our scouts got captured, the Army has him now."

"Where?"

"They grabbed him in the Vice Block. He's at their base at the airport now."

"Then our location is compromised," Torres said, the cold commanding tone back in place. "Evacuate immediately, activate the purge protocol. Make sure everyone is out and all sensitive equipment is secured or destroyed. Have field teams move to secondary locations and await further orders. We need to move up the timetable and get in that mine now. Go." His subcommanders ran off to deliver his orders. He turned to Sam and Rob. "You two are critical to the mission here now. I need you to go to the safe house in Taylorsville where Sub-commander Akers will have further orders. I'll contact you once it's safe. Your job now is to hold the enemy back and disrupt their advance for as long as possible while we get into that mine."

"You can count on us, sir," Rob said.

After Commander Torres left, Sam turned to Rob. "Hey, I'm sorry," she said. "I didn't . . . I mean, you should've been up here, too—"

"Don't," Rob said. "You earned the honor. You're Joseph Graham's Chosen, it's honor enough for me to watch your back. But we don't have time for feelings now, we have to go before the military closes in."

"Right," she said, feeling foolish, like none of this was how she expected it to go, then buried the thought as they took off through the tunnels and escaped into the city.

12
TIME TO GET SERIOUS

Markus sat in the shade thumbing through the inventory report Vircon sent to his tablet. Luckily their armory had plenty of weapons, which at first seemed odd for a mining company until Sellers had explained that after having lost several sites in other war-torn countries, it became standard practice for the company to have security equipment on standby. When asked why Vircon didn't just fully staff its own special security department, Sellers scoffed and said something about avoiding retirement and benefits costs. He'd said it was much more economically sound to contract it out.

Markus looked up as Dieter pulled up in one of the Prowlers and leaned out the window. "Reyes got intel to go over, Chief. I'll give you a ride."

The vehicle bay had become something of a command center for their operations. They'd brought in a conference table from an unused office and set it in back, mounted a bulletin board to the wall, set a weapon rack close by, and had a customary coffeepot on the counter. Reyes stood at one end of the table now, hands splayed over a map spread out before them. He had his own second-in-command there with him, a square-jawed officer named Weatherford.

"Contacts in Copperton passed some info," Reyes said. "Seems the troops are pushing out their checkpoints, but limiting patrols to specific areas within two hundred meters of the CPs. Still some contested areas here, here, and here," he said pointing to several spots on the map. "The heaviest fighting is here where the military's trying to spread further through the city."

"Any more word from the RF?" Markus asked.

"As of now we haven't seen or heard anything else from them."

"Which means they got plans for us," Tripp said.

"Plans we won't like," Dieter added.

Reyes nodded. "I think we need to assume something's coming and it's coming fast."

"Biggest threat will be from Copperton," Markus said. "It's the frontal approach, easy to hide, plenty of civilians for cover, which seems to be the rebels' MO. That's where they'll hit us first, but it won't be the point of infiltration. They'll draw us in at the gate, then try to slip in . . . probably here." He pointed to the north gate by the smelting facility. "We know they're in the mountains, easy enough for them to come down and try an assault. If it doesn't work, they just slip back into the hills. No threat from the military, easy retreat."

"Word on the net is they've got a serious sniper element now, too," Reyes said. "Those hills are going to be a problem. They've probably already got us scouted out by now." He looked at Weatherford. "Just like Nepal."

Markus rubbed his forehead. "We need to mask our movements in the open and be aware that we're under surveillance. Tripp, I want you to scope those ridgelines and identify the most likely problem areas."

"You got it, Chief."

"One more thing," Reyes said. "Apparently these

snipers are of enough concern to the military to convince the US government to issue a bounty on the heads of any RF sniper, dead or alive. Ten thousand American dollars a pop."

Dieter and Tripp looked at Markus. Markus shook his head. "We're still for our own interests here. We haven't committed to their fight yet, but if we go after their snipers we'll have chosen sides. No two ways about it."

"Not for nothing, Chief," Tripp said. "But we're in the profession of risking our lives for money. I know you don't like to hear it that way, but it's true. We're broke until this job's done and the only thing we're good at is fighting. I mean, how long can this gig with Sellers really last? It's only a matter of time before Vircon hightails it outta here and the rest of our contract goes with them." He glanced at Reyes. "No offense."

"Look," Markus said. "If it comes to it and we're forced into a situation then we'll see about claiming a reward after the fact. I want everyone to be aware of the consequences, though. The RF will not take kindly to us making money off their dead. We'll be fighting all of them."

Dieter leaned forward in his chair. "Chief. They want this compound. We're going to be fighting them all soon enough."

The strop of rotors, pulse wave reaching out, swatting the bird from the sky. Bright flash. Man in a chair, the bag over his head sucking in and out with each panicked breath. Elsewhere, an old rotting ship sinking into the mud and Devens is there, alive again. "Ain't no sense in all this anymore," he says, staring out into the bay. "You're alive," Markus says. Devens doesn't look at him. "Ain't worth dyin' for the wrong cause, brother."

Markus blinked awake, rubbed the sleep from his eyes, the images from the dream fading into the blue-gray of approaching dawn that seeped through the window. Been a while since he'd dreamt at all. Couldn't say he much cared for it, nothing but ghosts of a pointlessly violent past demanding to be remembered. He rolled over, cot creaking under his weight. The years were catching up to him, harder each morning to get up and get going. He was pushing through the tail end of his forties now, gray starting to show at his temples, old injuries—and old memories—making themselves known.

An explosion from outside. Close.

The walls shook, the windows rattled. In half a second Markus was off the cot and in his boots, shirt, and tactical vest. He snatched his rifle and bolted through the door.

The rest of the crew were in the bay already tugging on gear, clipping ammo belts, lacing up boots. Outside, sporadic gunfire broke out as the Vircon security posted on the walls started shooting.

"Alright," Markus said. "Head to the walls and stay in two-man teams. Dieter, Tripp, take the AX-7 to the north tower and watch that access road. Keep an eye on that ridge. Temple, Len, to HQ and secure Sellers and VIPs. Rourke, you're with me at the front gate. Comms on channel two."

Tripp popped open the rifle case and plucked up the AX-7. Dieter nodded. Temple slung a medical bag over his shoulder. Len racked the slide on his sidearm and tucked it into a holster. Rourke hefted the

M37 machine gun, two-hundred-round ammo drum locked in place. They all had their Vircon-issued civilian model MXs. Markus looked each man in the eye.

"Ready, go!"

They split off.

Markus and Rourke left the bay and ran down the road toward the main gate as the gunfire continued.

They met Reyes and his men on the walls, where they were returning fire at targets out beyond the perimeter. Tracers streaked overhead, the crack and bang of rounds punching into steel and concrete.

"They dropped a mortar on the gate, but stopped," Reyes shouted over the noise as Markus and Rourke joined them. "My guess is they don't want to fuck us up too much because they want to move in."

"Good, that's our advantage," Markus said. "I need to get a look."

Reyes handed Markus the range finder. Markus glassed the area.

Several groups of rebels were moving along the access road coming out of the Copperton slums and heading toward the gate, maybe two hundred meters out. They were taking cover behind berms on both sides of the road, moving cautiously, gesturing to each other with hand signals and moving in unison as if they'd been practicing, each clad in dark-colored clothing and weapon vests with Chinese rifles and M4s. They didn't look like random civilians. Markus handed the range finder back to Reyes.

"That's serious RF," he said. "Rourke."

The big man slid out the bipod and hoisted the machine gun onto the wall. "Let them get in close," Markus said.

"You got it, Chief."

"Figure their mortar team is in that ghetto," Reyes said. "Probably staged there with reserves and more equipment we haven't seen yet."

"I wonder why they're not coming at us with technicals," Markus said, referring to the truck bed–mounted machine guns used by rebel forces around the world. Despite their usually makeshift designs, they were proven deadly weapon platforms that could quickly and easily overwhelm stationary positions.

"Probably because they know we have these." Reyes reached down and pulled a handheld grenade launcher from a weapon crate. Beside the crate was a box of projectile grenades. "They tried bringing two pickups in close but I hit them quick and hard. Took the rug out from under them."

Bullets buzzed by, shattered a window in the tower.

"Hundred meters, Chief," Rourke said.

"Light 'em up."

The M37 came alive, ripping up the RF, the muzzle flash bright in the gray morning. Rourke fired and swiveled, keeping the pressure on the approaching enemy. Markus fired his M4, Reyes took up the grenade launcher and began thumping rounds downrange. Weapons roared from the walls as they tried to drive the enemy back.

Dieter raced the Prowler down the dirt road, hitting turns at full speed, punching through the straightaways, leaving plumes of dust in their wake. Tripp struggled with the mount for the night optics on the AX-7 as he bounced in the passenger seat.

They came to a skidding halt at the north tower.

The flimsy sliding gate hung before them, hardly a barrier at all. They climbed into the small guard tower next to it and found a lone Vircon employee there with a handheld radio. He was hunkered down, apparently rattled by the sound of gunfire.

"You see anything out there?" Dieter asked.

The man shook his head. "Was quiet all night until just now."

Dieter and Tripp watched the road. It stretched out into the hills until it disappeared up a steep slope straight into Revolutionist territory. Tripp found a sandbag and set it in a window back from the edge of the wall, then tipped over an empty MRE crate and used it as a seat. He settled into a shooting position, set his eye to the scope, and adjusted the light filter. Dieter took a small thermal imager from his cargo pocket and scanned the road.

Sure enough, about three hundred meters out was a squad of fighters moving through the dark toward the gate. Their movements were controlled and apparently practiced. Not too bad, actually, except they didn't account for Dieter and Tripp's low-light visual capabilities.

"Got a squad of fighters moving toward us about three hundred meters out, left side of the dirt road," Dieter called.

"Got 'em," Tripp said.

Dieter knew they could pick fighters off all day from a distance, but if there was a focused assault on the gate, there was just no way the two of them would be able to keep the RF out. If they brought technicals it would be over quick.

Dieter picked up the radio and called Markus.

The chief answered, the static crackle of gunfire in the background.

"We got RF advancing on the north gate. About fifteen foot-mobiles. We're going to need help here."

"Copy that."

"I'll keep you posted. Out."

"Got a guy looks like he's prepping some kind of ordnance," Tripp said. The AX-7 barked. Startled the shit out of Dieter, and the Vircon guy almost jumped out of the tower. A second later, there was a *whump* from an explosion somewhere outside the gate. "Got him," Tripp said.

Then Dieter went to the phone on the wall. There was a laminated directory pinned just above it. He picked up the phone, dialed the number for the hauler bay. It rang several times before a terrified-sounding worker answered.

"Listen," Dieter said. "We need one of those haulers brought over to the north gate, like five fucking minutes ago."

"Who is this?"

"We don't have time for this," Dieter snapped. "Get a truck down here now and park it right against the gate."

"Is that authorized?"

"You listen to me," Dieter said. "Unless you want to be overrun, you get a hauler down here right the fuck now."

"Uh . . . okay. You'll have to give us a minute to power up. We can be there in five, maybe."

"Alright, good."

Dieter slammed the phone on the hook and went to help Tripp pick off the enemy, rifles working in tandem, a pair of precision tools doing their violent work.

Annika Sellers lifted her head from her pillow and squinted through the darkness. She was normally an early riser but the clock on her nightstand said it was only 4:56 A.M., which was an hour and a half ahead of her normal schedule. She closed her eyes and let her head sink back into the pillow, hoping she'd be able to fall back asleep.

A rumble of thunder sent a vibration through the walls of her room and her eyes shot open once again. The executive private quarters had noise-canceling baffles built into the walls to help keep out the sounds of heavy machinery from the mine, but every once in a while, one of the ore haulers would rumble past and the vibrations would come up through the floor. But it was too early for the haulers to be active. This had to be some kind of storm then, and it must've been right overhead because another rumble of thunder shook the walls.

Annika sat up. Something didn't feel right. She couldn't pinpoint just what it was but she was fully awake now and feeling the slightest bit concerned, and maybe somewhat foolish for being afraid of a little thunder. But going back to sleep was out of the question now so she got out of bed, threw on a tank top and gym shorts, and hit the power on the coffeepot.

An urgent knock at the door caused her to nearly drop the mug she'd grabbed from the cabinet. This was not how she preferred her mornings to start.

More forceful banging at the door. Annika set the mug down and marched across the room, annoyed beyond reason for such an early hour. She disengaged the lock and ripped the door open.

"Who the hell—"

The sound of gunfire and explosions forced their way into her room.

Her eyes went wide. "What—"

"No time, Miss Sellers. We gotta get you out of here." It was one of the mercenaries her father had hired. He was dressed in ragtag military gear and had a big gun slung across his chest. "Ma'am, we have to go," he said.

Annika blinked at him, completely lost for words. They were under attack? This couldn't really be happening. Guns and fighting and rebel terrorists were for soldiers, not corporate employees.

Another explosion, somewhere too close for comfort. Annika flinched.

"Miss Sellers," the mercenary said as he reached for her.

She recoiled instinctively, and the gesture was enough to get her moving. She went back into her room, threw a button-up over her tank top and slipped into a pair of sneakers, then followed the mercenary out into the hallway where a second mercenary was ushering her father and Phil Orsten from their rooms. Outside, the gunfire continued.

They were herded down to the main lobby where one of the mercenaries went over to the front door while the other went to an equipment locker behind the desk and started pulling out spare bulletproof vests and protective helmets.

"Put these on," he said as he shoved the gear into everyone's arms.

In a daze, Annika slid the vest on over her head and

fumbled with the clasps. Her hands were shaking so bad she was barely able to get the helmet strap clipped under her chin. Another explosion made her flinch. The shooting outside was relentless. This *couldn't* be happening. She tried to remember what they'd said at the mandatory six-hour conflict zone preparedness seminar she'd taken before coming to the mine.

Stay low, stay calm, control your breathing.

Annika closed her eyes and sank to the floor behind the desk, doing her best to maintain control.

A hand closed around hers. She opened her eyes. Her father was crouched in front of her, clearly just as frightened as she was, his knuckles white as he squeezed her hand.

One of the mercenaries came around the desk and knelt down beside them. He put a hand on her father's shoulder but looked at them both as he spoke. "It's going to be alright. We're professionals. Just stay calm, trust us, and do what we say without hesitation." The radio on his belt was going nuts. Annika couldn't make out any of it. She had no idea how these mercenaries understood each other, or how they could be so calm right now.

"We have to get out of here," the other mercenary called out from the other side of the lobby where he was looking out the front doors.

"Listen," said the one crouching in front of the group huddled behind the desk. "Stay together and follow us. We're going to the safe house, okay?"

Ned and Philip's eyes were wide, flinching at every detonation that thrummed through the walls. The mercenary turned his gaze on Annika. She wasn't used to being helpless and didn't like the feeling at all. This was not her element. But still, she had to do something or they'd end up like the team in Colombia who'd been caught by the rebels, and *that* was something she did not want. The fear was so great that it became almost unbearable, and then a strange calm washed over her. She looked the mercenary in the eye and nodded.

The mercenary nodded back. "Alright, let's go."

Annika felt like she was outside her own body, like she was on autopilot. Before she knew it, they were outside following the mercenaries across the courtyard. The gunfire was louder out here, the crisp snap of bullets ripping through the air urging them on. The sky was brightening as day approached. Red flashes streaked the blue-gray hue. Tracer rounds, Annika thought, recalling the testimony of one of the Colombia site survivors. Looked like lasers out of some kind of science fiction movie.

Something whistled overhead, close enough to make even the mercenaries flinch. Annika watched as what must've been a missile or rocket arced off into the distance. Her father's hand squeezed around hers and pulled her on, nearly dragging her down. The mercenaries shouted. It was all complete and utter chaos.

Then the rocket disappeared into the gaping maw of the mine. A moment later the sound of an explosion came up to meet them.

They ran on, stumbling, flailing, trying desperately to reach the safe house just ahead.

A terrible rumble shook the ground, so powerful it drowned out the sound of shooting and explosions. The ground heaved like an earthquake. Annika's bones vibrated, her ears hummed. Still clutching her father's hand, she stopped and they both looked toward the mine.

A great cloud of dust and dirt rolled upward as a massive section of the mine collapsed, an entire wall sliding down into the bottom of the pit. Landslide sirens blared across the compound, orange warning lights flashing in time with the wailing horns.

Annika stood in the middle of it all, staring, unbelieving. This wasn't happening. This *couldn't* be happening. Her heart was hammering. The world was coming down around her.

"Come on," shouted the mercenaries, urging them on. They were about to move when two haulers rumbled past, then split off at an intersection, one heading east toward the main gate and the other heading toward the north gate.

Ned Sellers stopped and pointed. "Hey, what in the hell are they doing?"

"Nothing," said one of the mercenaries as he shoved everyone up the steps of the safe house and through the door.

It was a cramped space, more like a break room than a safe place to hide from an attack. Annika was vaguely aware of the fact that there wasn't enough for any of the other staff.

Her father sank onto the leather sofa that dominated the small room while Phil Orsten went straight to the cabinet along the wall and poured himself a glass of scotch, slugged it back and poured another. Annika settled in next to her father and took his hand in hers. She could still hear the gunfire through the walls.

One of the mercenaries was at the comms station in the corner punching at the controls and speaking the tense, hyperfocused dialect that military types always used. She thought she heard the word "May-day" more than once. She squeezed her father's hand even harder.

The other mercenary appeared in front of them suddenly, imposing with all his filthy gear and weaponry. His cold eyes looked at her father, who was staring off into space and shaking his head in a daze. Then the eyes slid over to Annika. Not wanting to appear weak, she tried to put on a brave face.

The mercenary glared at her before thrusting a pistol in her face, handle first. "You ever used a gun before?" he asked.

She stared at the pistol for a moment before meeting the former soldier's eyes. She nodded. "Standard training for operations in conflict zones," she said, recalling the seminar.

"Good. Here. It's loaded." The mercenary gave her the gun. It was a lot heavier than the training pistol they'd used at the corporate retreat. "I'll be by the door," the mercenary went on. "Don't shoot me in the back."

Staring at the cold, heavy piece of steel in her hand, Annika nodded, wishing she was anywhere right now but here.

Markus was covering the south side of Bingham Road. The RF were using the field with its dips and trenches to sneak in close. Rourke held down the road itself. They'd been trying to get pickups to the gate, speeding out from the cluster of shacks in Copperton, trailing clouds of dust, picking up wounded. And there were a lot of wounded. This wasn't some impulsive attack, this was a carefully planned assault. The only thing keeping them back was the sheer number of bullets going downrange. It helped that the compound was surrounded by open fields, too.

Markus could tell by the RF's movements and the way they used their rifles that they'd been training, but they were still regular people with no military background for the most part, just farmers and store owners and pissed off Americans too poor to afford the cure for their disease.

A pickup truck with a heavy machine gun mounted in the bed sped onto the road, firing wildly. Another pickup followed close behind. The truck slewed sideways, a cloud of dust rising from the rear wheels. It stopped in the road while the gunner continued to pump rounds at the compound. The second truck scooped up a few wounded, then both trucks turned and sped off.

Then it was quiet.

The firefight was over. The RF were gone. A few burning cars and several craters were all that were left outside the walls. The Vircon volunteers let out a cheer. Markus clapped Rourke on the shoulder.

Reyes appeared beside them, looking out over the battlefield. "That was a test," he said.

"Next time will be for real," Markus said.

Rourke spat. "They're in the fucking mountains, the city, they're all around us. The fuck are we supposed to do?"

"We protect this compound," Markus said. "As we've been paid to do. The military's on its way, we just have to hold out until they get here."

Temple arrived by the gate. He saw Markus on the wall and called up. "Hey, Chief, wounded?"

Markus pointed to the guard shack where two wounded Vircon security officers were laid out and holding pressure on non-life-threatening wounds. Reyes nodded and Temple ran inside with his med bag.

Markus called Dieter over the radio.

"Go ahead, Chief," Dieter answered.

"Status?"

"They pulled back, quiet here by north gate. We're all good."

"Copy that," Markus said, relieved. "Stand by until we can reinforce the perimeter."

"Roger."

The RF had lost the day, but Markus had a feeling they wouldn't take it lightly. Like Reyes said, it was a test. The fight had only just begun. Throughout the compound, the landslide alarms continued to blare.

13
ON THE MOVE

"What do you think's going on?"

"I don't know," Trent said from his perch in the guard tower. He was trying to pay attention to the street out beyond the perimeter and couldn't care less about whatever O'Malley was concerned with going on in the camp behind them. The kid couldn't stay focused to save his life. Trent ignored him and scanned the crowd through the binos. On any given day the streets were crowded, but for some reason they seemed exceptionally dense lately. It was hard not to focus on just how hopelessly outnumbered they'd be if all those people suddenly came together and decided to fuck them up.

"Something's up," O'Malley said, pressing the issue.

"For fuck's sake," Trent snapped. "It's probably just the 488th guys fucking off again. Would you please keep your eyes on the perimeter so we don't end up on one of Graham's execution videos?"

"Seriously, man. Look, that's the LT right there just brought all the squad leaders outta the war room."

Trent dropped the binos and finally gave in. Indeed, Lieutenant Vickers was marching off toward the column of APCs parked by the incinerator towers and Sergeant Creon was rounding his team leaders up.

There seemed to be a sense of urgency in their body language that turned a knot of fear in Trent's guts.

"Ah shit."

"See? I told ya," O'Malley said, smacking Trent on the arm.

Not much later two soldiers from the 488th came to relieve them from guard duty and Trent and O'Malley raced to meet up with the rest of their unit. By then everyone was scrambling into teams, checking gear, tossing packs into the APCs.

Trent caught up with Bodine by the vehicles. "What's going on?" he asked.

"Fuckin' rebels attacked the mine this mornin'," Bodine said. "We got orders to move out. Leavin' this place behind."

"Fuck."

"Yup. Here." Bodine thrust a crate of ammo into Trent's arms and he helped load them onto one of the APCs. "Go git the rest of your stuff and git back here quick, Ser'ant Creon said we're movin' out ASAP."

"Shit."

Trent ran to his get his stuff. First Platoon was racing around causing general chaos throughout the Area of Operation. Team leaders were shouting for everyone to hurry up, leave this, take that, move faster. Trent fumbled with his pack, checked his MX and loadout on his armor, left the cot since it belonged to the 488th anyway. Creon was waving the squad into an APC as Trent ran up the ramp and managed to press himself into a seat. Creon followed the last man in and the ramp folded shut, the APC shuddered, and they were moving.

Creon stood hunched by the door gripping one

of the overhead straps to steady himself. "Here's the deal," he said, drawing everyone's attention. "CID got that rebel scout to give up the location of their cell. Turns out it's being run by a man named John Torres." He pulled a touch screen out of his cargo pocket and passed it around for everyone to see, displaying the image of a middle-aged man in a green shirt. "He's one of Graham's top field commanders and he's a priority target. We know the general location of his base of operations but it's touch and go. The RF stay mobile and move often so time is of the essence here. Furthermore, as of zero six this morning the RF—presumably under the command of John Torres—conducted an assault on the Vircon mining facility. They were unsuccessful thanks to the efforts of Vircon's private security, but they can't be expected to hold out much longer. The more we push into the city the more desperate the RF get. We'll keep op-tempo high and keep these fuckers backpedaling.

"We're moving into enemy-controlled territory here, Headhunters. We'll be the forward-most unit in the southwest sector. We're the tip of the spear. That being said, the RF have been supplying the locals with weapons and propaganda and it's expected that the civilian population will be less than thrilled to see us. Adhere to the rules of engagement, don't just fucking shoot at everyone you see, but be ready to fight when it becomes necessary." He took the touch screen back, shoved it in his pocket.

The APCs eventually came to a stop. The command frequency chimed and Creon grabbed a handset, presumably getting orders. He confirmed and hung up the radio.

"Our ride's being redirected," he said. "First Platoon's getting off here. Prepare to dismount."

A ripple through the line as everyone made ready. "Fuckin' shit, they can't get anything right," Ramirez grumbled.

Bodine leaned toward Trent. "You remember how to use that thing, right? Round in the chamber an' all."

"Fuck *off*," Trent said, getting ready to exit the vehicle.

"Fuck off, *Corporal*," Bodine said and bumped Trent with his fist. "Stay on my six, let's do this."

The ramp dropped open and they poured out.

Trent raced behind Bodine as the squad got out of the street. He expected to be running under fire but was surprised to find the block relatively quiet once they got to cover and took in their surroundings. There were civilians about, but that was expected. What Trent didn't expect was the sense of complete normalcy about the scene. The civilians weren't shooting or running away, just watching, mesmerized by the soldiers suddenly in their midst. People were hanging laundry out windows, shooing feral dogs from their stoops, gathering in groups on the street corners. Trent watched as a garbageman took a break from throwing bags into the back of a truck to pause and wave. Tentatively, Trent waved back. He felt ridiculous all of the sudden, standing out in the crowd laden with heavy combat gear in an otherwise peaceful setting. *Antagonist* was the word that came to mind.

The APCs turned back and left First Platoon alone in the supposed enemy territory. Creon checked his GPS and confirmed they had another twelve kilometers to go before they reached the neighborhood they were supposed to be in. He mapped a course and they moved out on another midafternoon march through dense urban decay.

"Where exactly is this RF base?" Jones asked from somewhere behind Trent. "How we gonna assault it if we don't know where it is?"

"How the fuck should I know?" Ramirez said. "They don't tell us shit. They probably don't even know. Look how quick they threw us out here and left us without armor. They don't have a fuckin' clue, man."

Specialist Sawyer came up beside them. "They tell us what we need to know and that's good enough. Sergeant Creon said we'd be clearing and searching, so shut the fuck up and search. I'm sure we'll know when we've found it."

Trent wasn't thrilled by the implication. Any minute things could turn to shit and then it'd be nothing more than luck to survive. The tension ratcheted up as they marched and little things started to get to him. The heat coming off the pavement made him feel twitchy. Pissed he'd gone and altered those weapons instead of saying no and being back at the FOB. Wondered what Alley was doing right now, wished he'd been able to call her. That nagging feeling she was with someone else crept in, made him feel a million miles away. Worry slowly turned to bubbling anger that clung to him like his sweat-soaked shirt.

Before long they moved past the towering apartment blocks and into the sprawl of low-lying slums. Pavement turned to dirt, graffiti-covered ramshackle huts tucked tight against each other hid shadows of vaguely human forms sliding through the periphery. An abandoned school came up on the right, surrounded by chain-link fencing with random bits of trash snagged in it. Bullet holes marked the side of the school, the old bulletproof windows spider-webbed with impacts. A testament to the violent days before the war, and the chaos that followed. Now, a group of thugs hung out near the playscape, smoking and drinking and watching the soldiers. Trent didn't see any weapons, but he kept an eye on them anyway.

On a street to their left a propane truck idled at the curb, the big square grille facing in their direction. It concerned Creon enough to halt the squad and check it out. Wouldn't take much to hit the gas and drive the potentially devastating vehicle-borne explosive right into their ranks. That sure would put a damper on their mission.

People were still watching them, lounging shifty-eyed, apparently not concerned with their well-being enough to warrant getting a job. Lazy fucks. And here Trent was marching straight at the enemy to defend these lowlifes. For what?

So you don't end up like them, he reminded himself. He tamped down the discontent and lifted his hand to wave. They didn't wave back.

Then suddenly things went south.

Gunfire ripped the afternoon apart, snapping and whistling, yanking Trent right out of his daze. First Platoon ducked behind whatever cover they could find, parked cars, media dispensers, telephone poles, and returned fire. Trent found Bodine and slapped him on the shoulder to let the big guy know he was behind him. Ramirez came up behind Trent.

The quiet street scene had turned in an instant; the lazy people Trent had been busy despising were now shooting at them. Some were jumping out of alleys, letting out bursts of bullets then jumping back behind cover. A few people were standing in the middle of the street firing Russian AKs from the hip. Others were on the rooftops of the houses and shacks. Rounds whistled past, splinters of concrete pelting Trent's face.

Creon reported the contact over the radio and was apparently told this wasn't the fight they were looking for. The LT ordered them to push through and move on, air support would be inbound as soon as possible. With the APCs long gone they were exposed and wouldn't be able to retreat under cover, so Creon got the squad into teams to cover interlocking sectors of fire while they got out of the kill zone. He wanted to get away from that propane truck ASAP.

They leapfrogged back to the road and past the school, the thugs long gone. Trent fired a few rounds at a guy who kept stepping out of a doorway, saw the wood frame splinter, and the guy spun around and out of sight. No way to know if he'd hit him or not but it didn't matter. Trent turned and sprinted to catch up with the rest of the platoon as they made a mad dash down the dirt road.

It seemed like gunfire had erupted throughout the city, the crack of incoming rounds not getting any farther away, like it was following them as they ran through the cramped ghetto. Trent, Bodine, and Ramirez stuck together, checking corners, making seemingly random turns. Trent couldn't see the rest of the squad, let alone anyone else from the platoon. How Bodine knew which way to go was beyond him. *If* Bodine actually knew which way to go. There was too much adrenaline for Trent to feel fear, but somewhere in the back of his mind he thought about POWs and execution videos.

Then suddenly they were together again, all of First Platoon holding both sides of a main paved street, the LT on the radio with Command getting SITREPs from the team leaders. The immediate area was clear of civilians now but Trent could see swarms of people moving past the intersections some ways off, following and surrounding them.

Someone shouted for the medic and Sawyer went running over to one of the guys from Third Squad whose left arm was soaked dark red. The soldier was ambulatory though, despite the wound, and holding his MX in his right hand like an old-school action star.

Creon broke off from the LT and came over. "Mission's scrubbed for now, we're being redirected," he said. "Check your ammo and get ready to move. Once we get our wounded patched we're linking up with Bravo Company and heading to the Valley Regional Hospital where local police are being overrun."

"Is this the RF, Sergeant?" Ramirez asked.

"Doesn't fucking matter who it is, Private, if someone's shooting at you, you shoot them first."

Five blocks later they met up with Bravo, who luckily had some armored Prowlers and an APC with a turret gun. Slightly more confident with the increased numbers and firepower, they pushed through the city and came to the hospital.

Nightmare would be a good way to put it.

Cars jammed the small two-lane road leading to the front of the hospital in both directions, horns blaring, people screaming, getting out of their cars to yell at each other and push stalled vehicles out of the way, which only made the traffic worse. Cars were driving on the sidewalks, inching past crowds of people who pounded on the hoods. Trent heard police sirens somewhere but couldn't see them. The 117th moved into the crowd, shifting from high-strung combatants to compassionate caregivers too fast for the body to catch up with the mind. People came at them not with guns now but wounded, crying, begging for help as Trent and the others pushed their way toward the hospital. The Prowlers got caught up in the press, external speakers set to area dispersal ordering people out of the way, which of course they didn't listen to. Bravo got bogged down and set a perimeter as Lieutenant Vickers took First Platoon ahead toward the hospital.

The lot at the main entrance was crammed with cars and ambulances. Police were there trying to organize the chaos, waving vehicles on. People were dragging injured on red-stained blankets. Others carried small bundles in their arms. Many were covered in dust and rubble, streaks of red cutting through gray. Medical staff were in the crowd, moving from injured person to injured person, scrawling things on their foreheads in black marker. Some were ushered inside the facility, others turned away.

Someone grabbed Trent's belt. A woman holding a child, blood-matted hair crusted to her forehead. "I . . . I'm sorry," he muttered, then she was gone and someone else was in her place looking for help. Trent felt something in him crack. He clamped his jaw, forced whatever he was feeling out with a deep breath. Didn't help, only made him focus on the scent of blood and smoke and sweat.

First Platoon pushed its way through the crowd, past the screaming parents and walking wounded and idling cars, past the police hollering orders that no one listened to. They made it to the front of the hospital where Lieutenant Vickers found the chief of police and pulled him aside to get a SITREP. Sergeant Creon got the rest of the squad into position to hold back some of the crowd and give the medical staff some room as they treated people by the lobby doors.

"Who the fuck are we helping?" Ramirez snapped. "These the same people shooting at us a minute ago?"

"I don't know, man," Trent said, waving back a group of men suspiciously close to military age.

"Of course they are," Jones said. "Thought it was a good idea to shoot at us and then they got fucked up. Now they want us to help them. *Fuck* that."

"Yeah," Ramirez said. "And why do we need to secure this hospital anyway? Not like we're going to use it."

"Of course we are," Jones went on. "It's all about control, man. We take this hospital, these yokel fucks will think twice about pissing us off if they hope to use it. Just like Vircon. This whole fuckin' mad dash through the suck, man, it's all about control. Think about it, bro. Vircon's a fuckin' gold mine, like for real. We just gotta get there before it's all shot to shit."

Sawyer came through with his medic pack in hand, MX clipped to his chest. "Shut up, will you?" He nodded toward all the civilians well within earshot, watching, listening. "OPSEC for Christ's sake." Then he was off helping the hospital staff.

Trent, Ramirez, and Jones shut up and focused on pushing the crowd back. They remained like that for several hours until more troops arrived from other units and moved the crowd on. Many went home cradling untreated wounds.

And even though the 117th hadn't captured the RF stronghold or any enemy commanders, at least now they owned a hospital.

14
A SHOW FOR THE TROOPS

B ravo didn't stay long.

A few days after taking the hospital they were
sent to blockade the north end of Interstate 15 and
stop the RF from retaking the rear, but they'd signed
some of their Prowlers over to Alpha before leaving so
at least there was that. Engineers showed up two days
later and took over the assisted-living facility across
the street, linked it with the hospital, and built the
place into yet another fortified military camp. Heavy
equipment trucks brought in tall blast columns that
were hoisted into place by crane rigs, the walls rising
fast while morale was falling even faster.

As far as everyone was concerned, babysitting the
hospital while the engineers did their thing was just
another delay in the hunt for the RF cell and First
Platoon's objective of reaching the Vircon mine. The
more they were sidetracked, the longer it took to ac-
complish the mission, which of course meant the longer they'd have to stay in the valley. There seemed to
be a sense that once the mine was secured First Platoon would be allowed to go back to FOB Spearpoint
and call it a deployment.

Trent was starting to believe otherwise.

The more he thought about going home the more
he thought about Alley with someone else, and the an-
grier he got. It ate at him, wore him down and left

him with a poisonous mood. And he wasn't the only one getting irritable. Fights were breaking out among the squads; some of the younger, more spiteful soldiers were starting to test the NCOs' authority. Not a good situation for anyone as far into enemy territory as they were.

So the higher-ups had the brilliant idea of having a Morale and Welfare night. Mandatory fun, if you will.

Someone had acquired a holo-vid projector from one of the engineers and set it up in the hospital cafeteria. They'd taken blankets from the storeroom, sprayed them black, and hung them on the walls behind the projection as a backdrop to the glowing holographic USO show being live-streamed from FOB Spearpoint, complete with near-naked ultramodel dancers, pyrotechnics, and celebrity hosts taking turns on the mic to suck up to the troops. They were on a stage built inside one of the FOB's empty hangars to get them out of the rain since a storm had rolled in earlier that day and showed no signs of letting up any time soon. The rain dumping on the metal roof of the hangar played havoc with the audio, and every time a peal of thunder shook the atmosphere the feed flickered and threatened to cut out.

Trent was one of the lucky ones who'd managed to avoid guard duty this night and was able to find himself a seat near the front next to O'Malley. The kid was focused intently on the show, looking much like a toddler first discovering the wonders of TV. The image of a dancer spun into frame right before them, angling her body just so, curves twisting, bending, snapping taut. Hair flipped back exposing her neck, a smile plastered to her face. The cafeteria erupted in cheers, catcalls, ear-piercing whistles. Trent glanced at the female soldier from the engineer unit operating the feed, surrounded by all these cavemen, and suddenly felt embarrassed to be associated with such primitive company. The 117th certainly had females in their ranks, but not in First Platoon and it showed. The NCOs in the room let the soldiers have their fun and just stood around with arms crossed, trying not to look like they were enjoying the flesh show too much, either.

"Ah, man," O'Malley said. "If I could just have an hour with one of those girls . . ."

Bodine spat a string of dip into a cup. "Shit, you wouldn't last ten fuckin' seconds, assumin' you even knew what to do in the first place."

"I know what to do, asshole," O'Malley said under his breath.

The band playing for the dancers was one of those overproduced, corporate pop-rock cash machines called ProtoDriver, who pumped out overplayed cookie-cutter hits you couldn't escape from on the airwaves. The hologram was edited with effects to merge real-time feed with stock images of East Coast America probably meant to inspire the troops: the towering skyscrapers of New York, aircraft roaring through the clouds, the silhouette of a soldier standing atop a tank with the sun setting behind him. They reached the end of the song, the dancers broke into a sort of improvised final bow, and moved off-screen as ProtoDriver's front man, Cade Carver, took center stage.

He grabbed a microphone more for nostalgia than necessity since he'd already been miked up for his performance, maybe just for something to do with his hands as he looked out into the crowd back at the

FOB. The marvel of modern technology made it seem like he was looking directly at the troops in the hospital cafeteria.

"How you doin', Camp Spearpoint?" Cade Carver said.

"It's *FOB*, you asshole," someone shouted. Laughs rippled through the room.

"Thank you so much for havin' us out here," Cade Carver went on. "We couldn't be more honored to be here with all of you." Typical pandering bullshit. Trent wanted the dancers to come back. "We just want to let you know how much we appreciate the sacrifice you're making out here for us. You have the hardest job in the world, protecting the union of this great country, and you're doing a hell of a job!" He paused, the sound of the crowd back at the FOB coming through the audio. "Your mission is so important to the people out here, even if they don't seem to realize it just yet. Without you to fight for them they'd be lost to chaos and anarchy, and that's not what America stands for. We're better than that. It may seem sometimes that that's how it is, though, that the world is such a mess there's no way to put it back together, but we know that's not true. We know, all of us here back home know that the world *will* be right, that our great country will once again be back on the world stage, and we know that it's because of people like you, brave men and women who will never give up, who put their lives on the line every night and day to protect us."

"This priss don't know shit about what we do," Jones said.

"It may seem like an impossible task at times," Carver went on, "like the road ahead is never-ending, but it will end and you will prevail, and America will prevail because of you. God bless."

"Fuck you and fuck the rebels," another heckler shouted at the holographic image. Then the dancers were back on, another song revving up, and the room broke into cheers, laughter, hooting, and whistling.

Thunder shook the walls, a bright flash of lightning and the feed suddenly cut out. The merriment turned to jeering and hollering. The NCOs came off their posts and started hollering back, trying to control the chaos. The poor engineer was struggling to get the holo-vid back up but she was shaking her head in obvious surrender. Trent wondered if the feed had really cut out or if she'd just gotten sick of the macho caveman routine. Either way, the show was over.

"Welp," Bodine said. "I'm gettin' outta here before Ser'ant Creon gets us for some stupid detail." No one argued with that logic.

But outside, the mood hadn't changed. The amped-up horde spilled out of the cafeteria to light up cigarettes and break into new arguments. Two soldiers got in a scuffle for who-the-fuck-knew what. The rain was still coming down; people huddled in groups under cover, others couldn't care less and stood in the open. The engineers were still working, bright halogen lamps casting beams of light through the soaking dark, their machines thrumming and belching diesel exhaust to the backdrop of distant lightning.

Trent, Sawyer, and O'Malley stood under a tree some ways away from everyone else. They watched the madness spread across the hospital compound.

"Morale seems much better now," Trent said, lighting a cigarette.

Sawyer shook his head. "It's a joke. The whole fucking thing."

"Yup."

"No," Sawyer said, "I mean it. All of this. Everything we think we stand for is a joke."

"Here we go," O'Malley said.

Sawyer waved him off. "That's what I'm talking about. That's exactly what we're expected to say. We all have a script to follow and most of us don't even realize it. And those that do just ignore it."

Trent felt something about the comment hit close to home, but wasn't quite sure why. "Of course we have a script," he said. "We're in the Army."

"And that's just it, right?" Sawyer said. "We don't have to be held to account for anything because we're all just brainless automatons following orders. It's the same for civilians. Society has a script. I mean, what are social norms but prescribed expectations of people?"

"That the kinda shit they teach you in college, Sawyer?" O'Malley asked.

"If we'd been born here you better believe we'd have different views of what's going on, and how we feel about the Army kicking down our doors."

"Well what good does it do to worry about that shit out here," Trent said with just a bit more venom in his tone than he'd intended.

"So you're saying that if we were from here we'd agree with the rebels?" O'Malley said. "Like, for some reason we'd suddenly be okay with destroying the government and ruining the country?"

"An oversimplification," Sawyer said. "But, yes. Something like that. Think about it. What the fuck are we doing out here? We're killing fellow Americans.

And even looking at it like *that* is a prescribed view. Humans, they're humans. Just like you, just like me. It's too easy to keep our heads in the sand and do what's expected of us."

"If the rebellion wins then everything goes to shit," Trent said. "All it'll do is prove that chaos is the answer to our problems, not law, not order, not the democratic process. Beating the rebels is the best hope for return to order," he said. "At least, that's what I have to believe, because what the fuck else can we do?"

Sawyer stared out into the pouring rain for a while. "One day we'll be called to answer for the things we've done," he finally said.

O'Malley scratched his head, clearly struggling to add to the conversation. "Yeah, well, fuck that," he said, flicking his cigarette away.

Jones came over and joined them then, a welcome distraction from the depressing conversation. He leaned in close and pulled a flask out of his cargo pocket, a smirk plastered across his face. "Ya'll want some?"

"Where'd you get that?" Sawyer asked.

Jones took a sip, sucked his lips. "Bought it off some lady on the street while I was on patrol yesterday. Might take a bit of that edge off." He offered the flask, the sharp smell of alcohol in the air. Smelled like whiskey. God only knows what kind or where the woman on the street got it from.

"No man, not out here," Trent said, suddenly worried someone would see. "Creon catches you and you're fucked."

Jones shrugged and took another sip. "Yeah and the rebels can get you, too. Fuck 'em. I ain't gonna live my life scared of everything."

"I'm not scared, fuck-face. Just cautious."

"Yeah, yeah, same thing, bro."

"I'll have some," O'Malley said and took the flask. He tipped it back and made a face like he'd just swallowed a mouthful of angry hornets, much to the group's amusement.

Jones snagged the flask back. "Fuckin' kid doesn't know how to handle a drink!"

"Are you even old enough to drink?" Sawyer asked.

O'Malley struggled to compose himself. "I'm old enough to come out here and fight," he choked out.

"That's fair," Jones said.

Down by the parking lot someone stepped out of one of the latrine stalls waving something above his head. "Hey Brigham, I'm done with this picture of your wife!" he shouted. Another soldier—presumably Brigham—came over and grabbed at the picture and the two of them ended up in a wrestling match as others cheered them on. Someone else snatched the picture off the ground and ran into the stall, slamming the door shut behind him.

"Back home they call us heroes," Sawyer said. "Look at us. We're nothing but fucking animals."

15
A REASON TO FIGHT

The military had taken over the Valley Regional Hospital and put the surrounding neighborhoods on lockdown. Sam and Rob had been harassing their patrols, shooting and scooting, trying to hold them back in order to give Commander Torres time to orchestrate an assault on the mine. The disruptive tactics were working for now, but it wouldn't last forever. The military machine just kept grinding. So the RF were trying a new tactic, one Sam wasn't so sure she agreed with, but it wasn't her place to question orders.

They were in a warehouse now, hidden from drone observation and hoping to secure a potential—albeit questionable—alliance. RF circled the interior of the warehouse while Sub-commander Akers met with a man called Tez, a grimy street thug who led a local gang in West Jordan. Tez had his own crew behind him.

"You doing a number on them government boys," Tez said. "Got 'em running around scared now." Tez's crew nodded sagely. "Whatcha need us for?"

"Numbers," Sub-commander Akers said. "There's still a lot of fight left before we clear the city of those *government boys*. You know these streets, you have systems in place to monitor everything going on; who's who, where they go, who they talk to, what they say.

You have eyes everywhere. You have assets . . . you *are* an asset. We'd like to tap into that."

"Tap into that," Tez said, stroking his chin. His bloodshot eyes shifted over to Sam. "I heard that." He let his gaze slide down, then up. Slow, deliberate. Fucking sleaze. He saw her rifle. "You a sniper?" he asked, tilting his head back to look down his nose at her.

"I'm good with a rifle," Sam said. She remained still, collected.

Tez tugged at the crotch of his pants, sucked his teeth. "Yeah, I bet."

Rob's hands dropped to his side. Tez's men tensed. Sam kept her eyes locked on the gang leader. She had a reputation now, had to play it cool.

Tez swiped a thumb across his nose. "You know there's a bounty out for rebel snipers," he said. "Ten Gs dead or alive, twenty-five for the Reaper of Kill-zone Valley. What incentive we got to keep us from taking your pretty white head up to them government boys?"

Rob shot forward, snatched Tez by the shirt and jammed his pistol under the gang leader's chin. Weapons bristled throughout the warehouse. "How about I just fucking kill you here, you gang-banging piece of shit," Rob snarled.

Tez yanked his own piece out and shoved it against Rob's temple, his men had their pistols drawn and were waving them around. The RF pointed their weapons right back.

Akers took a step forward. "In order to drive the greater threat from this valley we need to work together. If the current government wins, what do you think will become of this place? Have you seen what's happening in Dallas? Or Denver? The government's *pouring* resources into the fight in those cities and the resistance is losing ground. Captives who aren't shot in the street are sent straight to General Schroeder's prison camp in Jacksonville and paraded around as traitors and criminals. Once the government takes those cities where do you think they'll go next? I'm sure you've heard about President Haymond's stance on gang activity. Not much room for forgiveness under his rule. So like it or not, we have to work together here. Either you're willing to do that or you're not. Regardless, you'll make no more threats toward our people. This is not a request."

Tez thought about it for a minute then pulled his pistol away from Rob's head. Guns disappeared back into waistbands and beneath shirts. Rob holstered his own pistol and took a step back. Sam stood locked in place, rifle in her hands. Her heart was racing, but she was doing all she could to play it cool. She let out a silent breath of relief as weapons relaxed.

"Very good," Akers said. "We'll arrange further plans to establish a liaison between our organizations and see that you're properly equipped. Now, resist any military presence in your area. Do whatever you must." With that, Akers turned her back on Tez and marched off.

Tez smirked at Sam, sucked his teeth.

She stared him down for a moment, wondering if this really was a good idea, before she too left the warehouse.

Outside, a car was waiting for the sub-commander. Sam and Rob walked her over while the rest of the RF fighters spread out through the parking lot to provide security.

"Is this really our next move?" Rob asked, still noticeably upset.

Akers whirled on him. "Don't ever act out like that again," she snapped. Rob froze, clearly caught off guard. Akers went on. "And don't ever question Joseph Graham's orders, especially in front of others. This resistance is built on shaky ground as it is with a dozen different factions trying to defend against a better organized military while a new capital with a new government takes root in California. That takes time and resources. The Coalition is barely holding out in Denver and we are in danger of losing ground." Akers narrowed her eyes at Sam and Rob. "You're soldiers of the Revolutionist Front. Others look up to you, both of you. Keep your impulses in check. The further we push into the city the further we stretch our lines," she said. "That means supplies, weapons, ammunition, communication, reinforcements. Those guys in there already have that established. We need to use their systems. We need to hold this city. In this war, we do what's necessary to win. The enemy of my enemy, right? Will you have any trouble following your orders?"

"No, ma'am," Rob said.

Sam said nothing.

"Cross?"

"No, ma'am," she said after a beat.

Akers nodded, then climbed in the car and was gone, leaving Sam and Rob in the empty parking lot.

"Fucking scum," Rob said, sinking into the lawn chair. He reached into a cooler and pulled out a Modera, popped the cap and drained half the bottle. "I can't believe we're actually aligning with those pieces of shit."

Sam lounged on her back, hands behind her head, looking up at the sky as the first stars of the evening winked to life. They weren't on duty, so to speak, but they still found themselves drawn to the rooftops. The safe house below was filled with fellow rebels so they could afford to relax. Most of the block was occupied by the RF, anyway.

Sam wasn't sure what to think of the whole thing, so she said nothing.

"You think this'll work? You really think we can trust them?" Rob asked.

"I don't know what I think," Sam said. "It ain't up to me to think about it anyways. Like Sub-commander Akers said, we follow our orders. If it means we hold off the military and buy time for the resistance to build something new, then that's what we do. I mean, we surprised them at first but reality is we just don't have the strength of numbers yet. It's only a matter of time now before they take Denver and send troops here. But I don't like it either."

Rob finished his beer then got up, grabbed two more from the cooler, and handed one to Sam. She took it, scooted upright against the wall along the edge of the roof. Rob slid down next to her.

"You see the way he looked at you," he said, apparently unwilling to let it go. "If we were regular people out on the street they'd have . . ." He trailed off, staring at the ground. He shook his head, then sipped his beer.

Sam looked at him. "I can handle my own. Always have."

"Yeah, but that's not the point. Imagine it wasn't you, but someone else, someone who isn't a fighter."

"Can't think like that."

Rob plucked up an old rusted nail, twisted it in his fingers, then tossed it away. Something was eating at him. Was he being protective of her? The thought sent butterflies fluttering through her belly.

He let out a breath like he was clearing his mind. He looked at her. "So you've always been tough, huh?"

"I wouldn't go that far," Sam said. "I grew up on a ranch outside Amarillo, Texas. My father owned two hundred head of cattle, had to run 'em across three hundred acres every day to keep the land from turning to dust. Down to Bonita Creek and back. Sunup to sundown. Dad taught me and John to shoot, camp, survive. Everything, really. You gotta be tough."

"John?"

"My brother. Older brother."

"Had a lot of coyotes on your ranch?"

Sam nodded, sipped her beer. "Yeah. That and raiders." It seemed like such a long time ago, she'd been so young, helpless. Not anymore. She realized suddenly that she'd drifted into silence. She cleared her throat. "Always someone out there trying to take from those who can't keep their own. Raiders never got the best of us, though. The terrain was too rough for vehicles so they'd show up on foot. Could see 'em coming from a mile away. One shot, one kill, Dad always said. I guess it was just fate that brought me here."

"Your family still at the ranch?" Rob asked. "You going to go back there after the war?"

Sam drained her beer. "Ranch is gone."

"Shit, I'm sorry, Sam."

She shook her head. "Nature of war. Wasn't the raiders in the end."

"We don't have to talk about it if you don't want."

"It's fine," she said. "I . . . like talking to you." That feeling again, sliding through her belly, excitement, fear, anticipation. She looked at Rob. He was staring back at her, his blue eyes intense even in the fading light. There was something in his face, not pity or sorrow. Something she couldn't pin down. She felt like talking. She felt like telling Rob about herself, even if it wasn't a pleasant story. She got up, brought a fresh round of beers, and sat back down.

"I was fourteen," she said. "Dad taught me and John the rifle but made us swear to never use it for someone else's dirty work. This was back when the fighting was just starting to break out on state lines and he'd snap off the TV when he caught us watching the news. Forbid us from ever joining any kind of fight. Thing was, I became obsessed. I started sneaking military magazines and field training manuals from Mr. Lyle's Pawn 'n' Supplies. I kept 'em in a box in the barn where I'd sneak off to read 'em. Never even told John about that." She shook her head. "I wanted nothing more in the world than to be a Recon sniper. I was young and stupid though.

"I was the first to hear 'em coming when they finally showed up. Heard the engines, knew it was more than one vehicle. The only other people nearby were the Darbys and they only had one truck, so I knew it was the government. I remember the cloud of dust they kicked up, like a sandstorm. Dad went out to meet 'em. Said they came for able-bodied folk to defend the Constitution. John was older'n me and the right age for conscription. Dad didn't want to hear it, told 'em they had no right. They claimed Texas was under federal jurisdiction and subject to its laws."

Sam sucked down her beer, felt the edge sliding off. She'd played the memory over and over so many times she wondered how much of it was true anymore, and how much was inflated by her hatred. "They took John by force," she said. "Dad got his rifle. This rifle." She patted the stock of the Remington propped beside her. "Before I knew it, our house was all shot up, John taken away. . . ." She felt tears well at the corners of her eyes. She clenched her jaw, fought it down. She thought she'd had control of this by now, but saying it out loud for the first time felt . . . raw. "They shot and killed Dad on the front lawn. Mom died in the house. And I ran like a coward. Ran off into the fields where I knew I could hide. They shot at me, too, but weren't any good. None of 'em came close. They made a half-assed effort to come after me, but gave up assuming I wouldn't be any kind of trouble for them. I just kept running and crying like a little girl."

Rob scooted closer, put his hand on her knee.

"I spent the next few years living with different folks," Sam said. "People kind enough to take me in. People like me, with no place to go. Learned a lot of new things. Got better at what I already knew. I even tried to find out what happened to John . . . to see if he was still alive, somewhere out there, but I never found . . ." Her voice trailed off. "I'm sorry," She said wiping her eyes. "I just . . . sometimes I hate myself for leaving like that. After everything Dad taught me and I just ran."

"But you're alive," Rob said. "And you're here now taking the fight to them like they've never seen. Sam, you're the Reaper of Killzone Valley. You're making them pay for what they did and helping liberate probably millions more who'd suffer the same as you have."

"You don't have to say that."

"It's true. I'm from California. The war hasn't ravaged my home. I don't have a reason to be here."

Sam reached out, placed her hand on top of his. "Yes you do."

"Well, maybe. I guess I'm just afraid of not having a greater purpose in life. And Joseph Graham has given us that purpose."

Something moved in Sam, a feeling that seeped through her body. She welcomed it, all the sadness, all the hatred, the loneliness, the satisfying sense of retribution. And Rob, here with her now, helping her, sharing it with her. She plucked his hand up, pulled it to her face. She felt his fingers brush her cheek, slide through her hair. He felt so close. There was a brief moment of uncertainty that hung between them like opposing magnets, until the polarity shifted, was made right and locked together.

Rob's mouth met hers, his stubble scraping her lips, her chin. He tasted of beer. She breathed in his scent, like sweat and skin and smoke. His hands pulled her in tight, their bodies shifting, pressing together. Sam lurched against him, grabbed at his shirt, fingers working the buttons. Her hands moved down his chest, undid his belt and tossed it aside, ammo pouches clattering. Her fingers hooked the top of his pants, popped the button and opened the fly.

Rob tugged her shirt up and over her head and tossed it aside. She pushed him down, threw a leg over him. She looked down, watched him watching her. His calloused hands slid up her bare waist, over her breasts, cupped her face.

"Sam . . ."

"Shut up."

She moved his hands, put them where she knew he wanted them. The storm of emotions inside her threatened to burst at the seams, not willing to be repressed any longer. She gave into it, let go. For tonight, the only thing that existed in the world was her and Rob.

16
ENEMY CONTACT

Alpha Company began reaching out from the hospital, setting up traffic control and checkpoints farther into RF territory like feelers, testing the waters before making another long march beyond the help of support. First Platoon had left the hospital behind and moved into a part of town colloquially known as "The Turf" because of the gang activity in the area, and was currently holding down a checkpoint at a traffic circle in the middle of a usually busy market square.

Trent stood guard at the gate, which was nothing more than an opening between a couple concrete barriers with some sandbags and trash stacked in piles out front. There was no actual gate to close in the event things went south, which was why Creon had given orders to act with extreme aggression in regard to force security. Street vendors came by every so often pushing wheelbarrows of useless trinkets with hopes of selling the garbage to gullible soldiers, but they were quickly driven away. The other day Trent watched as one middle-aged man of questionable intelligence failed to take the hint and kept pressing O'Malley for a sale. The man just kept smiling as O'Malley tried to shove him off. Creon came over and dropped the guy with the stock of his MX. The man crawled away and hadn't been back since.

Trent took a drag on his cigarette and scanned the street. Beyond the traffic circle there were a bunch of shops, an internet café, a satellite phone service, and some small general stores. There was usually a lot of activity; from sunup to sundown, the street was filled with shouting pedestrians, honking cars, and lots of sideways stares.

This morning, however, the street was empty.

That emptiness was accompanied by a deadly silence so palpable it set Trent's skin to crawling. He checked his watch. 1027 hours. Prime business time. Something was off.

"Hey, Bodine."

The corporal grunted. "What."

"Shouldn't there be more people out here?"

Bodine stood off to the side watching the north end of the traffic circle. "Ya know, I was thinkin' that."

Trent stubbed out his cigarette. "I'm gonna call it in." He got on the radio and sent it up. Less than thirty seconds later, Creon was at the gate.

"What's the issue?" he said, scanning beyond the barricades, rifle at the ready.

"This time yesterday there had to be a hundred people out there," Trent said. "Today it's a ghost town, Sergeant. Something's not right."

Creon stood silently, eyes narrowed on the street. Somewhere in the distance a generator purred, a dog barked, the breeze pushed loose paper down the sidewalk. But there were no voices, no patter of footsteps, no rumbling car engines or honking horns. The shops were open, doors propped and wares set out.

"How long's it been like this?" Creon asked.

"The whole morning," Trent replied.

"How long have you been on guard duty?"

Trent knew where the sergeant was going. He swallowed a lump in his throat. "Uh . . . since zero six, Sergeant."

"And you just now figured it worth reporting?" Creon said, eyes still locked on the street.

To Trent's surprise, Bodine actually stepped in. "Well, Ser'ant," he said, "sometimes they take a while to git goin' so we were keepin' watch. But it's not lookin' too good now."

Creon let out a long breath, then grabbed the radio and called the machine-gun nest. "Look alive," he said. "We might have activity."

To Trent and Bodine he said, "You two stay alert and call in anything you see. I'm going to get . . ." He stopped and cocked his head.

From somewhere down the street, Trent heard the distinct growl of an engine growing louder, closer. His heart sank.

Two blocks away a dented-up car screeched around the corner, turned hard in their direction, and started gaining speed. It flashed down the empty street, maybe a hundred and fifty meters away and closing.

"*Stop that fucking car!*" Creon shouted as he shouldered his MX and started firing at the vehicle.

Trent and Bodine dropped behind the pile of sandbags and fired. The car kept coming, swerving and bouncing over potholes, splashing through puddles of drain water. It was a hundred meters out when the .50 cal thundered to life, bright tracers flashing into the street, chewing up the pavement and climbing as the gunner walked the rounds into the car. The .50 tore into the engine block, sparking off the metal, then ripped through the windshield. The car veered hard and jumped the curb, sliced through a street sign, and slammed into the front of a shop. The machine gun continued pounding the car until the vehicle caught fire. It had stopped fifty meters away.

Creon gave the signal to cease fire. Trent's ears were ringing, adrenaline coursing through his veins. His hands shook. He wondered if any of his rounds had even hit the car.

There was a bright flash, a deafening explosion, and Trent was knocked to the ground by the shock wave, the acrid smell of burning chemicals and smoke filling the air. He lay there gasping, his hearing muffled like he was underwater. Something was screaming in his skull.

Then he was hoisted to his feet, gripped by the front plate of his armor. He tried to focus. Someone was standing in front of him and shouting but it sounded like distant trumpets. The hand shook him and clarity snapped back. Creon was shouting orders and pointing to the street. Bodine was crouched behind the concrete barrier, sweeping his rifle back and forth. Others had arrived, moving out into a defensive perimeter.

"Second Squad, on me," Creon shouted.

Trent had a sinking feeling as he and the other members of Second Squad formed a group around the staff sergeant. "They just hit us with a fucking car bomb. We're going out. Stay tight. Everyone else, cover the CP and call it in. Let's go." He darted out the passage through the barricade and led Second Squad into the street.

They raced across the traffic circle, leapfrogging to cover, rifles sweeping up, down, left, and right. They stacked along a wall at the corner of an intersection and Creon split half the squad off to cover the opposite side of the street, placing Bodine in command of the second team. Once they were in position, he gave the signal to move out and both teams pushed up the street in combat crouches, rifles at the ready.

There was nothing left of the car but a smoldering crater. The explosion had torn the front of the shop apart and set fire to the building. Twisted scraps of steel lay scattered about, black soot streaked across the pavement. A water line had been damaged and a pool of brown mud was forming in the base of the crater. Downed electrical lines sparked in the street.

Creon raised a hand, flared his fingers out and motioned them forward. They skirted the wreckage and pushed on, heading in the direction the car had come from. Across the street, the other half of Second Squad moved in tandem. They eventually reached a T-intersection at the end of the market, where a wide four-lane road cut across their path and a series of multilevel office buildings stood on the other side. O'Malley took point and made ready to dash across to cover the far side. Trent moved behind a parked car and took a knee to get a better vantage to cover O'Malley. He saw Bodine stack behind a corner a few meters away and get his own team in position to cross.

"Ready," Creon said, stacking behind O'Malley. He placed a hand on O'Malley's shoulder and said, "Go."

O'Malley darted out, head down, rifle gripped in both hands, charging through the open. The only sound seemingly in the entire city was the pounding of his boots. Trent scanned for threats as Ramirez from Bodine's team went to make the crossing, too.

One of the office buildings began to pop, flashes from several upper-level windows, and rounds punched into the street. O'Malley stumbled and pitched forward, collapsing in the middle of the road. Ramirez turned back and dove for cover. Trent watched in horror as bullets pinged off the pavement around O'Malley. Trent sighted on the muzzle flashes and returned fire. Soon the entire side of the building was pocked with bullet holes, shattered windows raining glass on the lot below. The enemy gunfire was inaccurate and undisciplined, but it didn't relent.

Creon called Jones over, who had a grenade launcher attachment on his MX. He ordered Jones to pound the side of the building while they went out to retrieve O'Malley. Jones slapped a grenade magazine into the chamber and ranged the weapon in.

"Trent, Sawyer, with me," Creon said. "On my mark . . . *go.*"

Jones's launcher thumped out grenades as Creon sprinted to O'Malley, Trent and Sawyer right behind him. Being out in the open made things feel suddenly unreal. Trent had the vague awareness that he was being sighted through some rebel's scope, but it didn't really seem that important. Right now he was just running, the pavement getting chewed up around him like in the movies. Just ahead, O'Malley was lying facedown in the street.

Creon was the first to reach him. He took position to provide covering fire and commanded Trent and Sawyer to grab O'Malley and go. No time to check for wounds, just get back to cover. Jones's grenades continued to smash the office building. It was a storm of gunfire, deafening and lethal. Trent crouched, grabbed O'Malley by the drag strap and hoisted him up with Sawyer's help. There was a puddle of blood on the pavement beneath O'Malley's body.

And then it didn't feel so unreal.

They each slipped an arm around O'Malley and dragged him back to the corner where the rest of the squad was holding back the enemy. Trent's legs burned as he tried to run with O'Malley's weight hanging off him, tripping, tugging, and pulling against Sawyer's own steps. Behind them, Creon emptied magazine after magazine into the building to cover their retreat. It felt like they were in the open for an eternity, like they'd never get behind cover. But then they were, tumbling past the rest of the squad, flopping down onto the sidewalk around the corner of a building and out of sight to the enemy. Trent eased O'Malley onto his back and saw the blood.

O'Malley had taken a round through the upper left shoulder, right in the gap between the armor plating of his vest, and another round through the hip. His uniform was soaked almost black. Sawyer dropped to his knees beside Trent, jammed two fingers into O'Malley's neck to check for a pulse, then opened his med bag. "Get those wounds exposed, Trent."

Trent froze, staring at O'Malley's seemingly lifeless form. His eyes were closed and his face was a grisly pale yellow. Sawyer punched Trent in the chest. "Hey," he said. "Focus. Open his vest and cut his clothes so I can get to the wounds, *now*."

Trent took a breath, swung his rifle around to his back and tried to steady his trembling hands as he unbuckled the vest and ripped the Velcro open. He fumbled with the buttons on the shirt, struggling to get them open one by one.

"Just fucking cut it," Sawyer said, ripping open a clot kit and sticking a gauze pack in his teeth.

Trent pulled his knife and cut the uniform top off,

then carefully sliced open O'Malley's T-shirt. Blood welled from a small hole in O'Malley's upper shoulder, just above the heart. Trent tried to recall anatomy class and whether or not any major arteries passed through that area. He felt like they did.

"Pants, too," Sawyer said as he poured a coagulant on the shoulder wound. "I gotta check that pelvis."

Creon hovered over them. "Is he . . ."

"He's alive," Sawyer said. "But he's in critical condition. He needs medevac now."

"Copy that." Then Creon was gone again.

Sawyer kept working on the shoulder, packing gauze into the hole in O'Malley's flesh. "How's that pelvic wound looking?" he asked, urging Trent to focus.

Trent reached for O'Malley's belt, cut the pants, and exposed O'Malley's pelvis. In any other circumstance it would have made for a good laugh, the private laying there with his privates hanging out, but there was nothing funny here.

"Here," Sawyer said grabbing Trent's hands and pushing them onto O'Malley's shoulder. "Keep pressure here." Trent pressed on the wound, blood soaking into the bandage. "It's alright," Sawyer said, "just keep pressure." Then he went to work on the pelvis.

Trent leaned into O'Malley. With the gunfight still raging just around the corner, he looked up and scanned the block. What if the RF were flanking them? Would those windows over there suddenly come to life with muzzle flashes? Would he be lying in the street bleeding out before the end of today? The thoughts raced through his head on replay, the dizzying storm of chaos numbing the edges, and Trent started to feel a thousand miles away.

Sawyer finished plugging up the bullet hole in O'Malley's hip. "Help me roll him on his side," he said. "Ready . . . one, two, three." They rolled him toward Trent so Sawyer could check O'Malley's back. The medic felt around, swiped his hand in and under the clothing and armor to check for blood. He found nothing. They laid O'Malley back down. "No exit wounds," Sawyer said. "The bullets are still in him. Probably tumbled. He could have severe internal bleeding. Trent, go see where Creon is with the medevac."

Trent climbed to his feet, thankful to get away. He went over to the street corner where Creon and the rest of Second Squad were still trying to hold off the enemy. A round buzzed past and punched into the brick, spattering Trent with debris. He ducked, whipped his rifle around and crouched behind cover. Creon was just ahead behind a concrete wall. Trent had to shout over the gunfire.

"Sergeant! Sawyer needs a timeline on medevac!"

Creon was shouting into a radio and stuck a finger up. "Headhunter Main this is Hound Two, we need air support at CP One-Seven. Heavy enemy contact with vehicle-borne explosives. One casualty, over."

Creon stuck a palm over his ear to block out background noise while he listened to HQ's response. "Copy that," Creon said, then threw the handset back to the radio operator. "*Fuck*." He punched the cinder block wall, then called Bodine over the squad comms. "This is Hound Two, fall back to the CP, over." He turned to Trent. "How's O'Malley?"

"Critical, Sergeant. We gotta get him out of here."

"Is he ambulatory?"

"Negative."

"Alright, you and Sawyer pick his ass up and carry him back. Go now, we'll cover your six."

"Roger that." Trent spun off and went back to Sawyer, who was pulling an adrenaline pack out of O'Malley's thigh.

The medic looked up at Trent. Something in his face spoke of desperation. Trent shook his head. "We gotta carry him back to the CP. We're falling back."

"He's not going to make it without fluids."

Bodine's fire team regrouped with the rest of Second Squad and began falling back, leapfrogging toward the CP. Just as Trent and Sawyer were getting ready to move, a Prowler arrived and came to a screeching halt in the road, the machine-gun turret blasting covering fire. Lieutenant Vickers jumped out of the passenger seat and ran around the back of the truck. Sawyer and Trent hoisted O'Malley up and dragged him to the vehicle.

Vickers opened the rear door and helped O'Malley into the back seat as Creon came over.

"Sir, there's a significant enemy force holed up in that office building. With the VBIED attack, there's no doubt they're planning an assault on the CP. AC-65s still grounded. If we don't get some kind of support we're going to lose the position."

Vickers closed the door with Sawyer in back to continue working on O'Malley. "Second Platoon is calling in APCs with support, but it's going to be a little while before they get here. We need to get back behind cover and hold them off until they arrive."

Creon wiped sweat from his eyes. "Copy that, sir."

Vickers nodded, then climbed back in the truck. The turret gunner kept up the heavy fire to cover the rest of the squad as they made a mad dash back to the CP. It was the longest sprint of Trent's life. As soon as he was behind the concrete barriers he bent over—hands on his knees—and retched. Nothing came up. His lungs burned, his legs were rubber. His gear weighed a thousand pounds. A few of the guys from Second Platoon were looking at him like he had two heads. Trent almost expected one of them to call him a bitch until he realized he was covered in O'Malley's blood. It saturated his armor, the sleeves of his uniform, coated his hands. He looked down at them, the creases of the palms filled with dark rivulets, bits of dried blood flaking off, buried under his nails. Beyond the walls of the CP the gunfight continued as the RF indeed closed in on their position. With no air support and ground support still far away, they would be surrounded, and their measly position wasn't really meant to withstand a full-on assault. It was a bluff and the Revolutionist Front was calling it. O'Malley's blood, Trent's blood, it didn't matter. The outcome was inevitable.

Oddly enough, it was in that realization that Trent suddenly felt relief. The fear and doubt and tension lifted like a fog burning off under a brilliant sun. There was nothing he could do to stop the end so why worry over it? Worrying was weakness; worrying about not getting hurt, worrying if he would get home, worrying if it would be him bleeding out next, worrying about Alley fucking some other guy. Too much fucking worrying for nothing.

He tilted his head to the sky, exhaled, and let the fearful and naive person he'd been dissipate in the wind. He didn't have the energy to be afraid anymore. Didn't have time to give that shit any attention.

Trent loaded a fresh magazine and went back to

the gate to engage the enemy and deal as much death to those motherfuckers as he possibly could before they took him. It was all he could do.

Backup arrived just after 1600. The armored vehicles rolled into the block with turret guns blazing. The ramp doors dropped and troops poured out, pushing the RF back. Give it to the rebels though, they kept fighting for two more hours after reinforcements arrived. Eventually, the shooting died down until it was nothing more than a few jittery soldiers popping off rounds. Then it was silent. The street was littered with debris, shattered storefronts, downed poles, small fires flickering in the alleys. About an hour after the shooting stopped, two AC-65 Wasps showed up, circling overhead, dipping down over the office building, then banked off and climbed away. A pointless show of force long after the fight had ended.

People came out from wherever they'd been hiding and filled the street, picking through the rubble. They smiled and waved at the soldiers, a little too emphatically. Cars began inching up and down the road, voices calling out trying to sell a few more goods before close. And just like that it was as if nothing had happened.

Trent stayed on the wall long after sunset. He could smell chow cooking in the mess tent, but wasn't in the mood to eat. The fight had done something to him and his hands buzzed with excitement. It couldn't be over. There had to be something more. He'd expected to die today so now that he was alive he wasn't quite sure how to feel.

Eventually he came down and lit a cigarette. He smoked and walked, trying to cool his blood. He came to one of the APCs that had stayed for the night parked in back in the shadows away from everyone else. Just where he wanted to be. He walked around the vehicle, admiring its dormant power. They'd dealt so much awesome carnage it gave Trent goose bumps thinking about it. Those 25mm turret guns pulverized the enemy right when they'd needed their help the most. He ran his fingers over the armor plating.

A female voice called out in the dark. "You're from the 117th?"

Trent jumped. "Jesus, I didn't know you were there." He sucked down his cigarette, trying to hide the shaking in his hands. "Yeah, I'm with the 117th."

She was leaning on the front fender smoking a cigarette of her own. How he'd missed her was beyond him. She didn't have body armor or a rifle, just a pistol strapped to her thigh. She didn't wear a helmet either and her hair was pulled back into a ponytail.

She watched him carefully. "You been out here long?"

"Feels like it," Trent said. "This yours?"

She took a drag off her cigarette and nodded. "Sure is," she said. "Been in theater for maybe a month. Been all over the city already. This place is fucked. Can't trust any of these people."

"No, I'd say not."

"They wave and smile and ask for handouts but as soon as you turn your back . . ." She nodded toward the city outside the perimeter. "They pull this shit. We should just carpet bomb the whole place and sweep up what's left." She paused, squinted at Trent's uniform. "Is that . . ."

"It's not mine."

"Oh. Well . . ." She hesitated, obviously trying to choose her words carefully. "Did you guys, like, lose anyone?"

"I don't know," Trent said. It was strange how empty he felt about the whole thing. "Some got hurt."

"Well that sucks. Hope they're okay."

"Yeah."

Her eyes went down to his rank and back up. "Hey, you wanna fuck?"

It took him a second to register what she'd just said. "What?"

She waved him off. "I know how it is, especially after a day like this. And I haven't gotten laid in forever. What do you say?"

Trent thought he must have heard wrong but she seemed pretty straightforward. His blood still felt hot, his mind was all over the place, and something primal was loose inside him. He thought of Alley, probably riding Brady at his beach house right now. He thought of how he almost died today and how nothing really mattered anymore but acting on instinct and responding to the moment. He had no use for concerns of the future, since realistically he didn't have one. He let the animal take over.

"Sure."

"Great." She came off the APC, flicked her cigarette away, and led Trent around the front of the vehicle, and out of sight. She unbuckled her pants, slid them down over her ass, and turned to lean on the armor. Trent fumbled with his own belt, then got his trousers down just far enough. He came up behind her, imagining the James Trent he used to know wave goodbye to the thing he was now.

She glanced over her shoulder as he entered. "Just don't let go inside me."

"Yeah. Sure," Trent said between breaths.

17
A HUNTER IN THE HILLS

Sam sat on the edge of her cot and watched Rob sleep. They'd been going hard assaulting outposts and disrupting patrols throughout the South Jordan District, and last night was the first time in a while where they could catch up on some rest. Of course, they stayed up most of the night catching up on other things. The thought put a smile on her face.

Chatter from outside the room, voices tinged with a sense of urgency. Sam rose from the cot, cracked the door and peeked out. Two men were standing in the hallway apparently having some kind of argument and looked up when they heard the door open.

"I told him you weren't to be bothered," one of them said. "He says it's important."

"It's alright," Sam said. "What is it?"

The other man was wearing jeans and a tank top, car keys dangling from his fingers. "Cross?"

Sam rolled her eyes, nodded.

"Commander Torres needs you and Barrett, now. There's a car downstairs," he said.

"Give me a minute," Sam said, then closed the door. She went to the cot where Rob was sprawled on top of the sleeping bag. She watched his chest rise and fall and thought of last night. She nudged the side of the cot. He didn't move. He'd been worn out.

"Hey."

He didn't stir.

As much as she wanted to pull him down to the floor and pick up where they left off, duty took precedent. She put a hand on his chest. "Rob."

His eyes shot open, hand went for the pistol beside his bunk, but Sam grabbed his wrist and held him still. Rob blinked through the fog of sudden wakefulness, then relaxed. He twined his fingers in hers. "Hey, you," he said.

Sam smiled, leaned down, and kissed him. Rob stretched, pulled her close. His hand slid down the small of her back. She felt his breath on her neck and she leaned into him and whispered in his ear.

"Torres needs us downstairs."

Rob sagged, arms flopping over the sides of the cot. "Dammit. I thought you were up for round two."

"Nope. It's time for work." Sam got up, started gathering her things. "And I don't think you'd survive round two."

Ten minutes later they were dressed, armed, and downstairs. The rest of the teams in the safe house were up and moving, cots and blankets tucked into corners, laptops opened and hacking into surveillance units thanks to the access codes they'd purchased off a few crooked cops. Sam hoped they hadn't been bugged to track their locations. The cops were about as trustworthy as the gangs.

The driver in the tank top saw them coming and ran over. He tried to grab Sam's pack but her vise grip on his wrist stopped him short. "Sorry," he said. "Just trying to help. This way."

He led them outside to a taxi parked at the curb.

Sentries in the street waved them on, indicating it was safe to be outside. They got in the car, Sam and Rob in the back seat, the rifle laid across the floor with a blanket draped over it in case they hit an unexpected checkpoint. The driver hit the ignition and spit gravel as he pulled away. They sped down the street, cut hard onto River Front Parkway, and accelerated into traffic. The driver swerved around a box truck, cut across the oncoming lane to get ahead of the lumbering vehicle, then yanked the wheel back in time to avoid a head-on collision. The engine revved high as the driver punched the gas.

"Hey," Sam said, gripping the back of the driver's seat. "You want to slow down? You're being obvious."

"You're driving like an asshole," Rob said.

The driver yanked the wheel to pass a car on the right, tires splashing through a puddle of foul-smelling water. Someone laid on a horn. "Commander said to hurry," said the driver.

Sam pulled her sidearm and laid it over the driver's shoulder. "If we get stopped," she hissed, "I'll put a bullet through your head."

The taxi slowed a bit.

Eventually they pulled into a warehouse lot, went around back, and parked behind a stack of shipping containers. The driver led them to a door where a guard met them with a challenge and password, got them through, and showed them to Commander Torres's field office, then excused himself to wait outside.

Torres sat at a desk striped by beams of dusty light filtering through the vented windows. In the gloom he seemed older somehow; hair grayer than before, bags under his eyes and sunken cheeks like he'd lost a bit of the edge to his cold command. "My sub-commanders tell me you're causing quite the havoc out there."

"We're doing our part," Rob said.

Torres gestured to a pair of chairs. "Please." They took seats while Torres stayed at his desk behind stacks of files and a few maps spread out with big red circles on them. He stared at the pages silently, fingers steepled, tired eyes scanning back and forth. He said nothing.

Rob glanced at Sam. "Sir," he said. "We were told you needed us in a hurry."

Torres blinked and looked up. "Yes, that's right." He wiped his hands over his face, gathered his composure. Sam didn't like the look of it. He looked like a man who was losing a fight.

"Government forces are pushing into our controlled territory no matter how hard we keep fighting," Torres said. "We surprise them initially and gain ground, but then they regroup and force us back every time. There's nothing we can do."

"What about the gangs?" Rob asked. "Local militias? The armed civilians? Are we getting any help there?"

"Sporadic at best," Torres said. "It seems they'll only fight if it's convenient for them."

"You mean if we're already winning," Sam added.

"Correct. Some of them even got the bright idea to turn sides at will and when I ordered them punished entire neighborhoods gave up the fight. Went right back to being helpless sheep. We can't count on them."

"Punished, sir?" Sam asked.

"Yes," Torres said with just a bit more bite than Sam cared for. "Those who agree to the righteous path and then quit and betray us are just as much an enemy as the pigs in Washington."

"Yessir," she said, breaking her gaze first.

Torres pushed a pile of folders aside and turned the map so it was facing Sam and Rob. "The government took control of sectors in West Valley, Taylorsville, and the Valley Regional Hospital in Murray now. They're carving a wedge in our lines. They mean to divide us, cut off our supply routes to the east, and when they do they'll have broken us."

"Broken our lines, maybe, but not our will," Rob said.

Torres nodded. "Indeed. But if they take this valley they gain control of the northwest. They do that, then the Revolutionist Front has no footing and the Coalition begins to crumble. It'll be only a matter of time."

"So what's the plan?" Sam asked. "What do you need from us?"

Torres pointed to a spot on the map where a yellow splotch appeared over the lush green of the western mountains. Sam recognized it immediately. "The Vircon Industries mining complex. We have been . . . unsuccessful in taking it. Their security element inside was too prepared during our initial assault and anything further risks damaging the facility. We're assuming they're former military, probably some form of Special Forces. They're no joke, even with their limited numbers. Which goes to show just how essential that fortification is. We need that facility and we need it now."

"What do we do about the Vircon staff that's

there?" Sam asked, not sure if she wanted to hear the answer.

"They'll have to cut their losses," Torres said, not bothering to go into further detail. "And unless their corporate headquarters in London wants to take sides in a war spanning the nation, that's just what they'll do. Bottom line is we need that facility, but we can't risk destroying the compound. A mortar strike already caused an avalanche in the mine that probably set back digging operations by a year or more, and we need the walls intact so the frontal approach is off the table."

"I see," said Sam. "That's where we come in."

"Yes, it is. I need the two of you to go into the hills and watch, report, look for weaknesses." Torres looked each of them in the eye. "Take out key combatants and weaken their numbers, as well as their resolve. Break them and they'll flee. Former Spec-Ops or not, they're in this fight for money, not martyrdom. You've done a hell of a job in the city, but I need you to be the Reaper in the hills now. Can you do that for the cause?"

"You can count on us, sir," Rob said.

Sam nodded. They'd spent long enough scampering through the dense urban decay. It was time to get back in the country, back into the hills. She could almost feel the dirt on her hands, smell the trees. Salt Lake was a rotten cesspool of human runoff; the mountains would be clean and alive and she wouldn't have to look in the face of all that suffering anymore. "How soon can we go?" she asked.

Commander Torres leaned back in his chair. "Right now, please."

* * *

The taxi came to a stop on a dirt road just outside South Jordan.

"This is as far as I can go," said the driver. He left the engine running.

Sam and Rob climbed out, strapped on their packs, and watched the cab drive off.

And then it was quiet.

Before they'd left Torres's office, he'd given them the radio frequencies for an RF camp that would serve as their QRF should they need support or extraction. Only problem was the radios they were using were old handhelds that operated on antiquated encrypted relays that were spotty at best, especially in the mountains. They'd have to scout a good location for a lengthy camp, somewhere out of sight of the mine or trails and roads, but close enough to maintain overwatch and communications with nearby friendly elements. Once that was established they'd be free to spend the next indeterminate amount of days living in the bush. It would be dirty, hard living, but it was what Sam grew up on. It was where she thrived. Sure, she'd gotten the hang of urban combat, close-quarters shooting, running and hiding in buildings, moving through crowded streets; hell, she'd earned the name Reaper of Killzone Valley for a reason, but out here she was truly in her element. She was unstoppable. Out here, she felt alive.

It was late afternoon by the time they were in position, the crater of the Vircon mine gaping in the distance. Sam had the Remington set and scoped the compound. Activity was down, fewer trucks driving around, fewer staff in the open. There were several of the large ore haulers parked near each gate like some type of last-ditch fortification. In the end, all that initial assault had resulted in was warning Vircon that the RF was looking to take the facility and gave them a chance to prepare.

"Five hundred thirty yards," Rob said, ranging the first target. "Two tangos on guard tower, three degrees north."

"Got 'em," Sam replied. "Gray uniforms, one sitting, the other leaning on the wall."

"You got it."

The breeze kicked up dust, rustled the leaves of a nearby bush. A bead of sweat tickled its way down Sam's brow and over her cheek. She timed her breathing with the crosshairs so they passed over the seated target at the end of her exhale. Her finger stretched over the trigger guard.

She waited.

"Sam?" Rob whispered.

She wasn't sure why, but something felt off. She stayed like that for a few minutes, watching the targets through the scope, wrestling with her thoughts. She realized this was the first time she was targeting someone other than the military. These were civilians working for a private organization. They weren't combatants. They weren't even her enemy, but they were holding back the RF from a much needed position. If she tried hard enough, she figured she could convince herself they were her enemy as well.

"Call it in," she said, still looking through the scope. "Confirm authorization for engagement."

She could feel Rob looking at her. "Okay," he said. She heard him unclip the handheld from his belt, paused. "I can take the shot if you want," he said.

"Just call it in."

"Alright." The radio beeped. "Outpost Six, this is Reaper."

The radio chirped. "Reaper, this is Outpost Six, go ahead."

"At least the comms work," Rob said before keying the mic. "Outpost Six, we need confirmation on authorization to engage civilian targets in sector Alpha-Four, over."

"Stand by."

Sam waited, blinking sweat from her eyes. She flexed her grip on the stock, tried to settle in the dirt. She knew they were calling Commander Torres on a LAN line. Some small part of her brain hoped he'd changed his mind. Maybe they could find a diplomatic way to get the compound. The whole thing seemed sort of . . . wrong.

The radio chimed. "Reaper, you have full authorization to engage any and all targets at will. Command would like to emphasize the importance of haste in this operation, over."

"Copy that, Outpost Six," Rob said. "Reaper out." He clipped the radio back on his belt. "You heard 'em."

"Yeah," Sam said. "I heard 'em." She eased into the rifle, slid her finger over the trigger. Breathe in. Breathe out. Crosshairs over center mass.

Fire.

The Vircon guard jerked, the white plastic chair exploding out behind him in a red mist. He toppled backwards, shattering the rest of the flimsy chair. The second target spun, saw his partner dead on the floor and dove to the ground. He was out of sight, hidden behind the wall of the tower. That was enough for now. He didn't need to die, too. The job was done. They knew there were snipers now. The rest would take care of itself.

She came off the rifle, slung the Remington over her shoulder, and packed up her stuff. Without a word, she and Rob slipped off into the cover of the forest and made their way to their next location.

18
CALLING IT QUITS

The RF's initial assault on the compound had been one thing, but then came the sniper fire. For the last several days no one could go outside without fear of losing their head. The RF had taken a drastic step in their attempt to conquer the mine, but Markus supposed it was inevitable. The local intel bulletins the military put out had reported the rebels were relying heavily on snipers, and there was one in particular that was proving problematic. A young woman by the name of Samantha Cross, aka: the Reaper of Killzone Valley. She'd proven such a threat, in fact, that the government had put a twenty-five-thousand-dollar bounty on her head. Markus wasn't entirely sure that that alone didn't make her more dangerous. He could see the worry in everyone's faces as they all wondered if they were in the crosshairs of the notorious Reaper.

Regardless of whose scope they were under, the damage had been to Vircon's resolve. The company had called it quits.

Markus watched the convoy of buses come through the gate and stage near the HQ building, where most of the remaining staff waited with packed bags. It wasn't really a hard choice for them: employment or death. For most people it was simple.

Hissing brakes as the shuttles stopped and sagged

to the ground. Doors slid open and Vircon staff filed in, and the better part of the security element left with them. They were abandoning the compound.

Everyone except Ned Sellers.

Sellers had argued with the board, who'd received an anonymous tip that they were being attacked and the war was no longer something they could ignore. Corporate headquarters arranged for EXFIL of the staff and offered the same to Reyes and his men. Most of them took it. Problem was Ned Sellers refused to leave, arguing that he had to finish cleaning company records and compiling data to the main servers and would need to be extracted at a later date. His dogged determination to ignore the danger had finally caught up with him and now, as the rest of the company fled, he was staying behind to unfuck the situation he'd created. Which meant Markus and his crew would be staying as well. It was what they'd been hired for and they weren't about to bail on an obligation. Markus told himself it wasn't about the money.

He turned his gaze to the mountains. Impossible to spot anyone up there at that distance without optics, but since the sniper fire had started he couldn't take his eyes off the hills.

Reyes came out of the crowd and joined Markus. His beret was gone and his face was clean-shaven. There was a look in his eye that spoke of determination and professionalism. He looked more SAS than civilian contractor. He gave a curt nod, stood next to Markus, and crossed his arms to watch the buses.

"You're not leaving?" Markus asked.

"Most of them are here for the money," Reyes said. "Let them go. A few are here because they're called to it. And not by money or orders from HQ. Some of us were born to be fighters. Can't deny it, can't change it. I don't know why."

Markus nodded, said nothing.

"This is personal for me now," Reyes said. He'd lost five guys in the last few days. Picked off by fucking snipers. Never had a chance to defend themselves. Never saw it coming. Hell, they probably didn't even know they'd died.

"How many are left?" Markus asked.

"Eleven, including myself. What about you?"

"Six of us total, and we're staying until the Sellers are extracted."

Reyes looked at Markus. "We'll need a solid battle plan if we want to own this compound."

"I've got my crew on roving patrols in rotating shifts. There's just too much perimeter to hope to secure. And since we're being watched right now they'll know we're down to a skeleton crew."

"We'll need to use every resource available. Fuck Sellers. We use what we need. We scrounge parts from old equipment, park a dump truck in front of every gate, including the inner compound, tighten our perimeter, turtle up. It's the only way we can hope to hold out."

"We can rig the pickups to use as a quick reaction force," Markus said. "Save the Prowlers for emergency EXFIL if we need to evacuate. We'll use the heavy equipment as mobile barricades. And we should get another count on remaining weapons and ammunition."

"Agreed. Let's get on that ASAP. The RF won't wait long after they're gone." Reyes inclined his head toward the shuttles, which were just now pulling away.

Markus watched as the convoy stopped at the gate and the steel doors slid open. The shuttles crawled through and left down Bingham Road. "We need to join the teams," Markus said. "This is gonna be a hell of a fight."

"Right. Hey, look alive," Reyes said as Annika Sellers crossed the lot toward them. "We'll continue this later," Reyes said, then left.

Annika arrived and watched Reyes walk away. "How's he doing?" she asked.

"He lost a lot of men," Markus said. "We're bound to lose more. Tell me it's not for nothing."

Annika looked at him. "I'm sorry for his losses, I really am, but they knew the risk when they took the job. So did you."

"I'm sorry to say, Miss Sellers, that doesn't fly. My *job* is to protect you and your father, my *mission* is to protect my men."

She smiled then, and it made Markus want to snap. "You see the irony in what you do, right?" She asked. "You're mercen—" She paused, changed her tone. "You're security contractors. Private military. Your job is to go around fighting others who are doing the same exact thing as you, only from a different vantage point. And your mission is to keep your men alive? Your lives by definition are contradictory to your desires."

"Miss Sellers," Markus said. "Why are we still here?"

"My father needs to finish the emergency data dump before we can abandon the facility."

"That's bullshit."

"Excuse me?"

Markus stepped closer. "We warned you of the

danger here. Reyes warned you. For Christ's sake, there's a war going on around us and Ned Sellers refused to acknowledge that fact. He pushed the company on, reaching for the next dollar, and now it's too late. Now he's scrambling to do what he should've done weeks ago. He's backpedaling to cover his own ass, that's why we're still here."

"I wouldn't expect you to understand the logistics of a thing like this," Annika said, countering Markus by taking a step closer. "It's not as simple as cut-and-bail when things get hot. This is a multibillion-dollar global enterprise, not some mom-and-pop hardware store. The fact that my father's staying behind while everyone else is fleeing to safety should garner him a little more respect than what you're showing right now."

Markus glared at her. She was showing her fangs. Ned Sellers was in the wrong here but the man was still her father and she didn't appear to be in the mood to admit the fault, regardless of how many people died because of the Sellerses' stubborn nature, and how many more were likely to follow.

"Truth is," she said, interrupting Markus's train of thought, "this isn't the first time something like this has happened." She backed off, lowered her voice. "Vircon had an account in Colombia a few years ago. Had to pull out when guerrilla fighters moved out of the jungles and started burning villages. Staff fled the compound to fend for themselves and get to their families. They had to get out fast. They had no security then, so you can imagine the shit show that was. The operation failed, accounts went south. Vircon lost a lot of money and some key investors. This time around, I urged my father to hire private security, even with Vircon's own team here. I don't know if that helps, but we won't suffer that kind of loss again."

"That kind of loss." Markus clenched his jaw. "Tell that to Reyes and his men. Now if you'll excuse me, I have work to do to make sure we don't lose any more." He stormed off before Annika could respond.

No more than an hour later, Reyes and Weatherford met Markus and his crew in the vehicle bay. Reyes set the remainder of his team on perimeter watch while they made their plans. They were seated around a table with notes and blueprints spread out before them.

"Alright," Markus started. "We're down to a skeleton crew here. The US military's still bogged down in the city and nowhere near close enough to provide support yet. We need to tighten up and use every available resource at our disposal to see us through this. We have no idea how much longer we'll need to hang around before Sellers is ready to go. So . . . what equipment do we have? What are the avenues of approach? Secondary defenses? Let's lay it out."

Weatherford pulled a notepad from his pocket. "Armory's getting used up, but we still have about eight thousand rounds of five point five six, two dozen forty-millimeter grenades, a crate of forty-five and nine-mil rounds, and two thousand rounds for the fifty."

"We can raid the mining reserves of TNT and C-4," Reyes added. "They won't need it anymore. Should be able to get enough to rig some improvised explosives."

"Good," Markus said. "I can have my guys work on that. Len's an ordnance tech, he and Tripp can rig them up and plant them along our weak points."

"Got it, Chief," Len said.

"Weakest points are the north gate and west perimeter," Reyes went on. "But they'll likely avoid going through the mine. When they come they're going to hit us at the east gate by the Copperton slums. Your guys could daisy-chain explosives along Bingham Road and clobber them when they get close."

"Alright." Markus said. "We should move any industrial equipment we can to the west perimeter in case they try something, focus the rest on blocking up those gates. We'll need a secondary perimeter to fall back on if it gets too hot. I think we should plant secondary explosives inside the perimeter as well."

Everyone looked at him.

Markus continued. "Should we need to fall back, the RF will be hot on our heels. Once they're in the compound, the fight will go quick. They won't expect it and hopefully they'll be too occupied pouring everything they've got at us to notice. We can hammer them hardest right when they think they've won."

"Dangerous game, mate," Reyes said. "Improvised explosives could go off and decimate us."

"It's a possibility," Markus agreed. "But Len's a master at this stuff. And we'll just have to orchestrate the fight to our liking. We can stack equipment to funnel them where we want. The odds are against us here, but we're the sort that thrive on this. The RF are rebel civilians with *maybe* a handful of defected military officers in their ranks. None of them have been through what we have. None of them can do what we can. We need to remind them of that."

Reyes nodded. "We'll make HQ our secondary post. I want all available weapons and ammo consolidated and moved there. Bring the haulers and Prowlers inside the courtyard for defense and emergency EXFIL. I also think if we're going to rig the compound, we need to rig the main gates. We know they're going to hit us there and try to get through. If that happens, we need to blow them and buy us time to turtle up inside the secondary perimeter."

"We could get trapped in here," Temple said.

"By then it won't matter," Reyes added.

Everyone took a moment to let the sincerity of the situation sink in. No one argued further.

"Good. Then it's sorted," Reyes said. "I'll get my guys on this right away."

"Rourke, Temple," Markus said. "Go with Reyes. Len and Tripp, I want you on those explosives right away."

Everyone got up, chairs grinding, blueprints rolled up, gear tucked back in pockets. All they could do now was hope there was enough time to prepare for the next attack. Because there was no doubt, there would be another and probably soon.

19
TARGET RICH

S am glassed the compound, adjusted the scope for elevation. They'd moved to a spot on a rise overlooking the western edge of the compound about 1,200 yards out where they'd watched as most of the staff left in a mass convoy. The compound was mostly empty now save for a few key personnel and a small detachment of security.

The mountainside buzzed with insects, a mild breeze hissed through the grass. Sam lay out in the dirt, rifle propped on her pack set in front of her, stock tight to her shoulder. Rob was next to her watching the compound through the range finder. She peered through the scope watching the flag in the courtyard flap gently and calculated the wind at three minutes left. She made another small adjustment and was dialed in. The sky was clear; the literal fog of war that shrouded the city remained trapped in the valley below. She breathed in, out. The rifle melted into her, became a part of her. She watched the compound.

Markus sat on the edge of his bunk rolling a bullet through his fingers, thinking about how things had gotten so out of hand. The smart thing to do would be to leave. Just go. Forget the job, forget retirement now. Climb in the Prowlers, drive through the gates, and leave this forsaken valley behind. But he'd never walked out on a job before and wasn't about to do it now. They'd made a commitment to protect the Sellerses and that's just what they were going to do. Reyes was committed now, too. He'd lost five men so far and, for him, it had become personal. Markus knew couldn't just take the crew and leave Reyes and his men alone in a country that wasn't theirs in the midst of a civil war. The whole thing was shit.

Markus watched the light play off the brass casing as he turned the bullet over and over. What really got to him were Annika's words.

You see the irony in what you do, right?

The message was clear. He and his crew made a living by putting themselves in harm's way, but his personal mission was to keep each of them alive and well. Contradictory actions. Like his whole fucking life was a joke. Maybe that was why he'd been dreaming about Devens again. Perhaps it was his subconscious trying to convince him to just let go of his pride and leave everything behind.

There was a knock at the door and Dieter popped in. "Chief?"

"Yeah, come in," Markus said.

Dieter closed the door behind him and pulled up a stool. "Got those explosives in place," he said. "Haulers at each gate, ammunition and weapons divvied out to the key towers, reserves stacked in the maintenance bay."

"Good," Markus said. He saw the way Dieter stroked his chin. "What is it?"

"How long do you think we're gonna have to hold up here, Chief?"

Markus sighed. "No idea. My hope is the RF don't

come back and the military comes and takes this place off our hands. Sellers pays out and we ride off into the sunset."

"And what does your gut tell you?"

Normally Markus had no problem confiding in Dieter, but this wasn't the time to show doubt. He was contemplating telling Dieter about his dreams when shouting outside brought their conversation to a halt.

"That sounds like Sellers and Reyes," Dieter said, reaching for the door.

Markus shoved the round in his pocket, grabbed his rifle, and went outside.

Ned Sellers was standing in the courtyard throwing his arms around while Reyes stood in front of him, arms crossed and stone-faced.

"What's the issue?" Markus asked as he hurried over, keeping an eye out for the reflective flash of a sniper's scope in the hills.

Ned Sellers whirled on Markus. "You goddamned mercenaries keep thinking my equipment is here for your fucking war games!" His face was red, veins bulging from his neck. The man was losing control, a position he clearly wasn't used to. He still wore his fashionable gray suit, which Markus had warned against since picking off high-ranking officials was sniping 101. And Sellers refused to wear the cumbersome body armor in this heat as well. The man was making Markus's job extremely difficult.

"Production may have stopped," Sellers screamed. "But this is still Vircon Industries property."

Markus stepped in close. "Mr. Sellers," he said as placating as he could manage, which was difficult, considering people had died because of Sellers's greed.

"The shit's already hit the fan. Vircon pulled their investment out just like in Colombia." A look crossed Sellers's face at the barb. Markus went on. "They've already written the equipment off as a loss. They'll come back after the fighting's done and retake what's left, but if we don't use what we have we won't be here to see that, and all your efforts to save your name and secure your place in the company will be for naught. Nothing left to do now but survive until we can get the hell out of here. That means using whatever resources we have available. That would be your equipment. It's going to keep us alive, Mr. Sellers."

Ned Sellers was about to enter another tirade when Annika pushed through the doors of the HQ building wearing her bulletproof vest and strapping on her helmet. Ned saw her and deflated. "You should've never come here," he said.

"I came of my own volition," Annika replied as she joined the group. She placed a hand on his arm. "And you hired these men to protect us, Dad. Let them do that. Let them do their job. We'll get out of here soon enough."

Ned rubbed his brow, shook his head. "Fine. Alright. We have a few more things to close up before we can go anywhere. I'll have to file a DA-6 with corporate. You know what that means, don't you?"

"I do. It's okay, Dad," Annika said, then traded a glance with Markus.

He nodded to her and then pulled Reyes aside while she talked some sense to her father. "How are we on your end of preparations?" he asked Reyes, trying to redirect his focus and ease him back from anger.

* * *

Sam watched the man in the courtyard engaged in what appeared to be an argument. He wasn't wearing body armor or a helmet, but he seemed to be in charge. He was waving his arms, obviously shouting at the others around him.

The remaining contractors inside the compound were limited in number, but professional. They'd fought hard during the RF's first assault, she'd been told, and were obviously prepared to defend themselves. She could admire that much at least, but Command wanted inside that compound and they wanted in now. The American military was pushing hard. The RF were losing ground in the city. They couldn't lose control of the valley. Anyone standing in the way was an enemy.

"Hey Rob," she said without breaking from the scope.

"Yeah?"

"What's the call on taking out key non-combatants?"

"If they're in the way they're enemies. Who's the target?"

Sam tried to steel herself. This wasn't the time for doubt. "Male, gray suit."

A pause as Rob scanned through the range finder. "Is that the guy that runs the place? That could be huge."

She made another adjustment on the scope. Wind was letting up. "I don't know, though. I'm not here to murder innocent people, Rob."

"You know what Torres will say," Rob said. "If this guy's holding this whole thing together, we could break their command system right now. And who better to do it than Joseph Graham's Chosen, the Reaper of Killzone Valley?"

"Yeah."

"That's eleven hundred yards out, though, Sam. Over half a mile."

She glassed the courtyard. A woman had joined the group now. She wore protective gear and seemed familiar with the man in the gray suit. Probably a second-in-command or lover, the way she touched him. It was a target-rich sight picture the likes of which a sniper rarely ever got. She couldn't let it go. But if she made the wrong call, it could set off an avalanche of uncontrollable outcomes. Two civilian officials, three men with weapons, all of them in positions of authority in one way or another. The contractors were clearly taking orders from the suit, but what if the suit watched his security detail die in front of him? Could sap his resolve right there without having to kill an unarmed civilian. With the lead security element out of the way they wouldn't be able to mount an organized defense and the RF could practically walk right in. But take out one soldier, another always stepped up.

The suit or the security.

Sam had to decide.

She breathed in, out. Rifle smooth in her hands. The flag on the pole stopped its flapping, indicating the wind had settled for just a moment. She made a quick mental calculation and adjusted for the shot.

Annika had never seen her father this vulnerable. All her life, all she'd ever known of the man was the stern, calculating businessman and the unwavering authority he exuded over others and had tried his best to instill in her so that she could one day assume the same authority in her own right. But watching him now as he tried to maintain control of this continually deteriorating situation was something no lecture or training seminar could prepare you for. It was discomfiting, and felt a bit like watching your heroes fail. Still, something about his desperation gave her strength. Every student had to surpass their instructor at some point, and for Annika Sellers, it seemed this was that moment.

"We'll get through this, Dad," she said, taking him gently by the elbow. "No one's blind to what's going on out here. We've done everything we could to protect the company assets, but it's beyond our span of control now. Corporate will understand. Better to file the DA-6 and save what we can than to lose more lives for nothing. The mine will be here when this war is over."

For a moment, Ned Sellers looked as if he might argue, but his eyes met hers and he deflated. "You're right," he said. "Of course you're right." He patted her hand gently.

It was as much of a compliment as Annika was ever going to get from him, and she delighted in it. For just a moment they were father and daughter, not corporate employees, not superior and subordinate. They were family, and all it took was a war to discover that small moment.

From the corner of her eye, Annika saw Markus break off from his conversation with Captain Reyes and come marching back over. A small part of her suddenly resented the aging mercenary for ruining the moment and bringing the conflict back to the forefront.

"Mr. Sellers," he said as he joined Ned and Annika. "You really should be wearing your protective gear. This place is being targeted by sniper fire, it's not even really safe to be out here in the open."

Annika spoke up on her father's behalf. "Thank you, Markus, but we'll be fine. They've only been targeting our armed security and we're non-combatants under the protection of national humanitarian law. I think the Revolutionist Front is smart enough to understand this."

Markus gave her a look that she didn't quite care for. "Miss Sellers, I think we can safely conclude after the last few weeks that the RF doesn't give a damn about anything but taking this compound."

Annika was about to argue but her father squeezed her hand, silencing her. "Rebel snipers be damned," Ned Sellers said as he took a handkerchief from his pocket and wiped the sweat from his brow. "This heat is killing me. Why don't we go insi—"

A crack tore the air, wetness sprayed across Annika's face. It was so sudden she barely registered what happened. For a moment it seemed like no one moved. Then her father let go of her hand and dove for the ground. But there was something strange about the way he moved. There was no control of his body, more like he just pitched forward and hit the dirt.

That was when Annika realized her father was missing half his face.

Before she could scream, she was tackled to the ground. Someone was crawling on top of her as she stared at the grisly details spewed across the dirt in front of her. Fragments of bone. Chunks of pink and red tissue. Her father, reduced to lifeless, broken pieces. Unbearable, undeniable.

A scream escaped her throat, raw and rattling, unbidden and unstoppable.

* * *

Markus covered Annika's body with his own as she screamed the terrible scream of one who'd never seen a loved one die. His biggest fear had come true right under his nose: his protectee had been killed by sniper fire. But that was already the past and he couldn't dwell on it. Right now, he had to figure out where the shot had come from. Ned's body lay facedown by the flag pole, heels twitching, blood and brains sprayed outward and away. The impact had come from behind, which meant the sniper was to the west. Markus twisted his head around while struggling to keep Annika down and glanced up at the western ridge.

Staying low, he dragged her behind a nearby truck. She was screaming so fiercely her throat had to be taking damage. Markus tried to turn her away from her father's corpse, but she was locked on. The woman was hysterical. There was nothing he could do about it now.

He keyed the mic on their secure channel and got Tripp on the horn. "Sniper fire at the courtyard. VIP is down and we're in the open."

"Got it, Chief. Be right there."

Reyes and Dieter were the first to arrive with their rifles up as they darted to cover. Dieter sprinted across the courtyard and slid next to Markus. "What can I do, Chief?"

"Take Annika to the safe house and stay down. We gotta do something about this sniper."

"Copy that."

Dieter moved next to Annika and placed a hand on her shoulder. He glanced at Markus, nodded. He had her.

Markus made a break for the truck bay. Reyes came out and fell in step beside him. "I'm going with you," he said. They got to the bay and shoved through

the access door. Markus ran for the nearest Prowler
while Reyes slapped a switch on the wall and the bay
doors opened.

Markus hit the ignition, Reyes jumped in, and they
sped off toward the north gate.

They found Tripp running along the road heading
toward tower seven. He had the AX-7 tucked in his
arms. Markus jammed the brakes, slid the truck to a
stop so Tripp could jump in, then stomped the accel-
erator and took off again.

"Who's down?" Tripp asked.

"Ned," Markus shouted.

"I want to find this son of a bitch."

"We don't have enough people to send a hunting
party," Markus said, knowing full well what Tripp's
response would be.

"I work fine on my own, Chief. You know that."

Reyes was in the passenger seat fighting with a map
that was flapping in the wind. "That shot must've come
from over a thousand meters out," he said.

Tripp leaned forward between the seats. "It's her.
Gotta be. This'll be a huge bounty."

"It's not about the money," Markus said.

"I got it, Chief."

Markus wanted nothing more at this point than to
keep his crew inside the perimeter. They hadn't even
had time to process what happened, let alone consider
what would come next. The man who'd given them a
job was dead. They'd failed. Maybe this was the only
way to finish it.

"Fine," Markus said. "We'll drop you at gate seven.
You can head out along the access road and flank that
ridge. The RF are out there so stay low and do your
thing."

They reached the gate and parked the Prowler out of sight. Markus, Tripp, and Reyes climbed out and made sure the coast was clear before helping Tripp slip through the gate.

"This is gonna be a bit of instinct and improv, Chief," Tripp said.

"No better man for it. I'll be here to pick you up when it's done."

Tripp nodded, then headed into the hills to go hunt down a sniper.

20
BATTLE AT THE BRIDGE

Private First Class Trent wiped down the bolt and slid it back into the receiver. He folded the MX closed and pressed the lock pin in place, racked the slide, pointed the barrel at a sandbag, and pulled the trigger. The firing pin clicked, and the weapon was cleared, cleaned, and ready for action. This had been his job once: fixing weapons for others to use. Seemed like so long ago now. But this one was his, and use it he did. Trent slapped a fresh magazine in the port, plucked the smoldering cigarette butt from his lips, and stubbed it out in the dirt.

Boot steps drew his attention to the end of the bunker where Bodine leaned in. "Trent, we're ready to roll in ten."

"Copy."

Bodine hesitated, then said, "No word on O'Malley yet."

"Okay." Trent didn't want to think about it. He couldn't. He didn't have time to let that shit get to him. Maybe if he ever got out of this he'd be able to deal with it, but not now. Not while he was still out here fighting the enemy.

Trent climbed to his feet, slipped his armor on. They were getting ready to move out and press even farther into RF territory, leaving the checkpoint behind to establish another outpost near the junction of

Interstates 15 and 215. According to Creon's briefing, they were going to be moving into a neighborhood where rebel commander John Torres was believed to be hiding. First Platoon would load up on transports with an advance assault team in armored personnel carriers to speed down Interstate 215, secure a bridge that Intel believed would be heavily defended and most likely rigged with explosives, then cross the Jordan River, overwhelm the enemy, and drive them from the neighborhood on the other side. This would give the military complete control of Salt Lake Valley airspace and essentially cut the RF in half, leaving any rebels that were east of Interstate 15 without support. Once that was accomplished the engineers would swoop in and build a new FOB to control the major highways, establish defensible logistical routes for forward units, and fucking finally be able to push toward the objective of the Vircon mine.

It all looked really good on paper.

The squads were loading up on transports, bulging rucksacks strapped to the sides of the vehicles making them look like a convoy of nomadic scavengers. First Platoon was filing into the APCs at the front. Trent didn't see the female he'd had a go with the other night, for which he was thankful. Simard would probably love to hear that story. But somewhere inside, as detached as he tried to be, Trent felt a stabbing guilt. He'd crossed a line and there was no going back. But really, this whole fucking war had crossed a line. What did it matter if he killed or fucked? At least he was still alive for now, and that was something.

Funny how he felt worse about fucking a stranger than killing one.

Shooting at people was becoming second nature, so

much so that he even dreamt about it. He was no longer surprised by the crack of gunfire or the whistle of incoming rockets, which was good because surprise led to hesitation, and hesitation led to death. No, Trent had learned to expect violence.

The door to the APC slammed shut and he realized with a start that he was already inside. The vehicle lurched and they were off. *This* was what he was growing to accept. The familiar smell of diesel exhaust, the hot, cramped confines, the angry red glow of lights. This was the staging place for battle. When the doors opened there'd be fighting, shooting, people would die. Coming to terms with that was the only way to ensure he was able to stay focused downrange. It wasn't easy. Anger helped.

Trent was lost in his thoughts and hadn't realized they'd stopped. Everyone was readying to move.

As soon as the door fell open, he heard the rounds coming in. Bullets rang off the armor as First Platoon poured out of the vehicles and dashed to cover. Trent stayed tight on Bodine's six while they cleared a guardrail and dove into a ditch. A rocket streaked past and impacted on the side of a building behind them. People were shouting orders trying to link up with their squads. Concussive blasts rocked the air. The APCs finished unloading and left in a hurry. More RPGs whistled by, leaving twisting trails of smoke to the points of impact.

Creon moved the platoon into an offensive posture, setting squads to flank the intersection that was getting pounded and to set up interlocking fields of fire. Trent was watching Creon when a hand slapped his back.

Lieutenant Vickers was lying prone beside him. "Cover me while I get a look," he said.

Trent and Bodine crawled up the ditch and pointed their rifles out while the lieutenant surveyed the block. The street was pocked with craters and littered with spent casings. Beyond the street was the Jordan River, and beyond that was a series of apartments that made up the neighborhood Intel claimed John Torres and the RF would be hiding in. Seemed they were on the money with that one.

Trent watched down his sights as windows sparked with muzzle flashes and rockets bent on wild arcs that slammed into the riverbank, tearing up the Army's side of the Jordan.

"Christ," Lieutenant Vickers said, scanning through the range-binos. "What are you waiting for? Return fire already."

Trent flipped the selector switch and fired. He was too far away to aim at anything in particular, but he sent rounds toward the apartment blocks all the same. Soldiers were shooting all down the line and the sound became a deafening roar. A few of the light machine guns ripped at full auto, carving into the neighborhood across the river. Trent could see movement on the rooftops as the RF tried for higher ground. He wondered suddenly if they were using snipers. He pressed himself into the dirt.

Sergeant Creon came over and met with Lieutenant Vickers. "Sir, we need to get out of this kill zone and establish a position along that bank or we're just gonna get hammered."

"Stand by," Vickers said. "Gonna soften these fuckers up with some air support. Get your men down." The LT went to his Prowler and got on the radio.

Trent caught movement on a rooftop to his left. Three people appeared at the edge working to erect something apparently heavy. A moment later a double-barreled .50-caliber machine gun opened up on their position. It thundered over the already explosive gunfight, tearing up the earth and devastating their position.

Then something hissed through the air, shot past their position, and streaked toward the apartments. One entire wall exploded, casting huge chunks of debris into the river. The building crumbled and a cloud of dust rose through the RF lines.

A pair of AC-65 Wasps cut through the sky, coming in low as their rotary cannons belched 20mm rounds down the line. The apartments shimmered, cracked, glass and stone shattering and spraying out into the streets. The Wasps banked in for another pass and fired a salvo of rockets at the west bank.

Soldiers cheered and pumped fists in the air as the enemy gunfire broke and First Platoon took the opportunity to advance its lines up to the bank of the Jordan. As the Wasps circled around and prepared for a return run, the RF had a moment to pop back up and open fire, only now they were clustering toward the bridge where the rest of the transport vehicles were unloading reinforcements.

The AC-65s dipped down almost to rooftop level and shot straight toward the west bank, releasing more rockets that screamed into buildings that were once people's homes.

Trent came off his sights and watched as a smoke trail shot straight up from one of the buildings and then veered toward the nearest AC-65. The attack craft's defense systems picked up the incoming missile and fired off a sparking shower of chaff while banking hard to get out of the way. It didn't do any good.

The surface-to-air missile hit the chaff and burst into a cluster of smaller detonations that broadsided the Wasp and sent it spinning off, trailing chunks of flaming debris and burning fuel. The second Wasp climbed high into the atmosphere as a second missile screamed up and after it, but the craft banked away and hit the afterburners, leaving the missile to sail off into some unsuspecting neighborhood.

Trent felt his stomach turn as he watched the damaged AC-65 fight for control before it disappeared behind a row of buildings deep in RF territory. A second later, a mushroom cloud of flame rolled into the sky.

The enemy gunfire picked up now that the threat from the air was taken care of. Lieutenant Vickers was on the radio trying to communicate with HQ while Sergeant Creon waited for orders.

"Copy that," the LT said, then tossed the handset into the cab of his Prowler. He turned to Creon. "Air support is gone but we can't cross that bridge under this heavy fire. Main's got a rail battery on standby, I need you to range those buildings for them." He pointed to the apartment blocks at the opposite end of the bridge.

"Roger that, sir."

"This'll be a combined effort. Support APCs and some armored Prowlers will stage here, then you'll call the artillery on my go. As soon as the guns stop, the support vehicles will cross and establish fighting positions to cover the rest of the advance." Vickers grabbed Creon's vest. "Keep it tight, don't damage that bridge."

Creon nodded. Trent spoke up. "Sir," he said, the two ranking men turning to glare at him. "Isn't the bridge rigged to blow?"

"A risk we're willing to take. Now follow your orders."

"Let's go, Private," Creon growled as he grabbed Trent, as well as Bodine and Ramirez, who had a long-range radio in his pack. He brought them around the back of the Prowler and surveyed the area.

"Alright," Creon said. "We need to cross the road and get up the bank. We should be able to see both sides of the bridge from there. Means we have to run for it. Ready?"

Trent fought to keep calm.

The RF sent volleys of RPGs over the river, blowing apart trees and shredding the front of a Prowler, scattering chunks of hot steel. The amount of munitions being dumped on First Platoon was astounding. The RF weren't just prepared for battle, they were counting on the win.

Creon stacked the team into position with Bodine in front to provide covering fire with the M37, followed by Trent, then Ramirez. Creon would go last. Bodine leaned around the edge of the Prowler, sighted on a building about two hundred meters out across the bridge. On Creon's mark, Bodine opened fire and Trent burst out into the open.

Never really a great judge of distance, Trent could have guessed the road was at least a mile across. Legs pumping, gear rattling, he fought for each step knowing he was going to get slammed any second. Boots pounded the pavement, helmet slid down obscuring his view. He leaned forward and let momentum carry him along.

Then he was at the guardrail, up, over, and down hard on the other side of the road. It took him a second to right his helmet, get into a kneeling position like he'd learned in Basic Training, and return covering fire for Bodine to cross. The big man took even longer than Trent to get over and thumped the ground hard before moving into position next to Trent.

Ramirez was next. His heavy radio pack almost shoved him over right in the middle of the road, but he kicked his legs and stumbled forward before diving headfirst over the rail. With all three riflemen in place, Creon made the crossing. By now, the RF had noticed the movement and rounds sparked off the pavement as the staff sergeant sprinted across. Trent sighted on the rooftop of a small apartment building where the RF had another machine-gun nest in place to cover the bridge. He knew he couldn't take it out, but he tried his damnedest to give them hell. At this point he wasn't even aiming, just shooting up buildings and pointing his rifle in the RF's direction.

Smoke from the wreckage of the AC-65 climbed into the sky. No doubt the RF were closing on the crash site, but judging by that explosion there wouldn't be anyone left alive. It was probably better that way. Better to die quick than at the hands of the RF.

"We have to move up to that relay tower," Creon said, gesturing toward the top of a hill just south of the bridge. Across the street, the rest of First Platoon kept pressing and shifting, trying to stay out of range of the RPGs.

Creon led the fire team up the hill and gained about fifty feet of elevation. There was an old chain-link fence at the top with sections cut away, most of the metal scavenged long ago. The relay tower leaned precariously toward the river, several dishes hanging like ripe fruit about to fall.

"Trent, Ramirez, up here with me," Creon said.

"Bodine, I want you covering those buildings on our six. I'll take the radio." Ramirez handed Creon the mic and went with Bodine down the hill to watch the apartments behind them. The staff sergeant gave the signal to get low and Trent pressed himself to the ground as they crawled into position.

"Don't touch the tower," Creon said, pulling out the range finder. "Might still have power running through it."

Trent glanced at the steel tubes, inched away from the wires that covered the ground.

From up here Trent could see down on top of the nearest machine-gun nest and the dusty lot behind the first row of apartments along the opposite side of the river and through the alleyways. To the north, the exchange of gunfire continued to roar between opposing lines.

Creon keyed the mic. "Hound Two Zero, this is Two. In position, over."

"Copy that," Lieutenant Vickers replied. "Stand by for green light."

A moment later, the scattered elements of First Platoon began to regroup, moving back and away from the river. Trent hoped the RF would assume they were retreating. In reality, the distance to the enemy was no more than two to three hundred meters. Anything within six hundred meters was considered danger-close for artillery. They'd be practically shaving with incoming ordnance.

Once First Platoon had regrouped behind the APCs well outside the range of the RPG barrage, Vickers gave Creon the go-ahead to call the fire mission.

Ramirez switched to the support channel.

"Bravo Three Seven, this is Hound Two, adjust

fire, over," Creon said into the handset while scanning through the range finder.

"Hound Two, this is Bravo Three Seven, adjust fire. Go ahead with grid, over," replied the artillery battery.

As Creon recited the grid coordinates to the battery, Trent scanned his sector along the south bank of the bridge. He swept his sights over the apartments and along the bank, and noticed movement in his periphery.

Someone was moving underneath the bridge.

He shifted to identify the target. Whoever it was down there was crouching in the shadows and making an effort to stay hidden. The target was maybe a hundred and fifty meters away at most. Certainly close enough for Trent to pick off.

Then the target stepped out of the shadows.

A boy who couldn't be more than twelve years old stood along the riverbank clutching an RPG. From that direction, Trent's position was completely exposed and the boy was looking directly at them. Trent's hands went numb as he watched the boy shoulder the rocket. Trent sighted on the boy, praying he'd get scared and drop the weapon, hoping against hope he didn't have to pull the trigger. Creon was still on the comms with the rail battery, and Ramirez and Bodine were watching the rear. No one but Trent saw the boy.

He held his sights over center mass, as small as it was.

The boy held the RPG, tucked his head into the sights.

No time.

Trent exhaled, squeezed the trigger.

The RPG fell into the river, the boy lay in the mud.

"Splash in five seconds," Creon shouted.

Trent could sense them getting down, but he couldn't move. He felt sick, sat up, let his rifle go limp in his hands.

The atmosphere ripped in two and the building with the machine-gun nest exploded, the shockwave thumping outward, throwing debris across the neighborhood, shattering windows and bursting Trent's ears. Something pinged off the relay tower and bits of shrapnel ripped into the hillside. Trent was thrown backwards, both from the force of the impact and the sudden shock back to reality.

Creon was yelling into the radio in muffled tones, sending the call for fire-for-effect. Seconds later, the neighborhood was pounded with a battery of rail gun rounds, obliterating the apartments, streets, and fighting positions of the RF.

When the artillery stopped, the enemy gunfire also died out. On the road below, the support element raced forward in APCs and armored Prowlers, crossing the bridge with guns blazing, shredding anything that dared to move after that salvo. First Platoon's escort rolled in after, pausing to regroup before making the crossing. After the first few vehicles made it over without the bridge exploding, troops began rushing across on foot.

Trent was on autopilot. His mind collapsed into itself to preserve what little was left to hold on to. He felt hands hoist him up, feet slipping down the hill. Soldiers stood around him, someone slapped him on the back. Then he was in the back of a transport. The truck rumbled forward and he was crossing the bridge. He shoved the fog of his thoughts to the back of his mind and prepared to enter enemy-controlled territory. Somewhere in the back of his mind, Jimmy Trent slipped beneath the surface and faded deeper into the blackness of oblivion.

Lieutenant Vickers was in the back of the truck, his voice coming suddenly into focus. "Good work, Head-hunters," he said. "That was serious resistance, but they can't stop the 117th!" A few people cheered. Trent listened from a million miles away. "We'll get medals for sure, men. And Staff Sergeant Creon, outstanding fire mission. You and your team rained hell on the rebels. Solid fight."

"Roger that, sir," Creon said, devoid of enthusiasm.

They cleared the neighborhood and set up base in a commandeered warehouse at a gas power plant. A unit from the Seventh Military Police Division showed up and teamed with a local police force to secure the area and root out any RF sympathizers. Word came down within the first hour that they'd found the rebel commander John Torres hiding in an old school build-ing half a block from the Jordan bridge. Apparently, the street gangs turned on him and decided to tip off the police in hopes of some kind of forgiveness for their previous actions against the government. Either way, Torres was now in the CID's custody.

After all these weeks, they'd finally captured Joseph Graham's number one.

As for the 117th, a detachment from Headquar-ters set up a field barracks in one of the empty ware-houses. Soldiers, exhausted from fighting, collapsed onto rows of cots in their filthy uniforms, their com-bat armor piled at their feet, boots still laced tight.

Trent stood outside smoking a cigarette. His eyes stung, his hands shook. He felt waves of heat pouring off his body, his uniform stained with sweat. His armor lay at his feet, MX leaning against the side of the warehouse. Fingers went to his mouth, drew on the cigarette, felt the bite in his lungs. It tasted awful. He watched the sun fall behind the horizon. The floodlights kicked on, the growl of generators a constant backdrop. There was a distant ringing in his ears. The image of that building getting blown to pieces kept going through his head. That, and the boy lying in the mud.

He kept replaying in his mind, imagining the boy lowering the RPG, dropping it into the river and running away fast enough to escape the incoming artillery. He tried to imagine it into reality, wishing that it had played out that way.

But it hadn't.

He'd shot that boy.

Trent felt his legs give out and he sank to the ground, buried his face in his hands, and wept. He tried to fight it but it would not relent. Regret and sorrow pummeled him, reached right in and twisted his shriveled heart. He was a monster, and worse, he was crying about it. How pathetic could he be? Whimpering and sniveling like a baby. At least he was alive, and that boy wasn't. That boy would never get the chance to grow up and experience life. Trent had taken that from him. What fucking right did he have to feel sorry for himself?

Trent's hands balled into fists, clenched so tight he hoped his bones would break. What the fuck was he doing? All this for a fucking University Scholarship? To impress Alley, who was most likely already on to some other guy? Would he go home and sit in bars drinking alone telling this story to strangers who didn't give a shit? No, Trent didn't deserve to go home.

"Get up, Private."

Trent looked up to find Creon standing over him. The man still had his combat gear on, rifle clipped to his chest rig, dirt smeared over his face. "You're making a scene."

This fucking asshole. Trent didn't have patience for his shit right now. *I shot a fucking kid,* he almost burst out, but checked himself. He couldn't bring himself to say it out loud, especially not to Creon. The man was a prick. No way would Trent confide in that asshole. He stood and stared at the staff sergeant.

Creon eyed him for a moment. "Good. Now go get the rest of the squad, we got work to do." He gestured to a supply truck that was unloading pallets of empty sandbags.

Trent sighed. He was exhausted, but rest would have to wait.

21
THE HUNTER AND THE HUNTED

It was late afternoon by the time Tripp reached the ridge. He moved slowly and was careful to stick to cover, staying downhill far enough to keep his silhouette from standing out against the sky. He made no noise as he climbed.

Now near the top of the ridge, he turned to face the mine far below him, raised the AX-7, and scoped the facility. From where he stood he could see the flagpole in the headquarters courtyard and gauged the distance in his head to roughly a thousand yards. He lowered the rifle, surveyed his surroundings. Cross had to have been camped somewhere in the area. It was a perfect shooting position: clear line of sight to the most central area of the compound, plenty of places to set up a nest and be relatively comfortable for days. This is where he'd shoot from. She'd been here. He just had to find her trail.

His attention went to the thicket of pines to the north. An excellent escape route: take the shot, slide into cover, and move locations.

He had to get out of the open. These mountains were crawling with rebels, and there was no way to know if Cross was still around.

Tripp wiped sweat from his brow, shouldered the AX-7, and made his way into the tree line. Cross—if it really was her—had been firing on the compound for several days from different locations. Her MO was shoot and scoot, like any good sniper. Odds were good she'd at least moved to another ridge, but Tripp was still cautious and maintained a slow, stealthy pace.

Branches swept over him as he moved through cover and he felt just a bit less exposed. If he stumbled on Cross or an RF squad, at least now he had some protection if it came to a firefight and stood a better chance of getting out. He didn't want to let the team down. Didn't want to let Markus down, especially.

The chief had been increasingly concerned for everyone's safety lately. Not like the team hadn't been in and out of the shit their whole lives, but Markus was getting older and sometimes that got to a person. Tripp was still about ten years younger than him, but was no stranger to the concept of death. None of them were. He was there when Devens was killed protecting a shipbreaking plant in Bangladesh for some slave-driving overlord. Markus had taken that particularly hard, and the years didn't seem to help. He also had the burden of command, which meant it was his burden if something happened to one of them. Tripp didn't know how the man handled it all. He certainly wouldn't want that weight on his conscience.

Tripp eased his way over a ledge and down onto what looked like a well-used game trail. He crouched and scanned the ground. Dirt and rock, here and there the telltale signs of wildlife.

Human beings were inclined to identify patterns in their surroundings and tended to gravitate toward the familiar. Lots of animals used the same trails and it wasn't much of a stretch to assume that Cross had come through here as well. Tripp stayed low and examined the path closer. Most of the prints were deer, but at one spot where the trail rose steeply over a tangle of twisted roots he found what he was hoping for.

A human footprint.

A mark about five inches across with obvious treads, the ball of the foot scraped the dirt where someone slid while climbing the trail. Next to it was a branch snapped at waist height. Not chewed like a deer would've done. He'd found them. But the footprint was larger than the typical woman's boot, indicating either the shooter wasn't Cross or she had someone with her. Made sense, actually, to have a spotter. The RF must've been upping their game if they were actually implementing military tactics.

The print looked about a day old so he knew he was close behind, but not right on top of them. He brought the AX-7 around to the low ready just in case, and kept going. He stayed low and silent as he closed on his target.

Dusk settled over the mountains. Sam and Rob slipped from cover and made their way into position on the ridge. They'd scouted an ideal spot earlier but stayed out of sight in case Vircon sent patrols out searching for them, but after watching all day, they'd seen no such party and wanted to get another look at the compound before the last of the daylight died.

They moved downhill until they reached a point where the grade leveled out and found several large boulders that made for excellent cover and concealment. Rob set his pack down and made a radio check with the nearest camp, which was about several klicks to the southwest. Sam crouched, swept away some stones, and rolled out her blanket.

While Rob was on the radio, Sam scoped the compound. She was overlooking the northwest perimeter near the back end of the administrative buildings and could see straight down the main utility road toward the front gate. She couldn't see the gate though because several long buildings like storehouses or maintenance bays blocked the way, but she'd be able to see anyone coming up or down that road. Close enough. She swept the scope over the rest of the facility. They'd parked more heavy utility trucks by the smaller gates and along the roads, stacked piles of excess materials in alternating clusters and reinforced the interior perimeter walls around their headquarters building. Most of the remaining staff stayed out of sight.

Rob was speaking in hushed tones over the radio. He ended the call and set the radio back on his pack. There was a look on his face that sent a chill through Sam, and not in the good way. "They got Commander Torres," he said.

"What?"

"The army took the Jordan River block. They used air support and artillery. Blew the entire neighborhood to shit." Rob was staring off in the direction of the neighborhood to the east. Impossible to tell if the smoke rising over the city was from the attack or not. The whole valley was a ruin. "They took the bridge, swarmed the block. Torres couldn't get out, apparently."

"Is he alive?" Sam asked.

"They didn't say." He ran a hand through his hair. "They're planning the second attack tonight," he said. "Sub-commander Akers is in charge now. She wants to hit the compound before Vircon has a chance to respond. No time specified yet, but I can almost guarantee it'll come after midnight. We're on overwatch from here."

Sam set the rifle aside. "How bad is it?"

"How bad is what?"

"Killing that civilian."

Rob was silent for a moment. "You did what you had to. You saw an opportunity to swing the advantage our way. We can't lose this valley, Sam." He paused, then added, "You did what you had to."

She sat up, leaned against the rock. "I killed a civilian, Rob. I did that. I had him in my crosshairs and I pulled the trigger. The military's retaliating because of what I did."

"You can't start doubting yourself now, Sam. There's nothing simple about what we do. This whole war is a mess. Commander Torres knew his life was in danger, as we all know, but that's the price we pay for our future. Things get messy, and sometimes we have to do things we wish we didn't have to, but we keep fighting and we keep moving forward. Remember Joseph Graham's words: we must remember our purpose."

"Yeah." She tried to believe him, but the more she thought about it the more she began to wonder. Was she doing the right thing? Was this even about doing the right thing? For so long she'd used hatred as motivation, hatred for the people who killed her family, hatred for anyone who victimized the innocent. But now she'd just killed an innocent person. She'd become exactly the thing she hated.

Rob got up, sprawled out his sleeping mat next to Sam. He put his hand on her knee. "It's a mess, Sam, no denying that. But it has to be this way in order to ensure a free and prosperous future, like Joseph Graham says. Bad things are going to happen, but in the end, good *will* come of it. I know it."

An emptiness was spreading through her and she needed to fill it with something pure before she lost her edge. Sam looked in Rob's eyes and let herself be swept into them, so full of sincerity and determination. He was a true believer, a beacon in the dark times, and she needed him now more than ever.

Her hand went to his, fingers laced. A spark lit in her belly, her blood tingling at the change in the way Rob was looking at her. She leaned into him, their mouths met, and before she knew what she was doing, they were sprawled on the blanket, tugging at their gear, tossing aside their inhibitions. Sam needed this. Needed Rob. She needed this moment to remind her what she was fighting for, that life still had its beautiful moments and that was all that mattered.

Afterward, they laid on their backs staring into the sky watching the clouds drift by. The breeze kissed the bare skin of Sam's belly and thighs. She stretched, laced her fingers behind her head. "I hope you're right about what we're doing."

She felt Rob inch closer. "There's nothing pleasant about it, and the fact you feel remorse or doubt or whatever you're feeling means you're still a normal, decent, morally grounded human being. This is tough stuff we're doing and I say there's no one better for the task. Sam, you're the strongest person I've ever met. To go through what you've gone through . . . I just can't imagine. But that's why you're doing it. It's why the Revolutionist Front came to be, to stop things like what happened to you from happening to others. To build a new state where we, the people, truly govern ourselves."

"I just hope you're right about some good coming from all this death," Sam said.

"It will," Rob replied. He got up, holding his belt in place, and walked out beyond the ring of boulders. He planted his feet with his back to her and began relieving himself.

Sam tugged her pants back up and buckled her belt, rolled over and looked at the Remington leaning against the rock, silent and still. Together she and that rifle had racked up a staggering number of kills. More than she cared to keep track of. Rob had the numbers logged in his little leather-bound notebook, each one accompanied by the specific details of time, date, temperature, distance. Maybe one day when this was all over and she had her head on right she'd look through the record. She wondered if she and Rob would be together after it was over. If it was ever over.

She was staring at the rifle when a sound ripped her from her thoughts.

A slap and zip, like something tearing the air, then a crack echoing off the surrounding rocks.

Terror seized her, turned her blood to ice. She knew instantly that they'd just been shot at by a sniper.

She dove for her rifle and scrambled to get tight against the rock, hoping she was behind cover. She scanned the far hillside trying to figure out where the shot had come from.

"*Rob*," she called out. He didn't answer and she couldn't see him. She hoped to God he was being smart and staying quiet. That shot had been close. She stayed low, crawled around the rock and slid behind some brush, working her way to a position where she might be able to find Rob's hiding place. He'd been facing the ridge to the south, so he had to be downhill from her. She whispered his name again. Again, he didn't answer. Panic now, she felt herself losing control. She called out louder. Still nothing.

She inched forward and rose into a low crouch, trying desperately to reach Rob. His rifle and gear were still in the camp. He had to be pinned down. Sam had the Remington. If she could find the shooter she could cover Rob while he got out of there.

The sleeve of her shirt caught on some brush and tugged the branches as she rose. Another round hissed past, the report of the rifle coming a second later. She dropped and scooted behind a rock just big enough to cover her. This time she'd pinpointed the direction of the shot. The shooter was definitely on that ridge. No way she could go back to the camp. Their gear, supplies, and radio were cut off. She was pinned down and she had no idea where Rob was.

She had to lock it up. Giving in to panic wouldn't get her and Rob out of this. She took several small breaths and tried to calm her racing heart. Then she rolled over, kept as low to the ground as she could, and peered around the rock.

The ridge was probably four hundred and fifty yards out. There were a few places where a shooter could hide, too many to be sure exactly where, but she knew he was there somewhere. The sun was slipping behind the ridge and the slope was shrouded in darkness, her side of the mountain bathed in the golden glow of sunset. The shooter had the upper hand.

As she scanned the distance, her peripheral vision caught something below her. She looked down and found Rob about forty feet away lying sideways in the dirt, arms sprawled in the kind of unnatural angle that only the dead could manage. The ground around him was stained dark.

"Rob," she cried.

He didn't move.

Her eyes watered, her sight compromised. She lay behind that rock for the better part of an hour as the sky turned full dark. Neither she nor Rob moved and she knew that he was dead.

Her body quivered. Fear, sorrow, rage, all fighting for control of her mind, and all somehow claiming an equal share. He was gone, she knew it. No matter how hard she tried to imagine things differently, the reality would not be altered.

Rob was dead.

Her gear was in the open and out of reach. All she had was her rifle. She lay in the dirt, not daring to move a muscle. Rocks dug into her skin, the cold seeped into her bones. She was trapped and alone. Rob was gone. He wouldn't have felt a thing. At least there was that. But now the shooter was just waiting her out. For the first time since she was a child, Sam felt helpless and alone.

All over again.

22
COMPOUND ASSAULT

"**M**ay I join you?"

Markus looked up and saw Annika Sellers standing next him. Even in the dark he could see her eyes rimmed with exhaustion, a distant expression on her face, numbed by shock and grief. A look he was intimately familiar with. He slid over and she leaned on the wall beside him, staring out at the darkness beyond, the faint light from the Copperton slums flickering in the distance.

"It's late," he said. "And it's not safe for you up here."

"Can't sleep," she said. "Is it safe for *you* up here?"

Markus shrugged. "Fair enough." It wasn't worth fighting. She'd lost her father just hours ago and as far as he'd seen, she wasn't the kind of woman who liked being told what to do.

"You okay?" he asked.

"I don't know," she said. "So much to think about. So much to sort through I don't even know where to begin. It's like . . ." She trailed off, lost for words.

"Hopeless," Markus offered.

She nodded solemnly. "Yes. Hopeless."

"That's what it feels like, but that's not how it is," Markus said. "There's always hope. Always a solution. The mission now is to figure out what that is then execute. There'll be time for grieving later." He paused, the silence of the night sinking in. "It takes time for the grief to really settle in anyway."

"You've lost someone before?"

"Yeah."

"How do you deal with it?" she asked. "How do you keep doing it?"

Markus took a moment to choose the right words. "The first step is coming to terms with what you're doing. We go into each job knowing the dangers, knowing full well any one of us could die. But you gotta push that thought down and focus on what needs to be done. Not for yourself but for everyone else around you. My main objective, always, is to keep my crew alive. So yeah, it hurts when we lose one of our own, but none of us can change the past. The only thing we can do is move forward and remember those who died. It's not easy, though."

"Dad knew what was going on here, he just didn't take it seriously enough. Neither did I."

"Sometimes it's hard to realize the gravity of the situation until you experience the worst of it."

Silence again. The cloud of smoke that hung in the valley blotted out the stars, made the lights from the city seem a hazy glow. He could see Annika trying to stay in control, but her head slumped and her shoulders twitched just enough to let him know she was trying not to cry. He struggled to think of something to say.

"You know most people die within thirty miles of the place they were born," he said, wincing at himself.

To his surprise, Annika took a breath, lifted her head and forced a smile. "That so?"

"Uh, yeah. I read it somewhere."

"And what about you, Markus? Where's home?"

"Right here."

She gave him a quizzical look.

"Wherever my crew is, that's home," he said. "Here, wherever, doesn't matter."

"Sounds like you really love them."

"They're my brothers. This crew is the only family any of us have left."

She brushed a strand of hair from her face. "How'd you guys come to be? You're a pretty diverse group, you know. I can't imagine you all grew up in the same neighborhood."

Markus didn't really feel like getting into the past, but he could tell that talking was helping her. "No, we didn't grow up together. We . . ." Again, he chose his words carefully. "We were part of a unit that worked . . . quiet missions. The kind they don't brag about. The UN passed the Disclosure Act, funding was cut, records erased, and we got shut down. Things kept going south in the US so we found our way back and kept going doing the only thing we know how to do. It's not glorious, but it keeps us busy and gives us a chance to try and do some good in this shithole."

"So that stuff's real, huh?" Annika asked. "Shadow ops and such?"

"Afraid so." It felt strange to talk about this kind of stuff with a civilian, but he was a civilian now, too. Had been for some time, no matter how hard he tried to keep up the operator persona. Truth was, he was nothing like what he'd been. "There's always something going on behind the curtains."

Annika stared at him for a few moments, not saying a word, her tired eyes searching. Markus went back to scanning the distance, but he could feel her gaze lingering.

"Have you heard from your guy yet?" she finally asked.

"Not since a few hours ago," Markus replied. "Tripp said he might've found the shooter's trail so he was going silent." Markus sensed Annika's unasked question. "He's good. He'll get her."

"*Her.*" Annika spat the word. "You really think it's the Reaper of legend?"

"No way to know for sure, but odds are good it is. And if there's anything I know, it's that legends are bullshit. This Samantha Cross, she's a person. Flesh and blood and she *will* bleed. Tripp will get her."

"I believe you."

Markus tried to believe himself. He didn't like that Tripp was out there alone in enemy territory, but desperate times called for desperate measures. They couldn't have a sniper harassing them any longer, and if anyone was capable of taking her down it was Tripp.

"Thanks, Markus," Annika said. "For listening—"

"Wait," Markus said, gesturing for her to be quiet. He was watching a vehicle move slowly through the outskirts of Copperton maybe half a mile away when the headlights cut out. He squinted to find the vehicle in the dark.

"There," he said. "See that? That vehicle just cut its lights but it's still moving."

Annika turned to look out over the wall. "I don't see anything? How can you tell?"

"Look there." He pointed to a dark shade sliding past lighted windows, drawing closer.

"What does that mean?" Annika asked.

"Means you get out of here and get your protective gear on. Go to the safe house now." Markus grabbed the radio. "All elements be advised, we have one victor inbound toward main gate, lights out, moving fast. ETA sixty seconds, over."

"Copy that," Reyes answered.

For a long, tense moment nothing happened. The world seemed to pause, frozen under the eternal blackness of night, every sense ratcheting up and reaching out.

And then the .50 cal opened up from the main gate, spitting tracers into the dark. The rounds sparked off pavement, found the approaching vehicle and ripped it to shreds. A second later it exploded in a bright flash, a cloud of orange and black expanding skyward, the shock wave rolling out across the fields.

Gunfire erupted from the darkness surrounding the perimeter. Rounds punched through the towers and clanged off the steel walls. A few spotlights shattered and winked out. Bullets zipped through the air, buzzing and cracking.

"Get out of here, now!" Markus yelled, shoving Annika down the stairs. She stumbled, heels slid out from under her, and she fell down the last few steps. There wasn't time to worry about it, better a bruise than a bullet hole. She sprinted off under the wash of sodium lights toward the safe house.

Markus turned his attention back to the fight. About a hundred meters away in the next tower Reyes and three more of his men were returning fire. Most of the RF were clustered along the main road coming out of Copperton as they'd done in their first assault, using the slums for cover and staging again. Markus didn't have night vision capabilities but he could see muzzle flashes spread out in a crescent near the main gate. They must've waited for the cover of dark then spent most of the night moving into position. It was hard to tell for sure but Markus guessed they were up against a platoon-sized element, probably forty or fifty enemy combatants.

With his crew and Reyes's, they numbered fifteen. It was about to get nasty.

Annika ran. It was all she could do. There was nothing else in her mind but getting away, even though she knew there was nowhere to get away to. She sprinted as hard as she could, the battle raging behind her as the handful of old soldiers stood on the wall fighting off the rebels as best they could. The crackling gunfire chased her across the compound, urging her on even as her body protested against the physical exertion. Annika stumbled, pitched forward and lost balance. Her hands shot out to break the fall and she scraped her palms on the rough gravel. Her teeth clicked as her chin bounced off the ground. She tasted blood in her mouth.

Behind her, she could hear people shouting between the bursts of gunfire. They sounded panicked. She forced herself up and kept running. Markus had told her to get to the safe house. That was her task. She certainly wouldn't do any good for anyone out here. She wasn't a fighter, not in the way these hardened mercenaries and security contractors were. The thought of standing on that wall and facing the storm of bullets made her skin crawl. It took a special kind of crazy to be a soldier.

"Annika!" Philip Orsten shouted as he came stumbling out of the headquarters building and raced across the courtyard. He must've been sleeping in his clothes because he was in slacks and a collared shirt and it was well after midnight.

Annika didn't slow her pace, just waved him along. "Come on, Phil, we have to get to the safe house!"

The snap and hiss of incoming fire followed them the entire way. They reached the safe house and fell through the door, then slammed it shut and pushed their way to the back of the small room in a feeble attempt to put as much distance between themselves and the fighting.

"Jesus fucking Christ," Orsten said. "What are we gonna do?"

Annika had no goddamn clue. But Orsten was hysterical and she couldn't deal with that level of panic in the room. "We hang tight," she said for lack of anything better to say.

"No shit," Orsten said. "What the fuck else would we do?"

"Then why ask," Annika snapped. Obviously, they were trapped. The rebels had done just what Markus had feared, just what he'd tried to warn them all about. But she'd known nothing of war before this and she'd taken his counsel for granted. Now her father was dead, and she would likely be dead very soon. If only she could go back and do everything differently. If only she had listened to Markus and the captain. If only she'd gone into healthcare like her mother had wanted. But wishing for a thing would never make it happen. And they were cornered in the safe house like rats in a cage as the rebel army closed in.

The walls shook as something outside exploded.

"What if they get in here?" Orsten asked, the whites of his eyes bulging from the sockets. "What will they do to us?"

Annika knew he was thinking of the videos the rebels were fond of posting to the net. She was fully aware of the horrible things some of the more violent factions did to those who opposed them. *No. No no no.* She forced the thought from her mind, then went to the gun cabinet and took out the pistol she had handled once before. Somehow it felt even heavier now. Maybe because it was likely she was actually going to have to use it this time if Markus and his team couldn't hold out against the rebels. And if they couldn't hold back the rebels then there was no way she was going to be able to. If that happened, there truly would be no way out.

She glanced down at the gun in her hand, turning it slightly so the light glinted off the blackened barrel. *No,* she thought. *There was one way out.* But she forced that thought to the back of her mind and prayed Markus and his crew would hold out.

Markus radioed Dieter and Rourke. "North gate, what's your status?"

"Enemy contact," Dieter answered. "Multiple foot mobiles with technical support, over."

The RF were hitting them hard, then. Markus had been counting on Rourke's M37 to be the big gun to the north, but if the enemy were coming at them with technicals, it would only be a matter of time before they were pushed back. But the longer they held out the better their chances of wearing the RF down and sending them into retreat.

"Stay frosty," Markus said. "Hold that gate."

"Copy that, Chief."

Markus was alone in his tower, but he'd prepped an arsenal of munitions that would make it seem like there was an entire fire team in there with him. He scooped up a flare gun, pointed it to the sky and fired. The illumination round streaked upward, a red tail arcing over the battlefield. It reached its zenith and popped, washing the fields in angry red, enemy positions suddenly exposed, long shadows betraying their movements. The Vircon security took advantage of the moment and let loose with return fire.

To the north, another flare burst in the sky. Gunfire echoed from every direction as the fight intensified.

Markus slung the MX to his back and grabbed the M203D repeating launcher, the drum magazine loaded with 40mm grenades. He arced the barrel up, thumped the first grenade into the chamber, and pulled the trigger. The grenade exploded a second later, a bright flash of white and red sparks expanding violently somewhere in the field beyond, about fifty meters from the main road. He held the angle, aimed a bit more to the right, and sent another round downrange. This one hit in the road and sent a group of rebels scrambling for cover. Spotlights from the towers lit them up as they ran in the open and the Vircon crew picked them off.

Markus continued to pump out grenades, sweeping the field, spreading the devastation. The last grenade thumped into the night and exploded near a ditch filled with RF. More rebels were closing in, with vehicles coming out of Copperton stopping just out of range of the grenade launcher, machine guns mounted in back. Tracer rounds streaked through the air and smashed into the compound.

After a few moments passed without any more grenade salvos, the RF began to press in, driving the technicals closer, covering the foot soldiers creeping along the ditches. They were focusing most of the fire on the main gate, presumably to soften it up before attempting a mad rush.

Markus loaded another drum in the grenade launcher, slung it over his shoulder, and brought the MX around to the front. He snatched the pack with spare flares and pistol magazines, slung it over his other shoulder, and took off down the steps of the tower, fighting to keep balance as he sprinted toward Reyes's position at the main gate. It was a short distance but felt like it took forever to get there, the gunfire crackling, more lights getting shot out, sparks off the towers. He could hear people shouting over the chaos.

Markus reached the stairs, grabbed the handrail to swing himself around, and took the steps three at a time. He met Reyes at the top, who was keeping low while returning fire. Markus clapped him on the shoulder. "I got the 203," he shouted. "Draw the technicals in to a hundred and fifty meters. I'll take 'em out before they hit the X."

"Copy that," Reyes said, not taking his eyes from the sights as his rifle barked.

Markus ducked behind the wall and moved down

the line. He wanted to stay out of sight so he had time to aim. It was critical that the technicals were disabled before they reached the stretch of road rigged with explosives so they could save that for the rebels who were on foot and unprotected in order to maximize the damage. The entire defensive plan balanced on inflicting enough damage to make the RF retreat. If they didn't, it would be over quick once they breached the gate.

The technicals were closer now, two moving up the road side by side and another following in the rear. The two lead vehicles were about two hundred meters out and closing.

Markus pulled the flare gun out, fired another illumination round into the sky, tucked the gun in his cargo pocket, and brought the grenade launcher up. The flare round popped and lit the battle space. The rebels were sprinting toward the gate, the two lead technicals just crossing the hundred-fifty-meter mark.

Markus aimed for a spot in front of the vehicles and fired. The grenade thumped out of the barrel and exploded in the road, spraying the trucks with shrapnel. The truck to the left hit the brakes and turned in to the ditch, the other veered off-road and accelerated, bouncing over the rough terrain. Reyes and his men poured everything they had into that vehicle as it tried to get away. The rear truck came to a skidding halt, then hit reverse and backed out of range.

The truck that was now stuck nose-first in the ditch was revving the engine, the tires spraying dirt but going nowhere while the gunner regained his footing and got back on the machine gun. The mount leaned at an awkward angle and caused the rounds to go low, which gave Markus time to adjust the next shot. He aimed and fired another grenade at the technical.

It detonated on the driver's-side door, ripping the metal apart, showering sparks and shrapnel through the passenger compartment. The gunner was thrown from the bed and disappeared into the shadows. The truck caught fire. Markus didn't see anyone climb out.

The RF in the field began moving away. "They're falling back," one of the Vircon guys shouted.

"Stay sharp," Reyes replied. "They're not done."

Markus took the lull to call Dieter at the north gate. "What's your status," he asked over the comms.

"Holding," Dieter called back. "But it's getting hot, Chief."

"Any injured?"

"Negative."

"Copy. Keep it up, don't let them near that gate."

"You got it."

Markus joined Reyes, switching the grenade launcher for the MX. "What are they doing?"

Reyes peered through the dark, the flaming ruins of the gun truck casting light in a small perimeter. Beyond that, blackness. The shooting had ceased but there was no way the RF would give up so easily. Something was off.

"Maybe they've had enou—"

A piercing whistle, then bone-rattling *whump*. *Whump, whump.*

Everyone turned to look behind them at the space inside the perimeter. Markus knew that sound. They all did.

Mortars.

The radio squawked and Dieter's voice came through. "Chief, that what I think it is?"

Markus keyed the mic, staring into the compound. "Stand by."

Another round impacted, a bright flash somewhere out by the crane staging area closer to the edge of the mine. Two more landed, each one walking closer to the main compound. Markus watched his worst fear coming true. The RF were so determined to take the compound they were willing to destroy it in the process.

Then it was raining mortars. They pounded the facility, smashing parked trucks, cranes, equipment, trailers. Something to the north detonated in a chest-thumping boom that Markus felt more than heard. A moment later, an angry, flickering glow illuminated the north end of the perimeter.

The radio beeped. "Smelting facility's on fire, Chief."

The mortars kept coming in, spreading all over the compound. Markus prayed they didn't hit any of the gates. His guys suddenly felt far away.

Markus keyed the mic. "Dieter, get the hell out of there before they hit the fuel tanks. Fall back to the secondary perimeter."

"Copy that." Markus could hear gunfire snapping in the background.

He went to grab Reyes when a blast ripped a chunk out of the wall ten meters to his left. He was thrown forward, bounced off the wall and tumbled to the floor, dust and pieces of hot steel falling around him. Someone was lying on his legs and his head was spinning. He pushed himself up, ran his hands over his body. Everything was there and in functional order, no bleeding or protrusions. He looked around, saw the others doing the same when the sound of enemy gunfire came back to life. Markus realized no one was returning fire and adrenaline pumped ice through his veins, forcing him to his feet. He thrust his MX over the wall, firing blindly into the dark. He hated wasting ammo without identifying targets but they needed covering fire or they'd be overrun. A few others joined him while the rest continued to recover.

One technical was racing up the road faster than the others, the machine gun in back belching on full auto. Behind it were several other vehicles and out in the fields, muzzle flashes told him the RF were converging on the main gate.

"We gotta get out of here," Markus yelled. He searched for Reyes. "We're gonna get overrun. We need to . . ." He stopped.

Reyes was sitting against the wall, head lolling, one hand pressed tight to his neck. Blood seeped through his fingers and soaked his shirt. The man's entire left arm was dark and wet. One of his men was trying to check the wound, but Reyes shoved his hand away.

"Jesus, Reyes," Markus said.

Reyes looked up, face pale. He grabbed at the wall to pull himself up. Markus went to help, ignoring the fight for a moment.

"We gotta get you to HQ, Temple can patch you up." Markus went to call his medic on the radio.

Reyes grabbed Markus's hand, stopped him. "Get out of here," he said, blood bubbling at the corner of his mouth. "I'm about done. Get to the secondary perimeter. I'll stay on the fifty until you're in, then blow the gate."

"Not leaving you," Markus said. "Not how I do things."

"Don't give a shit how you do things, cowboy. I'm done. Gonna take as many of those bloody fuckers with me as I can. Nothing else to do about it now."

Markus wanted to argue, wanted to try to save the man, but he knew it was futile. Blood was pumping through his fingers in spurts. He'd hit an artery. The man had moments left.

"Fuck," Markus shouted.

Reyes turned to his men. "Final order. Fall back, I'll handle this."

They nodded solemnly. Reyes handed his remaining magazines to the nearest man, then someone put the detonator switch in his hand. "Go," he said.

The enemy gunfire was pounding the tower now, so close Markus wouldn't be surprised if he came face-to-face with rebel fighters at the bottom of the stairs. He faced Reyes, extended a hand. "Good luck, it's been an honor."

Reyes blinked slowly, gripped Markus's hand. "Honor's mine, cowboy."

Markus nodded, then forced himself down the steps. The rest of the Vircon security were already sprinting toward the inner compound. He fought to keep up, his balance thrown off with the weight of the pack and weapons hanging off him.

Behind them, the shooting raged on, the sound of the technical and the .50 cal fighting it out just beyond the gate. The RF were right on top of them.

A second later, the first explosion ripped out into the night, followed by a cascading daisy chain of secondary explosions. The ground shook, the night sky lit with roiling clouds of red flame and black smoke. The two guard towers flanking the main gate blew apart, pieces of the wall flying outward, shrapnel digging furrows in the dirt road, chunks of the perimeter walls carved away. The pair of heavy industrial haulers parked inside the gate flipped up, listed in the air, then slammed down on their sides. The explosions rippled down the road a hundred meters through the RF lines.

Markus cleared the gate to the inner compound and turned to watch the ball of fire reach up into the night sky before the flimsy steel doors slid shut.

The rest of the men were sprinting for the headquarters building and Markus ran after them. As they crossed the lot, a Prowler and one of the Vircon pickups came racing through the north entrance and skidded to a halt. Dieter, Rourke, and Weatherford—as well as the rest of their fire team—jumped out, saw Markus, and rallied on the steps of HQ.

"We have a minute or two at most so listen up," Markus said. "Main gates are gone, the fifty is gone. They'll be coming at us hard, but they gotta go through those bottlenecks and cross open ground to get here. We need to focus fire on those points, hold them off as long as we possibly can. I need a fire team on those rooftops over there." He gestured to the Vircon barracks by the secondary gate. "A four-man fire team up top of HQ and two three-man teams covering everything else up there." He pointed to the long L-shaped maintenance bay in the center of the compound. It was a long shot, but it would give them the best possible position with interlocking fields of fire to cover their small plot of land.

Weatherford glanced around the remaining men. "Where's Reyes?"

"He's gone," said one of the contractors.

"He bought us this minute so let's not waste it," Markus said, keeping everyone focused. "Let's go."

They split off into groups and raced for the buildings, Dieter going with the Vircon teams to the maintenance bay, while Markus led Len, Temple, and Rourke up to the roof of HQ. They climbed the steel-rung ladder on the side of the building and took up positions facing the north end of the compound. The dark pit of the mine loomed off to the left, hopefully enough of a natural barrier to protect that side. The RF would funnel through the debris at the main gate and get hammered by the fire teams on the roof of the barracks, and when they came through the north gate they'd have to move around blockades that would push them close to the fuel tanks. Hopefully the remote detonator was still intact.

Too many hopes, not enough assurances. They'd learn the truth of it in a moment.

Markus made sure his team was in place then found Dieter. "I'm going to check on the VIPs. I'll be right back."

"Copy that," Dieter said.

"Hey, Chief." Temple called Markus's attention. "I managed to grab a sat-phone and list of relays from the tower. If I can find the right one I might be able to reach a government line, call for military support."

"Fantastic," Markus said. "Work on it, that's your priority. Make sure they know that if they don't get here now then this facility will belong to the rebels by morning."

Temple nodded, clipped his rifle to his chest, and set to working on the comms. The lights in the compound went out as someone pulled the breaker, concealing their positions.

Satisfied, Markus climbed down the ladder and crossed the courtyard to the safe house. The heavy steel-reinforced door was unlocked and he opened it a few inches. "Annika, it's Markus," he said before opening any further. The last thing he wanted was to get shot by a frightened executive. He pushed the door open a little further. Caution was eating up precious time.

"Markus?"

"Yeah," he said as he entered the room, letting the heavy door close behind him. "How you doing?"

She was hiding behind a desk in back of the room, pistol gripped tight in her hands and pointed right at him.

His heart skipped a beat, wondering if after everything this was how he'd meet his end, but she realized what she was doing and lowered the gun. "What's happening?" she asked, voice trembling. Philip Orsten climbed up from behind the leather couch, sweat pouring down his face.

"They're hitting us hard," Markus said. No sense in sugarcoating the truth. "But we've got the secondary perimeter locked down. Temple's trying to reach the military to call for support. We have good men in place to deal with the threat, but it's going to get noisy again any minute. I need you to stay in here and stay quiet. If we don't make it . . ." He paused, wondering if he should even bring up the possibility of failure. The RF were civilians, but there was no telling what they'd do once they were in. He decided to leave it alone. "Just stay down and lock this door when I leave, okay? We'll be right outside."

Annika nodded.

He left the safe house and went back outside. He'd only taken a few steps when the gunfire broke out. The team on the barracks building were firing toward the ruins of the main gate. A second later, several detonations went off to the north as the RF entered the exterior compound and tripped the explosives buried in the road.

Markus sprinted across the courtyard and climbed the ladder feeling more exposed than ever. He reached the top, pulled himself over and raced to Dieter's side. The man was kneeling behind the parapet walls of the roof, sighting out over the compound. In the distance, headlights closed in.

"Technicals, coming in close," Dieter said. "They had 240s and a DShK."

"Push 'em toward the fuel tanks," Markus said. "When they get close, light 'em off."

"Roger that."

Once the tanks blew, their explosive defenses would be gone. But they had to devastate the enemy. It was all they could try to do.

"How are the comms?" Markus asked Temple.

The medic was holding the sat-phone to his ear. "I got some cell provider in Denver," he said. "Getting routed to CENTCOM, waiting on verification."

"Well that's something," Markus said. He knew full well how complicated something as simple as making a fucking phone call could be with the military.

The technicals stopped about three hundred meters

out, still too far from the fuel tanks to promise destruction. The heavy machine guns opened up, hammering their position. They took cover and returned fire, trying to push the RF toward the fuel tanks.

The comms beeped and Weatherford reported they had a casualty on the barracks position. Temple's head snapped up, ready to run to their aid, but Markus thrust his fist out, telling him to hold. The radio for support was more important right now.

Loud booms pounded the eastern perimeter. Markus saw an RPG streak over the barracks building. The RF were pressing through the gap in the demolished exterior wall, on foot thanks to the debris left in the wake of the explosion.

More gunfire from the north brought Markus around. The technicals were moving, but not closer to the tanks. They were trying to flank around the open toward the mine and come up on the western edge of the compound.

"Rourke!" Markus yelled. "I need that 37 over here now! Push them toward the tanks."

"Copy." Rourke was up, lugging the machine gun like it was nothing. He dropped in next to Markus, using the bipod as a fore-grip to open up on the trucks. He walked the rounds into the technicals, forcing them back. Rebels were spreading through the battle space now, small-arms fire surrounding the area.

Markus thumped out a cluster of grenades and the technicals jumped back on the road and made for the gate. They were less than a hundred meters from the four massive fuel tanks now.

"Who's got the detonator?" Markus shouted, hoping to God someone still had it.

Dieter used his left hand to fish the remote from his cargo pocket and waved it while continuing to fire with his right, the rifle braced on the edge of the wall.

"On my mark," Markus said.

"Standing by for mark," Dieter said.

Markus watched the trucks gain speed and come broadside with the fuel tanks.

"Now!"

The earth shook. A massive explosion as the first tank erupted, a ball of fire billowing outward, followed by two more pounding blasts, then the last, adding its accelerant to the growing carpet of flame and super-heated debris showering the battle space. Balls of molten steel shot outward trailing black smoke, smashing through the ranks of the RF. The trucks disappeared in the wall of flame. Greasy smoke lifted into the atmosphere and bits of shrapnel fell earthward.

Markus, Rourke, and Len opened up on the devastated rebels. People were running around on fire while others lay facedown and smoldering. Thick black smoke blanketed the area. Those who were saved from the blast returned fire, the rounds coming in so close that chunks of cement pelted Markus's face.

This was where the RF would retreat if they were planning to at all, but they kept coming. More headlights came down through the north gate, more shooting over at the main gate. The RF were closing. Markus checked the knife on his belt, made sure it was ready for when it came down to that.

"I got through!" Temple shouted, waving the satphone. "They're contacting the air base and sending the nearest unit. We might make it out of this." He tucked the phone away and charged his rifle, medical pack over his shoulder. "Chief?"

"Go," Markus said, then Temple was off, over the edge and sliding down the ladder to go help with the injured on Weatherford's team.

Against the odds and out of time, Markus and his crew, with the rest of the Vircon team, kept up the fight as the rebels continued to close in on the compound.

23
HELL OF A NIGHT

Somebody's gettin' lit up," Bodine said, packing his lip with a wad of chew.

Trent lounged on the hood of the Prowler with his back against the windshield smoking a cigarette, listening to the firefight happening off to the west. Someone was indeed getting pounded. The gunfire in the distance sounded like muffled pops, a steady *tut-tut-tut-tut* that punctuated the night.

"That sounds like a fifty," Bodine said. Over the last few weeks the guys in the squad had made a game of identifying different types of weapons from sound alone. It was easy to tell the sharp snap of the standard military 5.56 round, but the rebels were using all kinds of foreign weapons in their hodgepodge army. Kalashnikovs, old M4s, Chinese stuff. Whatever they could get their hands on.

"That's a Russian DShK," Trent corrected. "*That,*" he said, pointing his cigarette at a different sound, "is a fifty."

Bodine spat a string of brown sludge. "How the fuck you know that?"

"Different rate of fire. Fifty's slower, deeper report." Trent took a drag off his cigarette. "I used to be an armorer."

"Oh yeah."

Ramirez whistled through his teeth. "He got you, Corporal."

"Shut the fuck up." Bodine swatted at Ramirez, who danced easily out of the way.

Sawyer came out of the darkness and joined the group by the truck. Like the rest of them, he looked like he hadn't slept for weeks. "What's up, guys," he said.

"Just listenin' to someone get their ass handed to 'em," Bodine said as a series of deep booms echoed over the valley.

Sawyer glanced toward the sound. "Yeah, well. I just wanted to let you guys know O'Malley's gone."

All eyes turned to Sawyer.

"What do you mean gone?"

"He didn't make it," Sawyer said. "Apparently he died in transport to the FOB. Took 'em this fuckin' long to let us know."

"Christ."

Trent saw the way the medic held himself. Hunched just a bit, shoulders sagged. He seemed deflated where once he'd been focused and ready for action. There was a slowness to his movements, like when you stayed awake for too long and the body stopped responding to the brain. Only this was more than that. "You okay?" Trent asked.

Sawyer blinked, turned from the sound of the shooting. He patted the hood of the Prowler. "Yeah. Good to go. Just wanted you guys to know," he said, then walked off.

"I don't fuckin' believe it, man," Bodine said, shifting his weight from foot to foot. He paced around the front of the Prowler, shaking his head.

Trent watched the corporal, waiting for him to snap. Ramirez said nothing.

"Sonofabitch. This was his first fuckin' tour. He shoulda never been out in front like that. What the fuck was Ser'ant Creon thinkin'? Kid never had a chance. Christ, he never even had a girlfriend!" Bodine was shouting, a quiver in his voice that threatened to crack.

"Can't think about it now," Trent said, knowing full well how stupid it sounded. What else was there to think about? They were in fucking Killzone Valley. Death was all there was. It was their fucking job. Kill or be killed, there wasn't time for sadness or regret.

Bodine stopped, was about to say something when shouting drew their attention. People were moving through the outpost, pounding on hoods, opening doors and waking everyone up. Diesel engines rumbled to life, lights came on. Trent saw vehicle gunners pop out of their hatches and rack their weapons. He stubbed his cigarette out on the hood and flicked it away.

Creon was calling everyone in the First Platoon lines to gather around the LT's truck. Trent grabbed his rifle, jumped down, and followed Bodine and Ramirez to the sudden briefing.

"Listen up," Lieutenant Vickers shouted. "At zero one hundred hours civilian contractors at the Vircon mine came under attack by a significant enemy force. There's no time to wait on logistics; we're moving out now as their QRF. We'll be clearing a slum called Copperton where the RF have been staging their assault. Second Platoon is taking point. Fall out to your squad leaders."

A collective roar of enthusiasm lifted into the early

morning darkness. They were finally going to reach their objective. High fucking time at that, and who gave a damn if they were driving into a shit storm; it was clear now that the firefight they'd been idly listening to earlier was the fight they were about to join. Soldiers scattered to their vehicles, squad leaders shouted orders, a few officers pored over maps on the hoods of their vehicles. The military machine was churning to life.

Moments later everyone was loaded up and they were off, racing through the streets on the last leg of their push through the city. Something pinged off the outside of the vehicle and the comms beeped telling them they were taking small-arms fire as they drove through gang territory and not to worry. The turrets thumped and they pushed through.

Eventually the APCs took a long, wide turn and shed speed. The comms beeped again.

"All units be advised, all personnel in area deemed hostile. AO is a free-fire zone. ETA sixty seconds."

Trent glanced at Creon sitting across from him. The staff sergeant made no indication he gave a shit about going into a town and wiping everyone out. People lived in Copperton, people who weren't part of the fight. People too poor and too stupid to leave. Free-fire meant murder. Trent had done enough of that. He wouldn't shoot civilians.

The APC stopped hard, jarring everyone inside. The turret started firing and the ramp fell open. First Platoon rushed out of the vehicles as they began to take small-arms fire. Trent stumbled down the ramp.

They were in the middle of a dirt road surrounded by dingy, run-down huts of plywood and corrugated steel. Trent stomped through a puddle of filth, raced for cover as rounds rang off the APC. He followed Creon into a narrow alley between a row of shacks, then cut right to flank the enemy. More APCs halted and dumped their squads into the street, and Second Platoon raced ahead to pierce through the enemy line. Several Prowlers shot past, turret gunners pouring rounds into the slum. Trent saw a few rebels dart from cover and get mowed down in the ditches. Huts were shredded by automatic gunfire, the flimsy structures collapsing in the dirt, knocking over neighboring homes, fires breaking out as people darted through the shadows.

Creon halted the squad as an enemy technical drove past in an attempt to escape before it was cut down by a turret gun. A cluster of foot mobiles ran past unaware of Trent's squad in the alley. Creon flashed a hand signal and the squad spread out into an offensive position.

Trent took a knee, realizing all too late that he was in another puddle of human waste and drew his sights on one of the RF. The rebel was glancing over her shoulder at the others in her group as they ran past mounds of smoldering trash. She noticed the soldiers in position behind them and opened her mouth to yell a warning.

Trent squeezed the trigger, felt the rifle kick, and watched her topple into a pile of garbage. Her companions dove to the ground and returned fire.

"Move right! Move, move, move," Creon shouted as the squad pushed around the attack. Trent rose, firing as he sidestepped behind the relatively useless cover of a wall of welded street signs. Everyone was shooting, overwhelming the enemy who were trapped in the open. The squad maneuvered into an L-shaped wedge, blocking the rebels in and hammering them to pieces. In a matter of seconds, the enemy shooting stopped.

Creon motioned the squad forward.

They slipped through the lot and checked the bodies. Five dead rebels and one wounded, gasping for air through a sucking chest wound. A middle-aged man with gray in his beard, his eyes searched but seemed to take in nothing. Sawyer went to work on him while Creon called it in so the man could be detained. He'd be questioned later, if he survived.

But the fight was still on and they moved quickly. Trent could hear the guns from Second Platoon moving around to the north, chasing down the squirters and driving the remaining RF off.

Trent and the rest of First Platoon pushed through lanes of muck, clearing huts and fragging parked cars, no idea if they belonged to the RF or civilians, but it didn't matter. Everything was destroyed. Creon split the squad into fire teams and sent them through a walled courtyard with more shacks inside. Trent took point on one hut, kicked the door open and slid in and to the right while Bodine covered left. A woman hid in the corner cradling two small children, all of them staring wide-eyed at the soldiers who just burst into their home.

Trent looked at Bodine. "I'm not shooting civilians. Fuck the free-fire order."

Bodine blinked a few times then nodded. "Clear," he said over his shoulder and slid out of the hut.

Trent looked at the mother and her children, pressed a finger to his lips, then followed Bodine back into the courtyard.

Creon led the fire teams around the back of an

old fueling station and found a rebel mortar team hunkered down behind piles of debris, three mortar tubes angled in the direction of the Vircon compound several hundred meters to the west. The rebels spotted the soldiers and opened up with M4s and Kalashnikovs at terrifyingly close range, sending the teams diving for cover.

Trent slid behind an old four-door sedan that had sunk into the ground up to the wheel wells. The windows shattered out, bullets hammer-punched the sheet metal, ripping up the ground around him. The rest of the squad was trying to maneuver into another L-wedge but the rebels were well placed to defend their position.

Bodine leaned through the busted-out windows and let the M37 go, spent casings raining inside the cab. Trent low-crawled to the front of the car, angled around so he could fire from the prone position. He sighted on the nearest fighter, maybe thirty meters away behind a row of oil drums. The rebel was shooting at someone off to the left and presenting a full side profile. Trent squeezed off a few rounds and the man dropped. He scanned for more targets but found none from that angle, so he rose to his knee and aimed over the hood of the car. Gunfire cracked so loud and close it felt like someone was boxing Trent's ears.

"Grenade out!" someone shouted. Trent had no way of knowing if it was one of their own or the rebels. He ducked behind the car and tensed, waiting for the blast.

A loud bang, bright flash, and several barrels flew away. Trent popped up and fired, no idea if there were any targets left. The weapon went dry, bolt locked to the rear. He dropped behind cover and loaded another magazine.

But by then the fight was done. The shooting stopped and the squad was already moving in to close. Bodine tapped Trent on the shoulder and they broke off from cover, swinging their rifles around every corner and possible enemy hiding place.

Eight more dead Revolutionists.

"Frag these fucking tubes," Creon ordered. The squad moved out of the station and someone dropped an incendiary grenade on the piled mortar tubes, melting them into useless scrap.

Fires had broken out throughout Copperton, the crumbling ghetto cast in flickering light, thick smoke choking the air. A few cars tried fleeing through the fields but were ripped apart by APC turrets. Trent hoped they were enemies, but knew they probably weren't.

Creon led them to a rally point at an intersection where they linked back up with Lieutenant Vickers and the main body of First Platoon. The LT said they'd cleared several mortar teams out and the remaining rebels fled on foot into the fields. They killed as many as they could, captured a few, but still some got away. The contractor element inside the compound reported over a satellite phone that the main force of the RF had retreated into the mountains. They were in desperate need of medical support so First Platoon was going in ASAP while Second Platoon held down Copperton.

The squads formed up on either side of Bingham Road with the APCs rolling down the center and made their way to the Vircon facility. Trent marched, suddenly exhausted from the fight and lack of sleep. He realized his hands were shaking again so he gripped his MX tighter to try to stop them. The first hundred meters of road appeared normal, but as they got closer to the compound things changed. A truck was in the ditch to Trent's left, filled with bullet holes and a body slumped over the steering wheel. There was a crater in the road and several bodies scattered about, clothes and limbs shredded and flung away. The APC's searchlights kept sweeping over the area, flashes of carnage that Trent couldn't help but stare at as he plodded along on autopilot. The pavement was torn up by heavy machine-gun fire. A truck was burning in the field maybe fifty meters out, the flames licking up around the ruined form of an old DShK anti-materiel machine gun mounted in the bed.

Trent marched on.

He almost tripped over a severed arm. It was thin and pale, torn at the elbow. Looked like it could belong to either a woman or a child. He hoped the rebels weren't actively recruiting children. He hoped the country hadn't sunk that low, but based on what he'd seen—and done—it was pretty likely. The rest of the body was nowhere to be found, but it didn't surprise him. The whole area looked like it had been carpet bombed.

It was nothing compared with the destruction at the gate, though.

The front gate had been blown apart, two guard towers on either side reduced to a pile of blackened rubble. The entire road was chewed up like it'd been hit with an air strike. Several trucks were tossed out into the fields, twisted and broken, scorched black from fire. Another truck was parked halfway up the pile of rubble blocking the gate, shot through from front to back, red smeared across white paint, a few bodies around it, one hanging halfway out the passenger door.

The APCs had to stop because there was just no way to get past the rubble.

Lieutenant Vickers got out of the lead APC and led the platoon through the gate on foot. Sergeant Creon stayed close by his side. Trent fumbled over the shifting piles of concrete and steel, slipping on transmission fluid and blood.

Inside the compound, things didn't appear much better. There was a secondary interior wall punched through with so many bullet holes it looked as if a single breath would topple it. The rooftops of several buildings poked up over the walls with more bullet holes. More bodies lying in the dirt. Thick clouds of smoke drifted through the compound. Farther inside the facility, towers of fire reached up into the sky.

Trent stopped when Lieutenant Vickers halted the platoon. Everyone scattered about the courtyard holding their weapons, casting nervous glances at every corner. The APCs idled beyond the gate, spotlights sweeping the area.

The flimsy metal gate set into the secondary wall rolled open, revealing a man standing in the middle of the lane beyond. Everyone tensed. The man was wearing tactical gear over civilian clothes and had several weapons hanging off him. He looked older, tired, his face covered in soot. Behind him were several other men in jeans and tactical vests, each with their own weapons.

The man in front lifted a hand. A tired wave.

The LT waved back and walked forward. Creon waved Trent and Bodine over and went with him.

"You Vircon?" Vickers asked.

The man glanced over Vickers's uniform then nodded. "I'm Markus, this is Weatherford," he said, indicating the man next to him in the gray uniform. "Thank you for coming, Lieutenant." He extended a hand.

The LT shook. "I'm Lieutenant Vickers with the 117th Infantry. You have wounded?"

"Three," said the man named Weatherford. "They're in HQ, this way." He had a thick British accent.

"Medic!" Vickers yelled over his shoulder.

Sawyer came running up lugging his medical bag. He had that determined look Trent remembered, as if he'd already put O'Malley behind him. That was good. Had to be that way. They followed the British contractor into the compound while Vickers and Creon got a quick debriefing on the events that happened. The man named Markus told it like he felt nothing about it, like he was made of steel, but Trent could see just the tiniest glimmer of regret in the man's eyes.

"You did all this with eleven guys?" Vickers asked.

"There were more when we started," Markus said. "We have one KIA, my medic's been working on the others."

"You put up a hell of a fight," Vickers said. "You can stand down now, we'll take care of it from here."

The contractor nodded then walked off with his crew. Lieutenant Vickers went back to radio Main while Sergeant Creon tasked the rest of First Platoon with securing the facility.

Trent stood in the courtyard taking in all the damage and wondered how anyone could've held out.

Looking at the fire and smoke, and the bodies and burning vehicles, he knew that if they hadn't arrived when they did this team of private contractors would've died in this place.

He walked back toward the ruined gate, climbed the pile of debris and twisted steel, and gazed out at the smoldering fields beyond, feeling a numbness sink into his soul.

24
THANKS, YOU'RE DONE

The US Army started moving into the Vircon mining facility before the dust had even settled. The Corps of Engineers began clearing the rubble, putting out fires, and rebuilding the ruined perimeter wall while Markus and his crew waited to be patched up. The soldiers worked tirelessly to turn the compound into their new stronghold. Reinforcements were already pouring in; a flatbed trailer was off-loading a delivery of portable bunk pods in the empty equipment lots and a patch of flat earth was being cleared for a landing pad. Two anti-materiel turrets went to the main and north gates. Could have used them earlier, but it didn't matter now.

Markus and the crew were gathered in the headquarters building conference room where they'd first met Ned Sellers several weeks ago. Somehow the place seemed different. The lights dimmer, the walls closer, the long table's polished finish hidden under a layer of dust. Markus imagined he looked much the same.

Dieter, Rourke, Len, and Temple filled the chairs next to him, each tapping a foot or drumming their fingers on the table. They hadn't quite come down from the edge yet, the thrill of battle thrumming like an electric current just under the skin. Even the most random gunfight would get the blood flowing, quicken the heart and shoot ice through the veins, but that hadn't been a random gunfight. That had been hell. And there was one element that was still unresolved keeping everyone on edge.

They still had a man in the field.

Tripp hadn't radioed at all since the fight ended. Markus hoped that maybe he'd missed a radio check during the chaos and that Tripp was closing in on the sniper. It didn't seem like the RF had any sniper support during that battle, most of the wounded and killed were from shrapnel and multiple gunshots. Had there been a sniper, there would've been more one-shot kills. It was slim, but enough to give Markus hope.

He rubbed exhaustion from his eyes, fought the urge to check the radio.

Dieter shifted in his chair. "No word yet?"

How the man was always able to read Markus was a mystery. "Not yet," Markus replied.

The conference room door swung open and an Army captain entered. She took a position at the front of the room, clipboard in hand and cleared her throat. "Gentlemen, this is Lieutenant Colonel Lowe." She gestured toward the door and an older soldier sauntered in, shoulders back, chin high, salt-and-pepper hair cropped short and neat, a silver leaf centered on his chest. The captain took a step back to allow the colonel to take center stage.

He clasped his hands behind his back, cast his gaze over Markus and his crew. "Which one of you is Markus?" he asked.

"Right here, Colonel," Markus said.

Colonel Lowe eyed him for a moment. "You boys are military? Or were?"

"That's right."

"We couldn't find any records of your service on file."

"And you won't."

The colonel smirked, set his hands on his hips. "Well ain't that high-speed. Alright, gentlemen, let's get to it. This compound is hereby commandeered by the American government. Vircon Industries no longer has a claim to this property for the duration of the conflict. Until the city is liberated of the Revolutionist Front and other rebel militias sympathetic to their cause, it will remain in the custody of the American military. Once peace has been established the property will be handed back to Vircon Industries. As for you and the remaining civilian contractor element, you are hereby relieved of the task of protecting this compound. It is now government property and you do not have clearance to be within the boundaries."

Markus felt the tension ripple through his crew. He had to say something before they pounced. "All due respect, Colonel, we have a man in those mountains right now hunting down a Revolutionist sniper we believe to be Samantha Cross. We're not leaving without him."

"Are you sure it's Cross?" Lowe asked.

"Sure enough."

The colonel rubbed his chin, frowned as he mulled it over. His assistant watched him closely, waiting for his answer. "Look, we appreciate what you've done here," he said. "You put up a hell of a fight. There's something to be said about that, but your contract with the Sellers and Vircon Industries is over. Gather your shit and move out. You have three hours."

Markus matched the colonel's stare. "And our man hunting down your Reaper?"

"Call him in. He's got three hours."

They stormed out of the meeting and went to the vehicle bay. Rourke kicked open the door and started tossing things into one of the Prowlers. "Fuck these motherfuckers," he shouted loud enough for the engineers waiting outside to hear. "We fought through hell to hold this place down. Now they're gonna kick us out into this shithole city? Fuck that." He wrapped a bear hug around a black tool chest and heaved it into the back seat. "I'm taking every god damned thing that's not bolted down."

The others spread out and went to gather their equipment.

Dieter came up beside Markus. "What do we do, Chief?"

A headache was starting to form in the base of Markus's skull. He rubbed his temples. "Can't risk calling him," he said. "We'll leave the perimeter, but set up nearby and wait."

"This is fucked," Len said as he lugged his pack into one of the trucks.

"Those pieces of shit only care about claiming property," Rourke said.

"This is a monetary asset," Temple added. "We're good Americans for doing our part to make sure that money goes back to the struggling government. Wouldn't want the wrong people to have the upper hand."

"Alright, that's enough," Markus snapped. It was too much, they were all on edge. "Check that shit and lock it up. We were hired to protect Ned Sellers and we failed. Now we're going to get Tripp and leave this place in the rearview. Understood?"

Rourke avoided looking at Markus. Len sighed,

nodded. Temple was busy stuffing medical supplies into his depleted bag. "Understood," Dieter said as he stood by Markus's side.

"Good," Markus said, feeling the weight of the universe on his shoulders. "Pack your things, collect everything you can. I want maps, batteries, any radios we can carry, and any we can't need to be zeroed out. Pack up the food, fuel, and water in separate vehicles. Check the trucks front to back. I'm talking tire pressure, fluid leaks, whatever we can do to top them off before we're gone, see that it gets done. We're on a time limit here so move with a purpose."

"Copy that, Chief," Dieter said. There was a hint of relief in his tone. The others bent to their tasks, happy to have orders.

"Hey, Chief," Len said, pointing to the door. Markus turned to find Annika Sellers silhouetted against the morning sun.

"Miss Sellers," he said, stepping outside and closing the door behind him. Didn't feel right having her in the bay while they looted Vircon for all it was worth.

Annika was worn out. She was still wearing the same clothes: dirty, sweat-stained, and torn at the seams. Her hair was pulled back in a loose ponytail, just enough to keep it out of her eyes. She looked like she'd been crying. Markus couldn't blame her. He knew she'd be haunted by the image of her father being shot right in front of her for the rest of her life. That wasn't something you just got over.

The two of them stood outside the bay looking at each other, neither one speaking.

"I want to thank you," Annika finally said. "For what you and your crew have done."

The words were a knife in Markus's chest. They

hadn't done what they'd promised to do. They'd failed. *He* had failed. "I'm sorry, Miss Sellers. We failed your father."

"No." Her mouth set in a hard line and she shook her head. "He knew what was going on here and didn't leave. You tried to tell him, but he was . . ." She trailed off, lost for words.

"I know," Markus said.

Annika stared at him for a moment. "It cost him," she said. "It cost all of us. I'm sorry."

"As am I." He felt the current ripple through him, then checked it. The image of Devens staring out into the bay, and the words he'd spoken in the dream, flashed through his mind. "Doesn't matter now that it's done. Can't dwell on the past."

"I suppose."

Markus saw the pain behind her eyes and knew she was fighting to keep control. Outwardly, she projected professionalism and confidence, but inside she was lost. It would take a few days for the reality of what happened to sink in, and she would come tumbling down like a tower slated for demolition.

"You gonna be okay?" he asked.

"Sure," she said. "They're taking me back to their base. They already took Dad's body. I guess I'll get a free flight home." She tried to smile. It looked painful.

There'd be much more than just a free flight home—which would be covered by the American taxpayers. She'd be questioned and debriefed. There'd be an inquiry into the events that led to the deaths of several company employees. Vircon would undoubtedly get pulled into a media frenzy unless some high-ups got involved, which was likely. They'd need someone to pin this on and since Ned was gone Annika was next in line. As much as Markus hated that kind of shit, he hoped it worked out for her in the end. There was a lesson in there, if she could see it.

Of course he didn't have the heart to tell her any of this. "Sure," was all he said.

"Have you heard from your man yet?"

"He's in radio silence right now. I'm sure he's closing on the . . ." He stopped before mentioning the sniper, but then it really didn't matter now. It happened and she'd have to come to terms with it. "We're going to get him as soon as we clear out of here."

"Listen," she said taking a step closer. "When you guys get out of this place give me a call. Vircon has assets all over the globe. No shortage of conflict zones where good, reliable people are needed." She handed him a small silver business card. Even in the face of all this chaos and misery, she was still playing the professional. A coping mechanism, Markus knew. Trying to cling to the way things had been before her life had been devastated by war.

Markus tucked the card in his pocket. Annika forced another smile, placed her hand on his shoulder, then left.

As she was walking away Markus said, "Take care of yourself, Miss Sellers."

She turned to face him. "Annika," she said.

Markus watched her for a moment, then nodded.

She left, off toward the headquarters building where the Army officers were waiting for her. Several Prowlers drove past, a pair of supply trucks following behind. The Vircon facility compound was bustling once again. How quickly things seemed to go back to normal.

Markus turned his gaze to a group of soldiers

smoking by the water tanks. Behind them were supply trucks loaded with military equipment that would tear the bay apart and make it into some sort of command center or barracks. They watched Markus in silence, eyes hard and narrow, quiet judgment passing between them. No love lost between soldiers and mercenaries. Didn't matter what he'd done before, only what he'd do next. The team was worn out, spread too thin. Perhaps it really was time to think of something else.

Ain't worth dyin' for the wrong cause, brother.

They were all lucky enough to have survived, he'd be a fool not to recognize the opportunity for something better.

He went back to help load the trucks.

An hour later, they were loaded and rolling, the three Prowlers leaving through the north gate to go get Tripp.

25
CONFIRM THE KILL

Sam spent the night crawling through brush and rocks in the pitch black. Probably only covered about three hundred yards, but it was enough to get out of the kill zone and give her better cover. The shooter was somewhere to the southwest so she went in the opposite direction, putting some distance between them. It was a long and exhausting crawl over the unforgiving mountain terrain, but the physical pain was nothing compared with the pain she felt at the thought of Rob's body lying in the dark, cold and lifeless. She knew it was her fault he was dead. She'd gotten careless. They'd made love while on overwatch for Christ's sake. Now he was dead and she was dragging herself through hell just to stay alive.

All night she listened to the assault she was supposed to be helping with while being hunted like an animal. The fight lasted most of the night then died out just before dawn. She wondered how many more died and if it had been worth it.

Now that it was daylight she could see her surroundings and moved into a patch of brush and tall grass along a south-facing slope. It was an obvious hiding place but she needed a moment to collect herself. The image of Rob kept flashing through her mind. She'd see him smiling, drawing in his notebook, see him leaning in to kiss her, felt his hands on her body, warm and alive. Then he was falling, pink mist spraying out behind him, his lifeless body collapsing in a heap. She hadn't actually seen him get hit, but she knew what it looked like.

It wasn't supposed to go down like this. Her eyes filled with tears, her throat tightened and her body threatened to heave. She bit her lip, pressed her hands and knees into the rocks beneath her, fighting down the storm. If she gave in, she'd be dead. And she couldn't avenge Rob if she was dead.

Sam rubbed her eyes, clenched her teeth, pushed the images from her mind. She let out a breath and felt the cold hatred slide back in. She wouldn't be the corpse today. She was the Reaper of Killzone Valley.

She lay in the grass, felt the cool breeze brush her skin and listened to the mountain. The world came into focus and Sam melted into her surroundings. She did an inventory check. Rifle on her shoulder, one magazine in her cargo pocket with four rounds, no sidearm. Wouldn't need it out here anyway. Across the ridge, the hillside rose up into rocky crags. The shooter had to be somewhere in that area, probably making his way to her camp to go through her things. He'd wait, using it as bait hoping she'd come back.

Sam didn't plan on being so obliging.

She watched the far ridge, looking for movement, and let the situation play out in her head. She was separated from her camp with limited means of defense and she was alone. The camp was a known location. The most logical thing to do would be to get to higher ground where she could scout it out and wait for the shooter to appear.

That was the logical thing.

Sam inched backwards, away from her hiding

place. When no shot rang out and no bullet came screaming in, she kept moving and eventually rose to a low crouch to make her way down the ridge. There was a tree line to her left, but it was a likely place for her to go, so she ignored it and kept heading downhill. It took her only a fraction of the time to cover the three hundred yards she'd spent all night crawling over, then kept going. She got down low again until she was pressed to the earth, dragging herself along. She reached the crest and scanned the distant slope. Her camp was above her now, about two hundred yards uphill. She needed to move just a bit more in order to get a better angle.

Sam slid through the grass, careful to blend with her surroundings. She eased the rifle off her shoulder and looped the strap around her hand so she could drag it with her. Her body was screaming, but it didn't matter. Couldn't focus on it. Then she was finally in position, tucked between a rock and an old fallen tree on an upward slope with a line of sight to her camp. She settled in, easing the Remington into her hands. Wind was maybe eight to ten miles per hour easterly. Fingers around the scope dialed in the angle. She'd be shooting upward so she'd have to compensate for that. A bit of Kentucky windage, but it would have to do.

Sam pressed her cheek to the stock, peered through the scope, and waited.

Tripp scoped the camp.

The sun beat down on the mountain, waves of heat lifting off the rock and making it hard to discern unnatural movement. He'd been on the rifle for hours now, his eyes strained, body felt melted to the earth. Beads of sweat were like a thousand tiny needles all vying for his attention.

Tripp came off the scope, rubbed his eyes, and took a moment to observe his surroundings. Vultures were starting to close in on the body of the man he'd shot, their black wings turning in the sky. No one had come back yet and the camp remained empty. From where Tripp was, he could still see the lower half of the man's body, his legs angled up the slope, head and torso hidden behind a rock.

Tripp's comms were still turned off in case Markus got antsy and tried calling. He heard the firefight going on all night, then it stopped before dawn. As badly as he wanted to check in, he had to make sure the ridge was clear. For now, all he could do was hope for the best. But sitting still was getting him nowhere and there were moving parts he just didn't have time to wait for. So he got up, swept away his tracks, and stalked over to the far ridge.

It took at least two hours. He still wasn't one hundred percent certain the enemy sniper was gone, so he took his time, choosing each step deliberately, easing over the terrain and back up the adjacent slope. He checked angles constantly, looking for places an enemy shooter might be waiting and made sure to put himself in defensible positions in case he took fire.

When he was about fifty yards from the camp, he crouched down behind a cluster of gnarled roots and grass, then drew the rifle up. The enemy snipers had chosen their placement wisely, surrounded by a series of large boulders with a clear view to the southeast. There was a blanket sprawled over the ground, a green pack with an antennae sticking up. He wondered if it was being tracked, but figured there'd have been reinforcements by now if that were so. On the blanket next to the pack was a small rectangular box with writing on it. He made out the words .308 MAG scrawled in black pen. The same ammo the Reaper of Killzone Valley was known to use. It was looking like he'd cornered the big prize.

He glanced uphill. What would he do if he were Sam Cross? He wouldn't leave a fellow soldier and valuable equipment behind, that's for sure. She had to be around somewhere. She was probably on the high ground watching the camp, waiting for him to be foolish enough to go dig through the spoils. Tripp scanned the ridge above him. Plenty of good positions up there among the trees and rocks. He had to get out of there and flank that position.

Tripp eased himself down and crawled backwards, moving down the slope. He couldn't just go right up. He knew she was watching.

Sam saw movement.

She perked up, fought to calm her suddenly pounding heart, which threatened to ruin a good shot. A single patch of grass had shifted. It was a fleeting glimpse, but enough to know it wasn't the wind. She slid the crosshairs over the area.

Nothing moved. The mountain was still. Then she caught the flash of a leg sliding in the dirt, then it was gone. The bastard was low crawling through the hills. At least now she was certain of two things: the shooter was still there, and he knew she was still there.

As she watched, she caught more glimpses of unnatural movement, a branch flicking, small rocks tumbling. It wasn't a lot, this sniper was good. Probably military trained. If it was a soldier he'd have a spotter somewhere. She had to be careful. But now that she knew the shooter's location she didn't want to move. They obviously didn't know where she was if they were still inching around trying to stalk her.

Whoever it was out there didn't give Sam a solid target so she waited, watching for the perfect moment. Luck was on her side as she realized the shooter was trying to work his way around to flank the ridge and in doing so was moving toward her. He thought she was on the high ground. Her gamble had paid off.

She sent a silent prayer to God to watch over Rob and tell him she loved him—something she hadn't gotten to say while she had the chance. Then she cleared her mind, focused on her environment, and let her finger rest over the trigger.

And it seemed God may have heard her prayer as the shooter suddenly crawled into the open. She watched him scoot out of some tall grass and settle into a kneeling position behind a rock, exposing his back to her. He was aiming a rifle up the slope, no more than three hundred yards away, completely unaware of her position. She eased her left hand up and made an adjustment to the scope. Brought the crosshairs down to his lower back, aiming for the base of his spine. A bit of a crosswind so she corrected her minute of angle. Sight. Breathe.

Her finger pulled the tension out of the trigger.

*　*　*

Tripp got set and braced his rifle. He had plenty of protection from up the ridge, plenty of angles of retreat should things go south and Cross tried to counter flank. There was still no movement up the slope. The sun was over his left shoulder, washing the far ridge in harsh sunlight. He tried to spot the glint of reflection off a scope. Nothing.

She was good, that was for sure.

He thought on that for a minute before something began to nag at him, something in the back of his mind. An instinct. A feeling. He'd told Markus this hunt would go down like this so he allowed himself to ease his focus off the scope and sort the thoughts in his head.

It came to him instantly.

She wasn't on the ridge. It was too obvious and the Reaper of Killzone Valley wasn't known for being obvious. He scanned the high ground one more time, then tracked down the slope looking for other possible hiding spots. There really wasn't anywhere along that ridge that would be conducive to shooting and scooting, which was what she'd have to do. Too much open ground, too difficult terrain. The only other option was . . .

His heart sank.

He knew where she was. He'd walked right into it. "God damned," he whispered. He turned slowly and looked behind him, downhill.

Before he could begin to make out the terrain, he was punched in the chest and thrown back against the rock. His body jolted and he sank down, the AX-7 falling from his hands. Despite the heat, he felt suddenly cold. He couldn't breathe. He knew he lost.

Tripp forced every ounce of whatever he had left

into moving his hand to the radio. He had to call it in. His fingers brushed the comm set.

He didn't hear the final shot.

He must've figured it out in the end because Sam watched the man pause, then turn to look right at her position. She fired before he had the chance to react. The round carried, hit him in the right breast. Must've punctured a lung. He fell against the rock, dropped his rifle. She chambered another round, aimed again. His hand was going for something on his belt. A radio.

She didn't give him the chance.

The next round punched through the man's left eye, spattering the rock with gore. He wouldn't have felt it.

The report of the rifle echoed off the hills, then was silent. She waited a little longer. She'd fired two rounds, so if the man had backup they'd be watching for her. After some time, when nothing else moved or made a sound, she scooted back and crawled to a different spot before climbing to her feet. No shot rang out so she stood a little taller, stretching her aching muscles. She brushed the dirt and rocks from her hands and knees. It was the first time she'd been upright in hours. With the rifle slung on her shoulder, Sam set out for the corpse of the man she'd just killed.

This was the first time she'd actually gone to confirm a kill up close. The body was seated against a rock, a puncture hole in his upper right chest, the left side of his face a ragged mess. She couldn't help but stare. This close, the grisly truth of war was undeniable, and she was held by terrible awe. No one lived forever—Sam knew that—but to know that she was critical in expediting the process was suddenly unsettling. Up to this point, she'd done her killing from a distance. It wasn't easy, exactly, but maybe *easier* to wrap her head around it from far away. This was something else. For some reason, she couldn't really believe that she'd done this.

Sam wiped the sweat from her face, crouched and checked the body. The man was in tactical civilian clothes; cargo pants, collared shirt, no fancy gear. Not military. A mercenary, then. The man had no loyalties beyond money. Something turned in her. Sam bared her teeth at the corpse and spat. The piece of shit had come looking for a payday and for that Rob was dead.

Because of *her* Rob was dead.

Sam wanted to cry, to scream. Every cell in her body wanted to quake, wanted to vent the storm inside her, but she fought it like she did everything else and distracted herself by rummaging through the dead man's pockets. She took a small canteen from him, sniffed the water, tipped it back to her lips and drained it in three gulps. Then she found two extra magazines for the AX-7 sniper rifle in a cargo pocket. A fine piece of equipment, expensive, customized, not easy to come by. This guy must've been serious. She thought about taking the weapon for herself, but couldn't fathom owning the weapon that had killed Rob. So she grabbed it by the barrel, lifted it over her head like a club and bashed it on a rock, over and over until the barrel bent, the stock cracked, chips of plastic splintered off. The scope shattered into pieces. She didn't realize she'd been screaming until she stopped and the mountainside went silent again. She let the broken rifle fall to the dirt.

As she stood fighting back the tears threatening to break, she noticed the radio on the man's belt. If he had a radio then someone somewhere else had one, too. For a reason she couldn't understand, Sam reached down and plucked it from the belt. It trailed a cord to an earpiece that popped out of the dead man's ear. She held it up, then clicked the radio on. Against her better judgment, Sam keyed the mic, said nothing.

A moment later a voice called over the channel.

"Tripp? You there?"

Sam stared at the radio wondering how she came to be in such a place, the horrors she'd endured, the horrors she'd inflicted. Rage, regret, and her grief manifested in a sudden bravado she hadn't expected. She keyed the mic again, and this time she responded.

"Tripp is dead."

Then she dropped the radio in the dead man's lap, leaving the channel open so they could find his ruined body and know they had made a mistake in trying to kill her. She threw the spare magazines off into the brush then left, climbing the trails back to her camp. Back to find Rob.

Watching her parents die in front of her had been one of the hardest things she'd ever endured, until she had to bury the body of the man she loved. Rob had stiffened overnight, which made touching him an ordeal of unbearable anguish. This wasn't Rob, it was something else, something alien. His eyes were glassed and wide, the pupils dilated. There'd been a soul behind them once, one that she'd been lucky enough to find. Rob had shown her that there was still more to life than fighting. He hadn't meant to, but he did. She could never thank him for that now.

Without proper tools, Sam couldn't dig a grave so she had to pile rocks over his body. She made a cross from some branches and tied them together with a length of cord and stuck it in the ground. When that was done she sat and allowed herself to cry.

But then it was time to move. She couldn't stay, she knew whoever was on the other end of that radio would be coming soon. So she gathered her things, strapped on her pack, and headed for the nearest RF camp several miles to the northwest.

26
NOT DONE YET

Almost overnight the Vircon mining facility had transformed into a legitimate military post. The only thing more impressive than the insect-like pace at which the engineers worked was the amount of shit being poured into the place. With Torres captured and more than half the city under military control some-one had decided it was safe to divert resources to this long-anticipated objective. And those poor sonsabitches who'd actually held off the rebels had been booted to the wind. Their contribution would be downplayed in the official reports.

Alpha Company didn't have any orders for the time being as the engineers did their work so Trent took the opportunity to wander off and find some COMMO guys from the Headquarters detachment where he traded a pack of cigarettes for a few min-utes on one of their sat-phones. He found a quiet place behind some shipping containers away from all the noise and construction.

He flipped up the antenna, punched in the num-bers, and tried to figure out what he wanted to say while it rang.

"Hello, this is Alley."

"Hey."

"Jimmy?"

"How are you?" He said. He felt like an imposter, like something inside was off. He realized he felt guilty.

Alley was oblivious and went on excitedly. "I'm good, Jimmy, how are you? Where are you? Are you safe?"

"Yeah."

"The news says we're winning out there. You guys must be kicking ass."

The boy with the RPG surfaced in Trent's memory. His hands started to shake. He ground his teeth, tried to ignore it.

When he didn't speak, Alley went on. "So, uh, my job's going well. Got a promotion, which is good 'cause it's better pay, obviously, and I actually have benefits now. I moved into a unit in downtown all by myself like a real functioning adult." Trent could tell she was smiling on the other end, trying to lighten the mood. Maybe she could tell something was wrong with him after all. Or maybe she was hiding something herself.

"Other than that, I've been spending as much time as I can at the beach," she said. "Just a . . . typical summer. You know."

"Yeah."

"Um . . . your dad called the other day. I missed it, but I'll give him a call soon. I think they're worried about you. You had a chance to call them?"

"No."

"Oh." There was a long, painful silence. "Jimmy, are you okay?"

"Yeah, I'm fine."

"Oh!" She perked up. "You'll never guess who I met last weekend. I was at a conference in Boston and Brady got us passes to this dinner gala with—"

"Brady."

A pause. "Yeah, he's my boss, Jimmy. It was a work conference."

"Spending a lot of time with him?"

"Jesus, Jimmy, come on. It's not like that. He's my boss and we're friends. I can be friends with other guys."

"Whatever."

"Look, Jimmy," she said. "You know you're the only man I want. In fact, I've been thinking about you every night. I've got something special for you when you come home. Something with lace I think you're going to like."

The image of the female soldier's bare ass flashed through his mind as he remembered fucking her against the APC. He closed his eyes, buried his face in his hand. He felt like a piece of shit. It was too much.

"Look, Alley, I gotta go."

"Oh. Okay. Well, be safe, Jimmy. I . . . miss you. And, uh . . . keep your head down."

"Yeah."

Another long silence. "Okay, well . . . bye."

"Bye." Trent ended the connection, folded the antenna back. He stood in silence for some time, staring at the ground. How had things gotten so backwards? He couldn't keep going like this. His nerves were fried, his mind was reeling. Everything sounded like gunshots. When he closed his eyes he saw death. He saw the bodies of enemy fighters, innocent civilians, his teammates. It didn't help that he wasn't acting like himself anymore. Or was he? Maybe this was who he was now. Everyone changes.

Trent fished an extra pack of cigarettes from his cargo pocket, lit one with trembling fingers. He drew the smoke in deep. Just one day at a time. It was all he could do.

He returned the sat-phone to the COMMO guys, then as he was leaving the bay a familiar voice called his name. Trent stopped and looked for the source.

Simard came off a bench in the smoking area and shook Trent's hand. "God damned," he said. "What's up brother?"

"What are you doing here?" Trent asked.

"Came with the HQ detachment. Looks like the 117th is moving in."

"That's great."

Simard frowned at Trent. "You alright, man? You look like you been through the shit."

Trent tried to think of an answer.

Simard went on, saving him from another awkward silence. "Well, I guess you guys been carving a path through the city. Any case, it's good to see you."

Trent nodded. "You heard about O'Malley?"

Simard blew a breath through puffed cheeks. "Yeah, man." His tone was somber now. "That fuckin' sucks. Bravo and Charlie lost some guys, too. They had a memorial service for everyone. Shit's fuckin' crazy. I'm glad I didn't have to . . ." He stopped himself.

Trent waved it off. "Ah, don't worry. It's a fucking crap shoot. I might die tomorrow. Fuck it." He took a drag off his cigarette. "Might die today."

Simard looked at Trent, a lost expression on his face. "Can't think like that, man."

"No other way about it," Trent said, then clapped Simard on the shoulder. "You stay easy, brother." Then he walked back toward First Platoon's staging area. There was nothing else to do.

As Trent passed through one of the inner gates,

Ramirez came running up to him in full combat gear. "Hey, where the fuck were you? Squad's loading up, we're getting ready to roll out."

"For what?"

"CID got Torres to talk. That motherfucker gave up the location of Joseph Graham's base camp, we're moving out to end this shit for fucking good!"

Christ, they didn't even have time to breathe. Trent followed Ramirez back to the vehicles and scrambled to throw on his gear as Lieutenant Vickers gathered First Platoon for a briefing. Trent was clipping his helmet on as the LT began.

"At ten hundred hours recon drones tracked a group of rebels fleeing into the mountains to what they believe is a significant enemy encampment. The coordinates synch with the intel CID got from John Torres. They have reason to believe this is indeed the location of Joseph Graham's base of operations, so we're acting quickly. Our orders are to locate the camp, close with, and exterminate the enemy. This is a decisive moment, our actions here could win this valley. This is what you've been fighting towards. Stay sharp, get aggressive, and fall out to your squad leaders."

Trent went through the motions and joined the rest of Second Squad as they gathered around Sergeant Creon.

"Headquarters was kind enough to lend us a few Prowlers for this one, but we're still bringing the main body in APCs. Team leaders in Prowlers, everyone else load up as usual. Keep comms on the squad channel. Once we make contact, we're to draw the enemy out. If you think West Jordan was sporty, prepare yourselves for the shit storm we're driving into today. Now, load up and let's fuck up some rebels."

Everyone raced to their vehicles, but Creon stuck his arm out and stopped Trent. The staff sergeant pulled him aside and leaned in close. "I know this isn't what you wanted, but you're here." There was something different about his expression, the hard lines and permanent scowl fighting against something beneath the surface. Trent stood and listened.

"I have a daughter," Creon said. "She's eight."

Trent blinked, at a loss for words.

"I don't take pride in some of the things we've done," Creon went on. "But you can't dwell on it. Not yet." He paused, searching for words. "There's time for regret later. Right now you may not care if you live or die, maybe you even feel like it's what you deserve, but you can't. It's not about you. It's about the men next to you. If you fall, you leave them exposed. When the shit hits the fan I don't fight for glory or medals or because I like it. Hell, I don't give a shit about President Haymond's agenda or bullshit politics. That shit doesn't concern people like us. I don't waste time wondering if the rebels might be right. When the bullets fly I fight for you and every other soldier around me."

Trent was stunned. Why the fuck was Creon going on about this right now?

"I know you saved our asses on that relay tower in West Jordan," Creon said. "I know what you had to do."

Ah.

Creon nodded. "I expect you to show the same kind of commitment to your fellow soldiers up there in the mountains. Forget everything else. Protect the men next to you."

"Roger that," Trent said. He really couldn't think of anything else.

"Good," Creon said. "Now load up."

Trent found his way to the APC in a daze. It was turning out to be one fucking strange day. And there was still so much more ahead. He felt like he wasn't really inside himself, more like he was watching from above. He saw his body move, his hands doing checks of his gear, counting the magazines in his pouches, tightening the ever-fucking-irritating chin strap on his helmet, looking over the guys around him. Everyone had the same tired expression, adrenaline the only thing keeping them going. Which could wear down a soul real fucking fast.

Soon the vehicles rolled out and headed for the hills. They hit the service roads snaking through the mountains, bounced and jolted and leaned at dangerous angles as they raced toward their target. Trent wondered how effective the assault would be in broad daylight. The rebels would see them coming from miles away. Maybe that was the plan, though.

After some time the convoy stopped and everyone off-loaded. Team leaders climbed out of their Prowlers as the drivers crept the vehicles along while everyone else formed into squads and marched on either side.

It wasn't much later when they made contact with the first of the RF.

27
THE FIGHT FOR SALT LAKE

A rocket screamed out of the forest and slammed into the lead APC, killing it on the spot. It blocked the trail, smoke seeping from the hatches. While the wounded were being extricated Trent and the rest of Second Squad maneuvered out to the right flank to engage the enemy ambush. Tracers cut through the trees, the atmosphere filled with the sharp hiss of passing bullets. Grenade blasts threw up plumes of dirt and ripped branches from trees. Trent was doing all he could to stay in formation, but it got harder the farther out they pushed. Behind them in the clogged mess the APCs' turret guns were shredding the mountainside. Trent hoped they knew there were friendlies downrange.

He heard shouting from somewhere ahead. People moved through the trees; people not in military uniforms. Couldn't be more than fifty feet away. Trent raised his rifle and fired. They disappeared behind cover, but more people moved into view.

Not people, Trent thought. *Targets.*

He fired again, saw one target stumble and fall to the ground. The rebel got up, clawed his way over some rocks and slipped behind cover.

The rest of the squad was shooting, rifles barking to Trent's left and right. Orders shouted over the noise, the radios trying to make sense of the chaos. He kept firing, kept sighting targets until there were too many to focus on. Muzzle flashes came from every direction.

Trent snapped his head around trying to get bearings on his squad. Bodine was leaning around a tree firing the M37. Ramirez and Jones were leapfrogging through cover, taking turns firing at the enemy as they advanced. Creon was just ahead, crouched behind a mound of rocks motioning the squad forward. Trent raised his MX, sighted on a target peeking around a tree and fired three rounds. The enemy fighter dropped to the ground. A salvo of return fire forced him back behind cover, splinters of bark showering him, deflecting off his helmet and stinging his face.

The shooting stopped only for a second, but it was just long enough for Trent to slip out from behind the tree and push forward. He sprinted as fast as he could through the brush, tripped and pitched forward, almost losing balance, but he kept pumping his legs until he slammed into the mound of earth next to Creon. The rest of Second Squad fell in beside them.

"They're dug in on that hill," Creon shouted over the gunfire while knifing his hand toward the enemy position. "There's a 240 nest a hundred meters below us pounding the trail, but these assholes are covering 'em. Third Squad's keeping them from gaining ground but we gotta get rid of that nest fucking yesterday!"

Trent heard it now, the rhythmic *chunk-chunk-chunk* of the old 240-Bravo machine gun. It wasn't much against the APCs' turret guns but was a solid enough weapon to inflict serious damage to the ground troops evacing for the wounded. Certainly enough of a distraction to allow more RPG teams to close in.

"Trent, Bodine," Creon said. "Hold this position

and fucking hammer 'em. Ramirez, Jones, you're with me. We're going up top, hit them with grenades." He gestured up the slope to a short rise that gave good ground for the pincer move Creon was going for. They'd close the RF squad in and hit them from two fronts.

Trent dropped his spent magazine and slapped a new one home, then he and Bodine popped up over the berm and opened fire, covering Creon, Ramirez, and Jones as they raced for the rise.

The rebels fired back, but not aggressively enough. They were trying to stay behind cover and stay alive, which was exactly how they were going to die. Off to Trent's left, the turret guns were raging, trying to hold the trail. He couldn't see the vehicles through the trees anymore. It sent a chill through him being so far away from help. But a moment later three blasts rocked the enemy position, followed by a storm of gunfire. Trent and Bodine joined in until the call for cease-fire came over the comms.

Creon scrambled back down the rise and Second Squad pressed forward, sweeping their barrels for anyone still alive. The rebel fighters had been shredded by the grenades. Ramirez got jumpy and pumped a round into an already dead body, but Creon calmed him and called Third Squad to relay that the enemy backup was done. The 240-B thumped for a moment longer then was quickly silenced.

Before they moved to regroup with the main body of the assault force, Trent paused over one of the rebel corpses. It was a young male probably about Trent's age, on his back, eyes open, his pupils black holes staring right through Trent. The rebel's shirt was soaked with blood and plastered to his belly. Trent glanced at the other bodies. All young, inexperienced civilians playing at war. Untrained, undisciplined human beings with guns and misplaced morals.

Deeper in the forest, more gunfire snapped and popped, voices shouted from somewhere below. Creon barked an order and they raced down the hill, back to the fight.

Sam scrambled through the forest cradling the Remington like a newborn child. She'd almost made it to the base camp when she'd heard the gunfire. And it wasn't a small engagement either, but a legitimate fight between significant forces.

Branches slapped at her face as she sprinted through the brush and came out on a ledge overlooking a dirt road packed with military assault vehicles. She dropped to cover and pulled up the Remington. Troops were moving through the forest on either side of the road, firing and moving; rhythmic, controlled, advancing into the tree line. One of their armored vehicles was in the middle of the trail pouring smoke from a gaping wound in the front armor. There was a cluster of injured soldiers being treated in a hasty triage behind two other assault vehicles with raging turret guns. She had no idea where the rest of the RF were but judging by the movement of the troops and the direction of the damage to the lead vehicle, she guessed they were to the north of her position.

She hooked her thumb over the bolt, chambered a round, and took aim at one of the turret gunners, then fired. The turret stopped. She chambered the next round, aimed, took out the second turret gunner. Troops nearby scrambled for cover.

Sam crawled backwards, rose to a crouch and ran northwest. She had maybe a minute or two to try to get around the leading enemy squads before she'd be cut off, and silence was no longer a concern since the battlefield was deafening.

Behind her, the turrets began firing again.

She darted right, slowed to a trot and knelt behind a tree. She had the high ground for now, but she'd have to go down into the draw, cross the trail, then scramble uphill to join the main body of the RF. Hoping, of course, that they didn't shoot her first.

Sam tucked her cheek against the stock and sighted down the scope. Not long ago she'd felt indestructible, but now, without Rob, she felt alone and exposed.

She spotted a soldier creeping through the trees less than one hundred yards away. He was moving slow, probably thinking he was hidden. He was mistaken.

Sam shot him in the chest. The soldier's feet shot out from under him and he hit the ground. She chambered the next round, went to find another target, but saw the soldier start to get back up. He'd dropped his weapon and was patting his torso in disbelief. He got up on his knees and looked like he was calling someone. By then, she saw the rest of the squad moving into view.

Sam scooted out of there and ran farther up the mountain until the trail bent east. Using the bend to cover her crossing she darted out, raced for the other side, and plunged back into the brush.

She plucked the radio from her belt and tried calling Command. No one answered, so she switched to the open channel and was hit with a torrent of incoherent radio traffic. Sam spat, put the radio away, and climbed a rocky ledge where she could see the military vehicles again. She took a knee, leaned against a tree and scoped the road. A Prowler was weaving through the larger armored vehicles stuck in the jam. The windshield faced her straight on and she hoped her .308 would be enough to punch through the thick glass. She aimed at the bouncing truck, leading the shot, then fired.

The Prowler accelerated then veered hard, flipped into a ditch and rolled down into a gulch.

Sam didn't have time to hang around as she watched a soldier pop out of one of the APCs, shoulder a rocket launcher, and aim in her direction. She raised the Remington and fired. The soldier dropped, the rocket streaked off into the distance. It was all happening so fast now.

Markus stood on the hood of the Prowler peering through a set of binoculars. There was gunfire to the north, maybe a mile or two away. Hard to tell exactly, but certainly farther in the mountains than he'd ever heard. They'd watched the convoy of armored infantry head into the Oquirrhs a few hours ago. Must've found what they were looking for.

They were parked on a dirt road about a quarter mile from the compound where they'd been waiting for Tripp, but then the call had come and they knew their friend was gone. Cross had been audacious enough to let them know herself. Markus wouldn't forget that. None of them would.

The gunfire continued to the north. Len was working the radio in the Prowler to tap into an open channel where someone was shouting through heavy static and background noise. The rest of the crew were waiting anxiously.

"Chief," Len said, leaning out the door. "Got a hit, it's the RF. Someone on an unsecured net, sounds like they're under assault."

"Cross's there, she's gotta be," Rourke said.

Markus lowered the binos. "Let's roll."

The crew climbed in the Prowlers and took off up the mountain.

Markus powered up the nav-screen while Dieter drove. The satellite image of the mountain range appeared, then went out of focus before going completely blank. It flickered back on, then off again. Markus punched the screen, then dug out a map from under the seat, tracing a finger over the crinkled page as the truck bounced over the trail.

"Should be an access trail ahead," he said. "There, turn right."

The Prowler took the turn at speed, sliding sideways as Dieter yanked the wheel. Then they were climbing, following a ridge until they plunged back into dense forest, turned onto a wider trail, and gained speed. Markus could hear gunfire over the engines now and knew they were close.

An APC appeared in the road in front of them. Dieter jammed the brakes, the truck slid in a cloud of dust.

The APC gunner swiveled the turret around to bear on them. Markus switched on the area speakers. "Easy," he said. "We're the contractors from Vircon. Heard there was a fight, we want to help."

The gunner looked confused and afraid. Markus could see his mouth moving as he spoke into his headset, relaying the situation to someone higher. There were other armored vehicles ahead of them, soldiers on foot moving through the trees. Looked like they'd been stopped in the road.

Not good.

"Jesus, look at that," Dieter said.

Markus looked over and saw several soldiers lying in the grass by the side of the road, a handful of others moving around them. Two of the soldiers had medic badges and heavy packs with gauze and shears strapped to the outside. A field triage. There were a lot of wounded.

"Christ," Markus said.

A soldier came around the back of the APC, said something to the gunner and the turret swiveled away. Markus climbed out of the truck and went over.

"What are you doing here?" the soldier said. He wore the rank of lieutenant.

"We want to help, Lieutenant," Markus said.

"This is a military operation, you're a civilian."

"Sir, we're all former operators. You know what we can do. How can we help?"

The lieutenant scratched his chin. Something up the road exploded, a thunderous boom rippled down the line. More gunfire and shouting. "We're bogged down. APC got hit in the road. Trying to press on but we can't get by with the rest of our armor. Tried sending some Prowlers up but we don't have enough to afford to lose them on their own."

"We got three solid vehicles," Markus said, then, "You guys taking any sniper fire?"

"Huh? I don't know, it's hard to tell. We're taking lots of fire." The LT looked up as Temple joined them, medical pack on his shoulder.

"Chief. Sir," he said. "I can help." He nodded toward the injured soldiers sprawled in the grass.

The LT thought for a second. "Yeah, we can use the help."

Temple ran off.

The LT turned back to Markus. "Medevac can't get up these trails and we can't afford to send men and equipment back down the mountain while we're engaged with the enemy. It's a mess all around."

"Let me talk to my guys," Markus said, then jogged back to the trucks. He gathered the crew around the hood. They kept their weapons close.

"We got a choice to make," Markus said. Everyone looked at him intently, waiting for the hammer. "Army's bogged down ahead, taking heavy fire. They can't push on with all their wounded, but they can't break from the fight either and their medical vehicles can't get out here. Gentlemen, we can either get in the fight and help them push back the RF, or we can load up their wounded and medevac them to base camp and actually do something good for once. I'll leave it up to a vote."

"We back out of the fight, we could lose Cross," Len said.

"We get in the fight and take our own wounded, and still lose Cross," Dieter added.

Rourke spat. "Much as I fuckin' hate it, we don't have much chance finding that bitch in this shit show anyway. But we can save some lives."

Markus watched the crew exchange glances, then turn to him in unison.

"Let's load 'em up," Dieter said.

"Alright," Markus said, then relayed their decision

to the LT. He waved their trucks up to the triage and Markus found Temple packing a gunshot wound in a soldier's thigh.

"We're medevacing the wounded," he said.

"You got it, Boss," Temple said, then he turned and grabbed one of the soldiers helping with the triage. "Separate groups by priority and assign color categories: Red for immediate, Yellow for delayed, and Black for expectant. I don't care about Green. I want Reds closest to the road for quicker loading. Find any available CLS-trained troops to ride with critical patients." He turned to Markus. "Back the trucks up and get 'em loaded. Save room for medical staff to ride with them. Make sure they call it in so we don't get shot when we get to the FOB."

"Got it," Markus said. "I'll get the comms up on their network and locate the rally point. Good work, Temple."

The crew set to hoisting bodies into the Prowlers, taking care to move the severely injured as gently as the battlefield allowed. It wasn't long before the trucks were slicked with blood. It was worse than Markus first realized and he knew the crew had made the right decision. His heart swelled with pride in his men.

Another explosion up the road.

They picked up the pace.

Trent emptied another magazine. "Changing!" he shouted as he loaded a new one. He popped back up, found a rebel running through the brush. Aimed, fired. The rebel fell midstride. Another was shooting at them from behind a tree. Trent stitched a three-round burst into it. The rebel felt the pressure, turned heel and ran.

Ramirez slid into the ditch beside Trent, gasping for breath. "My weapon's jammed!" he shouted.

Trent came off his sights to see Ramirez holding his rifle out to him. "Christ. Here," Trent said, letting his own rifle hang in the harness as he grabbed Ramirez's MX. He dropped the magazine, cleared the chamber. Did a quick functions check as bullets snapped around them.

"What's wrong with it?" Trent asked.

"I don't know," Ramirez said, ducking as another spray of enemy fire hit their position. "Bolt rides fine but nothing happens when I pull the fuckin' trigger."

Trent snapped the receiver open, checked the trigger assembly and spotted the issue. Someone had tried modifying the trigger: there were scrape marks on the metal face of the bolt catch and the spring hadn't been replaced properly. "You got a pen?" Trent shouted.

Ramirez gave him a look, dug through his pockets and handed Trent a ballpoint. Trent snatched it, popped the core, and used it to dig out the spring and hook it back to the mechanism. He slapped the receiver shut, reloaded the weapon, and handed it back to Ramirez. "That should do it," he said.

"Thanks!" Ramirez twisted around, opened fire. The weapon spat several rounds no problem. He turned to Trent. "Hey, fuckin' awesome, man! Thank—"

Ramirez's neck burst open, a spray of hot red pelting Trent's face. Ramirez flopped backwards, his eyes searching, mouth working like he was trying to say something. He clutched at his neck, blood ebbing between his fingers.

Trent stared, horrified. *"Medic!"* he shouted. His hands moved on their own, going to one of the pouches on his vest, pulling out a field dressing and pressing it to Ramirez's neck.

Creon ran over, Bodine right behind providing covering fire with the machine gun. "Jesus," Creon said, seeing Trent bent over Ramirez. The staff sergeant got on the radio and called it in. The LT said they'd send a runner to collect him, there were no available medics.

"Fuck." Creon sent some rounds downrange then crouched in the ditch. "We gotta keep moving," he said. "Move, move." Bodine peeled off with the rest of Second Squad following close behind.

Trent made to get up and follow but a rocket screamed past, blew a crater in the earth behind him and sent him sprawling.

Sam kept shooting.

She'd gone through three of her magazines and was quickly using up what little ammo she had left. She didn't have time to dig through her pack and reload the empty ones so she scooped up an M4 she found on the ground near some bodies and scavenged a spare magazine.

She could see the RF running through the forest ahead of her, but she didn't want to just up and sprint for them, afraid she'd get shot as she moved in the open. She'd catch up to them in a minute.

Sam dove to the ground as she was sprayed with rounds that punched into a tree and kicked up dirt around her. She rolled away and scooted behind a rock, then leaned out and lifted the M4. The red-dot sight wasn't zeroed to her own sight picture, but her targets were so close it didn't really matter. She fired a few quick bursts, dropped two as the others scrambled behind cover.

Sam took off up the slope, trying to stay with the rest of the RF. She was on autopilot. Position, shoot, move. Over and over. Each time she pulled the trigger, somebody fell. But with each shot, something in her withered. They wouldn't stop coming. They just kept dying.

Another group of soldiers appeared in the brush maybe fifty yards away. She aimed but couldn't see them, they were just blurry shapes in a wavering sight picture.

She realized she was crying.

Sam tried blinking the tears away, pointed the rifle and fired on burst. Her hands were shaking, the shots went wide. She wasn't sure if she was missing on purpose or not. The bolt locked to the rear, the magazine spent. She dropped the M4 and ran.

What was wrong with her? The middle of a damn battle was no place for crying, but there it was again, that terrified little girl beneath the surface. Her anger had turned on her. Nothing she did would change the past. She could kill hundreds of enemies, thousands even, and it wouldn't change anything. Rob was dead. Mom was dead. Dad was dead. John was probably dead. It was all too much. Her heart was being ripped apart. She only knew one way to respond, but it only made things worse.

As she stumbled through the woods she came upon a pair of RF hunkered down in a dug-out fighting position. They looked up at her in surprise.

She froze, clutching her Remington. "I'm RF," she

said, hoping they didn't hear the quiver in her voice. "Sam Cross," she added, to which they lit up as if the savior had just arrived. It should have been inspiring, but it felt like a crushing weight on her shoulders. They were the same age as her, but they seemed so much younger and had a look in their eyes that said they were new to all this.

Rounds snapped past.

Sam dove into the hole and scrambled to the edge. The two fighters returned fire, spent casings bouncing off Sam's head and shoulders. She eased the Remington out and blinked through watery eyes. Her crosshairs were nothing more than vague streaks across a spilled watercolor canvas. She was useless.

The enemy was so close now she could hear them shouting. The forest was roaring, snapping, booming. People were dragging wounded to cover.

One of the fighters in the hole had a radio that went off calling for everyone to fall back. He looked at Sam, terrified.

"We have to move," she said, trying to keep them focused. "I'll get up that rise and cover you."

"Don't leave us," one of them said, and Sam thought of that little girl so many years ago running through the hills as her family lay dead behind her.

"I'm not leaving you," Sam answered. "I'm going to cover you. It's what I do. I promise you'll get out of here." She put steel in her voice and fought back tears. "Now cover me."

The two fighters let loose with all they had left as Sam got up and scrambled for the high ground. Tracers flashed by as she made it into position. She plucked the magazine from the port, counted eight rounds. All she had left. She slammed it back, pulled the bolt and chambered the first round. She'd have to make these last shots count.

Stock tucked to her shoulder, eye to the scope, Sam glassed the fighting position.

The two rebels were in the bottom of the hole looking up at a pair of soldiers standing above them, MXs pointed down.

There was no time. Sam trained the crosshairs, eased her finger on the trigger.

Trent's ears were ringing, head spinning. He checked to make sure he still had his weapon. Muffled thumping faded to the sharp report of gunfire and his focus was back. The rest of Second Squad had cleared some distance and were moving toward the enemy flank, but Trent and Creon were still in the ditch.

For the moment, the ground around them had stopped churning as the RF turned their focus on the rest of the squad. Creon grabbed Trent by the drag strap and hoisted him up.

"Let's go," he said and took off out of the ditch toward the enemy position. Trent found his feet and raced to keep up, expecting to feel the punch of a round tearing through his body any second.

But then they were at the base of a berm, clawing up the face, then they were over and sweeping rifles down into the position. Trent paused next to Creon, the both of them standing in the open, looking down on two young Revolutionist fighters huddling at the bottom. They had weapons, but dropped them and held their hands up.

Trent saw the terror in their eyes, felt the terror in

himself, but he'd gone numb to everything else. He waited for Creon to take the lead. When the staff sergeant didn't move, Trent dared a glance.

Creon was frowning down at the rebels. His finger came off the trigger. The barrel of his rifle lowered just an inch. His mouth twitched open like he was about to say something . . .

There was a crack from somewhere up the slope and Creon's side puffed out where the armor left a gap, a larger hole tearing out the other side and splashing over the rebels as they scrambled out of the fighting position. Creon let out a grunt and collapsed into the hole.

Trent ignored the fleeing rebels and went to Creon's side. He put pressure on the exit wound, his hand slick with blood. He cupped the torn uniform, tried squeezing Creon's torso together. The entry wound was small but bleeding profusely. Trent couldn't apply enough pressure to both at the same time. Staff Sergeant Creon's eyes were wide open, fully dilated. Trent jammed his fingers under Creon's jaw, checking for a pulse. He found nothing.

Creon was dead.

Sam watched the soldier drop. She'd hit him in the ribs right where their armor was weakest. The man was dead, she knew that. Her round had passed through his torso, tearing out the bottom half of his heart. It was quick, at least.

Her thumb hooked the bolt, chambered the next round, and she brought the crosshairs down on the other soldier.

The RF had sprinted out of the hole and fled off

into the forest, but the soldier didn't bother with them as he was trying desperately to help his comrade. Something about it twisted inside Sam. She held the crosshairs over the soldier, drifted up to his shoulder, just off center of his neck. She could hear people screaming in the forest, didn't matter which side they were on. Complete chaos.

Her eyes welled up again. Her finger eased off the trigger.

She couldn't do it. The unbearable weight of all she'd done suddenly pulled her down, anchored her to the past, nothing more than violence on top of violence. None of it would bring her family back and now she just wanted to be as far away from it all as possible. She got up and joined the pair of rebels as they sprinted to the camp.

A hand clamped down on Trent's shoulder.

"C'mon, we gotta go!"

Trent looked up, dazed. Numb. Bodine was helping him out of the hole, others were running past. "Sergeant Creon . . ." Trent said, pointing at the body. He stared at his hand. It was covered in blood.

"Medics'll come back for 'im," Bodine said. "We're regroupin' on the LT."

Trent was already following Second Squad, running, tripping, climbing. They converged on Lieutenant Vickers by some trees opening onto a field. RF were sprinting across to defensive positions on the far side.

"Road's cleared," the LT shouted. "Armor's heading to cut off their retreat. Bravo located their base camp over that rise. They have eyes-on. They're calling in Harpies for an air strike."

Trent followed the lieutenant's gesture and saw the tall black spear of an old radio tower rising above the trees several hundred meters off.

"We need to mark our position before the fast-movers get here," Vickers said. "Have to get across that clearing and drop smoke." Tracers flashed back and forth, grenades blasted craters in the earth, more rockets screamed past.

The seconds ticked by as everyone thought about the implications of crossing that no-man's-land. Somewhere far away heavy ordnance was closing in.

They'd been fighting for hours now, the rounds kept coming and Trent wondered why he hadn't died yet. He was tired. He'd watched enough people die. His hands were stained in their blood. Creon's words came back to him, the words he'd said before they left the compound.

It's not about you. It's about the men next to you.

That's what he'd been missing the whole time. His entire military career had been about himself. What he wanted to do, where he wanted to go, what he hoped to be after all this. But this was it. James Oliver Trent didn't care if he lived or died because that detail didn't matter. He was right where he was supposed to be.

"I'll go, sir," he said

The LT looked at him. "This isn't about being a hero."

"No sir, just doing the right thing."

The LT checked his watch. "Harpies are already inbound, you got three mikes," he said. "Use red smoke, I'll call it in as soon as I see it."

Trent didn't waste time with any final words. No need, there was nothing else to say. He scrambled up and ran out into the field as the platoon threw down covering fire. He'd always imagined people had some sort of profound thought at times like this, but the only thing he was focused on was staying upright. The ground tried to trip him up, bullets hissed by, somewhere people were shouting.

With no idea how much time he had left and having gone as far as he dared, he stopped to fumble a smoke grenade from his kit, dialed it to red, and threw it toward the enemy position. A second later the field was filled with a cloud of blood-colored smoke. He could only hope he'd thrown it far enough.

He jerked backwards suddenly, head snapping forward, helmet sliding down over his eyes. The ground came up and hit him in the back, knocked the air right out of his lungs.

"Git your ass down," Bodine said, gripping Trent by the back of his armor. Gasping and short of breath, he added, "You're a fast motherfucker to keep up with."

They pressed themselves to the ground and then— faintly—over the sound of gunfire, Trent heard the distant roar of Harpy attack jets closing in.

Sam made it back to camp to find the place in utter ruin. Equipment scattered, armed rebels stacking crates in a last-ditch effort to fortify their position, while—to her horror—defenseless civilians were being ushered through their ranks. She saw mothers holding their screaming children, men being handed guns and pushed toward the perimeter, young fighters wrapped in bloody bandages dragged back behind cover. An elderly man came up to Sam and asked if she'd seen his wife who he'd come with. She'd been here a minute ago, he said. She bit her lip and shook her head, fighting back tears. The old man thanked her and wandered off, seemingly oblivious to the firefight making its way toward them.

There were people clustered by the command tent, a few armed rebels surrounding the group. One of the rebels saw the rifle in Sam's hands, recognized who she was, and brought her through the crowd. She went along in a daze.

Inside the tent Joseph Graham was speaking to an audience of terrified refugees. He looked up and paused midsentence when he saw Sam. His hands lifted, palms up, looking much like a preacher giving a sermon on any other Sunday.

"You see," he said, looking at Sam, "all will be as it must. Welcome back, Samantha Cross." A few of the refugees turned wide-eyed stares at her, apparently familiar with her name.

"Sir . . ." She didn't know what to say, didn't know what to make of this. "We have to get out of here. These people aren't safe—"

"These people are right where they belong, right where all of us belong," he said. "And now you are here with us. Everything is as it should be."

"Rob's dead," Sam said.

Joseph Graham put on a practiced face. "We've all lost in this fight, we've all suffered. But we are here now to cement our place in history, to lay the foundation that will be our future." He turned his gaze to the captive audience. "There is no salvation without pain, no success without loss, no path without purpose."

"Did you hear what I said?" Sam snapped. The awe she'd once had for this man was gone now and in its place was . . . something else. "Rob's *dead*! They killed him. Just like *I* killed all those people. Nothing's changed, there's no *purpose* to this. It's madness."

Sam felt someone move behind her, a presence looming over her shoulder. Heard the distinct rattle of a weapon. Her finger eased out toward the trigger of the Remington, wondered if she could turn fast enough.

Joseph Graham held up a hand. The presence eased off. "Samantha," he said. "It's alright. You've done great and terrible things, but times like these call for extraordinary people like you to deliver—"

"No. Save it." She'd had enough. She'd done enough. For too many years she'd let anger guide her, then Joseph Graham had used that for his own agenda. Not a single one of those people she'd killed in the valley had been the ones who'd taken her family from her. Not one of those kills had brought her family back. "I'm done. You keep your crazy shit to yourself. These people are in danger and you're—" She was going to say *feeding them bullshit,* but it hit her.

Graham was using them as human shields.

And if any of them died in the military's final assault they'd be martyrs and fuel an entire new generation of vengeful rebellion.

The rifle was up and pointed at Joseph Graham before she knew what she was doing. "You son of a bitch . . ."

"Trying times, Samantha," Joseph Graham said. "We must all do difficult things. Please do not ruin your legacy like this."

She could kill him, but the other two armed rebels behind her would gun her down before she could chamber another round, let alone turn and fire. And even if she killed Joseph Graham it wouldn't be any different from what she'd already been doing. No, Sam was done killing.

She lowered the rifle. "You can keep all this." Then she turned and pushed past the rebel behind her and out through the tent flap, through the camp, through the chaos, away from the fighting. She was done, and she meant it. What she'd do next was something to consider later. Right now she just had to get away from it all. Sam was about to slip into the forest when she paused and looked up at the sky. She thought she heard the sound of attack jets drawing closer.

The Prowlers came to a skidding halt outside the north gate of the mine. Medics came rushing out carrying litters and medical equipment, a casualty transport vehicle right behind. Markus jumped out and helped Temple unload the injured soldiers while the rest of the crew pulled perimeter security. The medics collected their casualties and rushed back inside the compound, then Markus signaled for the crew to load back up. A staff sergeant grabbed him by the arm.

"You can't go back out there," he said.

"The hell we can't, there're more casualties."

"No, I mean we got fast-movers inbound. We can't have civilians on the mountain."

"You can't be serious. They're right on top of each other up there—"

As if on cue, the sound of jet engines echoed across the valley. Markus and the staff sergeant looked skyward to see a pair of dark-gray Harpy attack jets clear the city and streak by overhead, deafeningly loud. They banked upward, climbed over the peaks of the Oquirrhs, and a moment later the mountain-side flashed bright white and burst into orange flames as clouds of black smoke unfurled into the sky. The boom rolled out over the valley seconds later.

"My god," Markus said as he watched the mountain burn.

28
AFTERMATH

They found Tripp's body five days after the assault.

It was hard to look at, having been left unattended up in the mountains for so long, but they wrapped him in canvas, built a pyre, and laid his body across the timbers.

They took turns making peace with their fallen brother, kneeling over the wrapped form and whispering their final goodbyes.

Markus went last. *It should've never been like this,* he thought. *You should have been with us. You shouldn't have died alone.* He clenched his jaw, fought back the storm. Devens, and now Tripp. Their way of life was claiming them one by one. And this time it wasn't some foreign threat or act of terrorism, it was at the hands of Americans. Americans he'd killed as well. The line between right and wrong had become too obscured for Markus to understand. It was exhausting. Maybe it was the years catching up to him, but he just couldn't find the energy to validate it anymore.

He stared down at Tripp's body. *You were a hell of an operator, one lethal teammate, and one of the best men I've ever had the honor of knowing. You rest easy now and I'll see you on the other side.*

Markus stood and joined the crew. Dieter handed

him a lighter. Markus flicked it on and tossed it on the pyre.

The fuel-soaked timbers burst into flame. No one spoke. There was nothing else to say. They stood vigil until Tripp's remains burned down to a pile of cinders.

They came down out of the mountains and stopped outside Copperton where the Army had begun bulldozing the slums to clear the hazardous area around their new base. The Army had been thankful for their help in medevacing the wounded and fixed their Prowlers up, stocked them with weapons, ammunition, fuel, and rations. Enough to see them on their way.

As for the Revolutionist Front, it seemed their rebellion was over. Joseph Graham had been confirmed killed in the assault and without proper leadership the rebels were being pushed out of the valley in droves. The air strike had been the coup de grâce to the enemy, but it had also killed thirty-six civilian refugees who'd been caught in the camp as they tried to flee west, and the media was all over it. The military had its hands full now trying to maintain order in the city with the entire local populace suddenly and overwhelmingly against military occupation. The US government won against the Revolutionist Front, but it came at the cost of killing innocent people. Needless to say, they'd lost the hearts and minds.

That's how things went. Markus had seen it before in countries far from here. But war's always the same.

Payment for their contract cleared the account Vircon had set up, and just like that they had more money than they'd ever seen at once. The excitement was short-lived, though, as they divvied out Tripp's share since he had no wife or children, and the reminder of what they had to do to earn such a living weighed heavily on them all as they planned their next move. Markus checked over a map, following routes to where-the-fuck-ever. They'd gone through enough. Problem was, this seemed to be all they knew.

Markus dug a knuckle in his eye to stop it from twitching. The valley was a blanket of smoke and fog, devastation and despair. That was the world now. The more the powers-that-be fought to control their domain, the faster it spread. Truth was, it was inevitable. Growth, expansion, the human race consumed the world like a cancer then turned on itself. This life was all he'd ever known. What else could they do? Be farmers? Philanthropists? Politicians?

"Hey Markus," Dieter said, pointing to a khaki-colored Prowler approaching from the road. The truck pulled up and Lieutenant Colonel Lowe climbed out with a file folder in his hand.

"Afternoon, gentlemen," he said.

"What can we do for you, sir?" Markus said. The crew stood around watching.

"That's the question indeed. The Pentagon's working to procure funding for the hiring of private security forces to support the war effort out west. There's a lot of paperwork to be done, some reallocation of monies, but it's in the works." He handed Markus the file. "This is just an outline of the conditional offer, but I'd like you to look it over, give it consideration. You and your crew are hard men. We'll need hard men as this war continues. You could do some real good around here if you stick around." He paused. "And, well . . . the federal government will remember what you did for their guys."

Markus opened the file, glanced at the document.

Typical government bullshit. Same old problems with a fresh coat of paint. He closed the folder, turned to look at his crew.

After everything they'd been through, after everything the military had done in this valley, after all the chaos the Revolutionist Front had brought down here, each man gave his answer with nothing more than a look.

Markus handed the file back to the colonel. "No thanks," he said. "We're done here."

29
THERE IS HOPE

Sam woke with a start.

Another restless night, the faces of the dead haunting her dreams. They kept coming back to show her what she'd become, to surround her, make sure she'd always remember. She'd been so eager to join the fight and punish those who'd wronged her she hadn't stopped to think about who she had been venting her anger on. Her own people, or at least what had been her own people at one time, before the war, before the country became so divided that the only path to resolution was through violence. And through that violence came names like Joseph Graham, President Haymond.

Sam Cross, the *Reaper of Killzone Valley*.

She wished she could say that it hadn't been about validation or vengeance; that it was about defending each person's God-given freedoms, the freedoms they were born with before the government slapped them with restrictions, but she knew that for the lie it was. She'd wanted to be a soldier once and had she not lost her family first, she might've been the one kicking down people's doors. The idea of purpose was nothing more than justifying the things you did to deal with the shitty hand life dealt you.

Sam rolled over, put her feet on the floor. It was still dark out, but the sun would be up soon and she had to get moving. She wanted to be gone before the farm owners came to check on her. They'd been kind enough to let her stay the night without any questions. As far as they were concerned she was just another teenage girl on the run. Probably seen plenty of them in their time. Still, she wanted to be up and gone from this place before they came back.

She rubbed her eyes, slipped her feet into her boots, and pushed herself up off the cot. It was harder these days to get up and go, her body protesting the lack of rest. But she couldn't afford to relax with a bounty still on her head and she had too many miles left before she'd allow herself to feel even the littlest bit at ease. Odds were good any surviving Revolutionists would have it in for her as well, the way she'd turned her back on them in that last moment. Not that she wanted to be a part of that anymore, but knowing she had *nowhere* to go was . . . frightening. No matter where she went she'd have a target on her back. She'd earned it. Probably never really be comfortable again. For now, though, she had to keep pushing. Rest would come later.

For her, the fight was done.

Sam set to gathering her things, clipped on her belt, checked her pack and made sure it still had the sat-phone, water, spare rations, and ammunition. She grabbed the rifle from the corner, slung it over her shoulder, and stepped out into the darkness.

It was cool outside, hinting at the end of summer. It would only get colder as she fled farther north. Some goats got agitated at the sight of her and started running circles in their pen, the bells around their necks clanging in the morning stillness. The air was thick with the musty smell of fur and hay. It was peaceful. Reminded her of home. She wished she could stay.

Sam took one last look at the mountains to the east, the sky turning light over their peaks. She thought about Rob resting in that place forever and the valley on the other side where they'd formed a bond through the chaos. She wondered about the cost of all that death, if it had made any difference, if the difference was for the better or not. She wondered if any good could possibly come of it.

Well, she thought, her hand drifting to her swollen belly, *there is hope.*

30
LEAVE THIS BEHIND

The 117th got its orders to go home.

They handed the mine over to some Intel unit no one ever heard of, which lit a fire under the rumors about secret ops in the valley. A detachment of Advance Scout operators had moved in with Intel, too, so it was no big leap to guess they were up to the usual spooky shit.

After the assault on the RF base camp, the rest of the rebels quickly removed themselves from the city. Like the fight had gone right out of them. The higher-ups got worried because they knew the rebels weren't done, and the lull suggested a regrouping and change in tactics, something that would bloody the Army all over again. Maybe that was why the spooks were there. Either way, it was in Trent's rearview.

Back at FOB Spearpoint, the 117th had an award ceremony for Alpha and Bravo's heroics on the mountain. They'd been forced into formation out on the pavement under the blazing sun in full gear. Stone still, thousand-yard stares, listening to Lieutenant Colonel Lowe prattle on about great deeds and acts of heroism and other such bullshit. The battalion commander clearly loved the spotlight and made a lot of comparisons to battles from old wars in countries on the other side of the world, their true accounts repackaged with movie-quality grandeur.

It was all utter bullshit.

Now, Trent stood at the shore of the great stinking Salt Lake, mounds of rotten foam sloshing in the surf, the vast sky reflected in the rippling gray surface. Soldiers on R&R sprawled on the rocky beach trying to catch a tan in the sun as summer began its change to autumn. Soft music played from somewhere. The FOB had been drastically upgraded and expanded since the fighting died down, becoming more of a self-contained city than the sparsely manned camp it had once been. Part of that upgrade was this MWR area. Supposed to be a place where soldiers could relax and pretend the war wasn't just over the wall. They'd even brought in fishing poles for those who enjoyed such archaic traditions, despite the fact that even fish weren't stupid enough to swim in that salty shit. The whole place was a joke.

Trent looked down at the medal in his hand. A Presidential Crest of Valor. Blue and red ribbon hanging from the bottom, a star cold-pressed into the center. He and a handful of others were awarded the medal for "*assisting in holding the enemy at bay*" while the air strike obliterated the mountainside. The Revolutionist Front had sustained significant casualties, but so did the civilian refugees that were in the camp. Intel did an investigation and cleared the military of any responsibility for their deaths, citing military necessity in bombing an established enemy outpost. The locals weren't buying it though.

The medal was supposed to be an honor, but it just felt heavy in his palm. Like a weight trying to drag him down. He didn't want it, but there it was anyway: shining permanent proof that he was here and he'd been a part of it. And from that he'd come to realize the hard truth. That everything he'd been through, all the horrors he'd suffered, the horrors he'd inflicted on others, had all been a choice. That was the bottom line. The one single thing that everyone had in common. Every last one of us had a choice.

This war was a choice.

And Trent had chosen to join the fight and do the things he'd done all for his own self-interest. He thought of the people he'd killed, the homes he'd invaded, the neighborhoods torn to shreds by artillery fire. The devastation on the mountain. He'd done that so he could go to college, maybe impress a girlfriend who probably wouldn't be there when he got back. What fucking right did he have to survive this nightmare?

But he *had* survived. And he still had a choice.

As for the Army, they were dug in for the long haul, a permanent resident in the sprawling, overcrowded city filled to bursting with angry people who were starting to look more and more like they were ready to embrace the idea of a new future, and a new government.

Salt Lake City. Killzone Valley.

Trent shook his head, closed his hand around the medal, then threw it into the lake. It sailed out over the shore, the ribbon trailing like a comet tail before splashing down with a tiny *splunk*. His tour was over. He wasn't going to bring this home.

Overhead, a TC-27 Chariot began its spiraling descent toward the airfield below.

ACKNOWLEDGMENTS

Although writing, itself, is a lonely endeavor, producing an actual full-fledged, publishable book is anything but. A good number of people helped bring this one to life and I owe each and every one of them an immense debt of gratitude.

First, I want to thank my mother for encouraging me to read from an early age. Our regular trips to the library were pivotal in fostering my love of books, and she never let me feel like my creative endeavors were a waste of time.

A huge thank-you to the brave souls who read earlier versions of this book and gave me invaluable advice on how to make it better: Ryan Monahan, Sean Monahan, David Bobola, Matt Guarrasi, Jimmy Pupillo, and Bryan Huntting. Their honesty and enthusiasm gave me the strength to press on.

I want to thank my agent, Joshua Bilmes, for taking a chance on a nervous Boskone attendee who could barely string together a coherent sentence. Joshua saw what *Wake of War* could become and with his expert guidance, helped an aspiring new writer shape it into what it is. This book wouldn't be in your hands were it not for his unwavering support.

Thank you to my editor, Christopher Morgan, who saw my vision for *Wake of War* and helped bring that vision to life. Thanks also to Oliver Dougherty and the rest of the team at Tor/Forge who believed in this book and made it happen, including Rafal Gibek, Ryan Jenkins, Peter Lutjen, and Heather Saunders. Thanks to my copy editor, Bill Warhop, whose sharp eye helped make this manuscript presentable.

A special thank-you to my wife, Susan, the other half of my soul. I wouldn't be where I am today without her love, patience, and support.

And finally, to you, dear reader . . . thank you. Stories are meant to be shared so that we may better understand the world around us, and perhaps, learn something of each other as well. We are all in this one together. It's important, now more than ever, that we take care to remember that.